Rhythm Bay Love

Rhythm Bay Love

PATRICIA A. BRIDEWELL

Paperback ISBN: 978-1-7321309-2-0
Ebook ISBN: 978-1-7321309-3-7

Publishing Assistance: Tymm Publishing LLC
Content and Copy Editing: Felicia Murrell
Cover and Book Design: Tywebbin Creations LLC

Acknowledgements

Where do I begin is the question? First, I want to lift my hands in praise, and thank my Lord and Savior for blessing me. He has brought me a long way in this writing journey. My novice experiences as a writer made me want to give up, but God has kept me confident in my ability to create stories that my readers have enjoyed.

Tyora Moody, THANK YOU so much for your talent and support in this journey, and thank you to your staff at Tymm Publishing. Blowing kisses to David Anderson. Thank you for the encouragement while I was writing this book. Donya E. Fenner, you keep me on my heels and toes and I am so blessed to have your friendship. My gratitude goes out to all who were instrumental in bringing life into this book — my editors, Felicia Murrell, Maxine Thompson, proofreader and friend – Marcena Hooks, Ella D. Curry for your awesome promotions of my books throughout the years. I want to send a shout out to my beta readers – Marsha Cecil,

Severine Bryan, and Cassietta Jefferson for your honest opinions and feedback.

Other special acknowledgements go out to Victoria Christopher-Murphy and ReShonda Tate Billingsley for allowing me the opportunity to become a best-selling author in the Brown Girls Books Anthology "Single Mama Dating Drama." Keep your eyes open for their next Anthology "Confessions Secrets and Lies Revealed." I am excited about being a part of this anthology as well. Thank you, Raye Mitchell. Cousin, your information on the Bay Area was phenomenal. Sending love to my cousin, Bernard Mitchell, and to the kids, Tierra, Damon, DeVon. Love y'all for reminding me to get some sleep during my all-night writing marathons. To all my readers, I appreciate your ongoing support, and God bless you!

In God I Trust,

Patricia A. Bridewell

Chapter 1

JADA

Los Angeles, Friday 2019

Jada Carson removed the burgundy coffee mug that she'd hidden in the KTLM Radio Station breakroom cabinet. The white letters read *"LOVE GOD AND YOURSELF FIRST."*A well-deserved gift after her breakup with Gordan – a part of her life that she chose to forget. Yet he'd hung around longer than a nasty cold.

She bought the mug during a short weekend trip to Vegas with her sister Celine. Jada inhaled, relishing in the memory of their brief getaway. She and Celine were workaholics. They fit the script well—neither had taken a real vacation in years. Celine, an R.N., darn near lived in the Emergency Room, working like her life depended on it, and she was in school pursuing a Bachelor of Science in

Nursing Degree. Jada cherished her Traffic Director position and the autonomy of coordinating and scheduling the paid commercials and promotions. She rarely asked for time off fearing the radio station would collapse if she was not there. And some weekends, whenever Griff, Simon, or Toni were out of town, she was the unofficial 'go to' person for concerns with the commercials. She released a sigh. It was time to remind management that she was not a salaried employee.

Jada stooped down to get the coffee can and a filter from the lower cabinet. After preparing the coffee, she leaned against the counter and stared at the mug. It always reminded her of the goals she hadn't achieved: taking better care of herself, dating again, attending church regularly, deleting Gordan from her life. For days, a somber mood that she couldn't shake hovered — it was the tenth anniversary of the tragedy.

LOS ANGELES – 2009

Spring augmented a full bloom of ripe peaches, and Momma promised to make peach cobbler when she got back from vacation. Jada was home from college on spring break, and that nagging sweet tooth craved her mother's cobbler. Her parents —Thaddeus and Ellen Carson —

devoted weeks of preparation for a flight to Montego Bay, Jamaica, for their twenty-fifth wedding anniversary. A trip that Jada, her sisters, and Aunt Dee had encouraged them to take. But year-after-year, both parents never failed to postpone their trip. Excuses ranged from not wanting to leave the girls to Momma feeling guilty about Aunt Dee running her dress shop alone.

At a red stoplight, Jada smiled watching the elation on her parents' faces. The light changed, and she whizzed down Century Boulevard to LAX Airport. Aunt Dee rode with her since their flight was at 5:15 a.m. and darkness still loomed over the city. Her aunt had also volunteered to stay with the girls for five days to help Jada.

"Now, Jada, be sure to keep a close eye on Charmaine," Momma said, removing her

compact. She powdered her mocha brown face and added a coat of candy apple red lipstick.

"Momma, don't worry about Char. I'll check her if she gets out of hand," Jada said.

A chuckle escaped from the back seat. "Yeah, baby girl is slick. When the parents are away, the mouse will play," Daddy joked, holding his hand to his mouth. Jada glanced in the rearview mirror at her father laughing at his own words. She didn't see much humor in Charmaine's behavior. Her sister was a little fast for her young age, and Daddy was lax at times since she was the baby. But when Momma spit fire, Charmaine slowed her roll.

Momma puckered her lips. "Well, she's a lil' better now that she's fourteen. But, I'm not beyond breaking off a switch and whippin' her behind if she acts up."

"Y'all have a good time and stop worrying about those girls. I'll handle Charmaine and the dress shop," Aunt Dee said with a serious look on her face, a replica of her sister's mocha brown skin and high cheek bones. They looked so much alike, everyone assumed they were twins, but Aunt Dee was three years older than Momma. They'd grown up in a rural area of Baton Rouge, Louisiana, where hard labor was no stranger to them.

Jada and Celine also favored their mother. Charmaine acquired their father's stunning black licorice skin tone. Although Charmaine was beautiful, she hated her skin color and never shared why.

"Yeah, she's gonna be all right," Daddy said. "Suga, get to your right; we're gettin' closer to United Airlines."

Jada glanced over her shoulder and swerved over, merging into heavy traffic. She pulled in front of a white truck, parked in front of the United Airlines terminal and popped the trunk.

Daddy hunched over the car seat, kissed Jada's cheek and squeezed her shoulder. Momma hugged her, and they both exited the car, leaving the aroma of their colognes lingering.

"Sweetheart, be good and take care of the girls. Dee, we'll talk to you," Daddy said.

"Expect a call after we get to the hotel. Probably tomorrow between two-thirty or three L.A. time," Momma said.

"Have fun," Aunt Dee waved and climbed in the front seat.

Daddy lifted the luggage out the trunk, and her parents said their good-byes before they walked up to the skycap station. Jada took a deep breath and sipped bottled water while she waited for the skycap to retrieve their luggage.

Aunt Dee stuck her arms inside the sleeves of her sweater. "What a relief. To tell the truth, I didn't think they was goin'."

"I didn't think so, either."

Finally, her parents were off to a much deserved one-week trip. Daddy had worked his way up from a bus driver at L.A. Metro to a management position, and Momma ran her Touch of Class Dress Shop. Their lives couldn't be any better. Every other day, they checked in to say hello, bragging about Montego Bay, fun under the sun, walking along the beach at sundown, partying until 12:00 or 1:00 in the morning, and sleeping in late. Surely, they could not be the parents who refused to take a vacation for six years. They sounded happier, more deeply in love than ever before. Until that fateful day.

Their plane was supposed to land in LAX at 2:53 p.m., but their parents didn't call. Jada assumed the plane *was delayed. Hours went by before Aunt Dee called the airport. Unable to obtain any information, the girls and Aunt Dee started panicking. The house phone rang. When Aunt Dee screamed, "No, Lord, please no!"*

Celine exited her bedroom first; Jada and Charmaine followed her to the living room.

"Aunt Dee, what's wrong?" Celine asked.

"The...the plane crashed. Oh, my Lord." Sobbing, Aunt Dee dropped her head, "Everyone on board died..."

For the first several minutes after hearing the news, Celine and Jada screamed, cried and clutched each other to keep from falling to the floor. Somehow, they found the strength to console each other. As Jada's world collapsed, she paced the room, numbness causing her hands to shake. Celine rocked back and forth, consoling Aunt Dee with one arm as they both wept.

Jada noticed her baby sister's stiff posture. Charmaine hadn't talked, whimpered, or cried since Aunt Dee told them about their parents. Jada walked over and gave her sister a hug, but Charmaine pulled away.

Aunt Dee mustered the energy to stand, "Girls, can we pray?" Celine, Jada, and Aunt Dee formed a circle and clasped hands, waiting for Charmaine to join.

Still sitting in a chair staring in space, she shook her head, then ran to her room.

The death of her parents propelled an influx of responsibilities and Jada struggled to help her aunt and sisters cope, especially Charmaine. There was so much to do, too much anxiety, less rest, but she mainly focused on her family and her mother's dress shop. Still, she managed to complete her last year of college and got a job at KTLM Radio Station where she interned. It was only through God's grace and Aunt Dee's devotion that she made it through.

Jada gazed at the coffee still dripping into the pot. This was taking way too long. She'd come back. As she walked into her office and picked up a folder centered on her desk, she wished for a positive day. She read the large note on the front of the folder and Denise's request about adding another spot for Gigi's Wigs and Weaves came to mind. Now, she'd have to go deal with that crazy DJ Ant.

Chapter 2

JADA

Friday

TWENTY MINUTES LATER – Rapping on the radio station's main studio window with a pen, Jada squinted. "Open the door," she said in a tone one notch below a scream.

A cocky grin swiped Antoine Bailey's mouth. He flat-out annoyed Jada, which was irritating. He lifted one hand with a scribbled note. *FIVE MINUTES.* Jada quickly jotted a note and pushed it against the window. *NO!! NOW!* He shook his head and swiveled the chair around to the microphone. *Who does he think he is?*

She shot the back of his head a daggered stare and watched him rock back and forth to the music, flinging both arms in the air like he was having muscle spasms. He just didn't know. If she could do anything except go inside the studio and deal with his stuck-up egotistical attitude, she would. She huffed a long sigh. "Go ahead. Just keep ignoring me," Jada said as if he could hear through thick glass windows and blaring music.

The door to Studio Two opened, and DJ Rocky Lopez exited. "Hey, how you doin'?"

"Oh, I'm okay. Trying to get in there."

"You can't get in?" he twisted the doorknob. "It's locked. Looks like he's busy."

"I guess I'll wait a while longer."

"Yo', hit him up on the red line. If it's work-related, he shoulda let you in to see what you wanted." DJ Rocky attempted to twist the knob again. Antoine wasn't giving either of them a first or second thought. "Good luck."

"I'm not worried, but thanks a lot." She appreciated DJ Rocky's advice, but she would not be the cause of any commotion. DJ Rocky already had a beef with Antoine and management about switching Antoine from nights to his dayshift.

Perched against the studio wall that was encased with glass windows, Jada tapped one foot, watched Antoine from the back, and waited for what seemed like forever to get his attention again. "Five Minutes? That's what he said fifteen minutes ago," she mumbled under her breath.

Why was it so hard to understand clients come first? When they buy a spot that's supposed to air at a certain time, it had to air. His problem? Antoine knew but didn't care if he could sit in there, play music, and make things hard for her. Well, she'd wait. And, whether he liked it or not, adding the spot was not an option.

Antoine had been at the station for over a year. A surprise to many, his rapid acceleration from newbie to one of the most prominent radio disc jockeys in Los Angeles was mind-boggling. The word was DJ Ant's popularity had put a spit shine on Simon, the program director's face. On the opposite side, his move to dayshift sent DJ Rocky Lopez and Jada on a tailspin.

"Wake up, wake up, L.A.! It's time to move to the groove. This is your favorite champ DJ Ant, the Prince of Romance, bringing you the first two hours of oldies but goodies and some spicy romantic tunes for your pleasure." Antoine lifted both hands. "More to come—musical joy at 101.3 KTLM on your dial. Here's one of my favorites." Running his hands through an acre of light brown dreadlocks, Antoine inhaled and leaned into the mic. In a sultry voice, he said, ""Keep Your Head to the Sky" by Earth, Wind, and Fire."

Jada's head tilted. She inhaled and exhaled to

remain calm. This was getting ridiculous. Watching him expediently multitask between the mixing board, paperwork, laptop, and sips of water, she shook her head. That man was so full of himself. Two months. That's how long she'd been dealing with his behavior.

Antoine turned, gave her a dimpled smile, saluted her like a sailor, and held up one finger. She almost held up her middle one, but she caught herself.

"Keep your eyes off my man," Denise snapped her fingers as she swayed over to the door wearing a pair of four-inch multicolored Jimmy Choo shoes. A scarf that matched the shoes was a perfect choice to accent the aqua blue dress that hugged her size sixteen pyramid.

"Hey, lady, I'd be happy to. He's not my type, and I'm about to report him to Simon. He won't let me in."

Denise stuck her tongue inside her cheek. "He's probably busy... or trying to get your attention."

"Oh, stop. He's not that busy. And why would he want my attention?"

"You never know," Denise said.

Jada's eyes swept over Denise's clothes. "Look at you. I like that outfit, and those shoes are dope." Denise and Jada had been close friends since meeting at Pepperdine University and sharing some required courses. Both grew up in urban communities and shared a lot of common interests. Jada lived in South Central Los Angeles and Denise in Compton. Jada respected her sharp friend and was thrilled when the station hired Denise for a sales position four years ago based on her referral.

"Well, I've chatted with him briefly. He seemed personable." Denise turned her focus to Antoine. "I've got to give him props, though...he's one *fine* brother." She faced Jada and leaned toward her ear.

"Some of the sistas around here got their eyes on him."

Jada shrugged, "All they want is the package in between his legs."

Denise gasped and placed a hand on her chest. "No, that didn't come out your mouth."

Jada fluffed her reddish-auburn kinky-curly hair. "What else would they want? He's way too arrogant. Add sarcastic and rude, too." Though she would never tell him, Jada's curiosity about the hype that stoked his fans' devotion forced her to listen to his shows on the way to work. She cut her eyes at Antoine.

"Well, I-I...Oooh, have mercy. What do we have here?" Denise fanned herself with one hand while checking Antoine out. He'd removed his jean jacket and tossed it on a chair.

Jada tried to dismiss her friend's comments, but like Denise, her eyes didn't stray from his well-toned tattooed arms. *Dang!* Those musical notes and clefts moved seamlessly every time he flexed those arms. Jada loved colorful tattoos and had a red rose tattooed above both ankles.

With her eyes stuck on Antoine, Denise said, "Uh, as I was getting ready to say, they can have DJ Ant. I love my buttercup, and he's all I need."

Jada huffed out a sigh and waved her hand to get Antoine's attention. "I like the tats, but my concern is why he won't open this door." She glanced at her watch.

"What are you trying to do?"

"Add your spot to his log," Jada lifted her paper.

"He already knows. Wonder why he didn't check with you?"

"That's what I'm saying. I've got to make sure the commercial airs on time," Jada checked her watch again. "I called the red line when I got in. He said he'd confirm with you. Just bang on the window after the song ends. He'll let you in." Denise shook her pen at Jada. "Cocky, sarcastic, whatever you wanna call him, I think he likes you." Denise tilted her head. "And you, my sister, standing out here lookin' in that window all this time? Just to add a spot? Give me a break."

Jada's mouth opened, but before she could speak, Denise's eyes widened as she jerked her head toward Antoine, who was facing them with one finger up. Jada looked at him and nodded.

"See? You caught him at a bad time. He'll let you in soon. I've gotta run; I'm expectin' a client." Her forehead wrinkled as she paused. "We haven't been to lunch or dinner in a while. Let's get together."

Jada flipped through the log. "I agree. It's been a minute, text me a time and we'll go to lunch on Saturday."

"Will do. Uh, I almost forgot," Denise waved her hand. "Ervin has plans for us on Saturday. Send me two Saturdays that you're free. We should hook up before the month ends."

"Why don't you send me yours? I'm free every weekend."

"True. It's about time for that to change."

Denise pivoted and headed to her office. From the moment Denise mentioned Antoine's possible interest in her, it weighed on Jada's mind. Denise loved to tease for laughs, and Jada suspected her comment about Antoine might have been just that — one of her tutti frutti jokes.

Or was her friend trying to play matchmaker again? Hopefully not with Antoine.

Antoine ambled to the window, lip-flapping words she couldn't understand, then returned to his seat again. With furrowed brows, she stuck her tongue out at him. *I could wring his neck. He knows I didn't hear him. The females in this place must be desperate. Am I the only one without shutters over my eyes?* She tapped lightly on the door with her pen. Finally, he rushed back to the door after a commercial break and opened the door.

"I apologize. I had to log my playlist before my shift ends, and I was behind. How's your morning going?" Antoine asked as though he'd done nothing wrong.

"Better. Now that I can do my job. Can I see your log?" She stepped back so he could take his seat. A violet aroma filled her nostrils. She searched for incense but didn't see an incense burner or vase.

"Sure, little lady. Go ahead." He placed his headset around his neck and handed the radio log to Jada.

Her first thought was to ignore the silly nickname he'd given her. She hated it, and her inner voice said *no way should she engage in this guy's rhetoric today.*

"I think you know my name. It's Jada, and I don't

like being teased about my height. I have no problem with being short." *I wish.* Between her five-foot one height and petite size five figure, people always assumed she was much younger than thirty-two. Jada had coped with being teased during her school years, but she'd reached a breaking point. Now a lot curvier, she often flaunted her bodacious legs in skirts and dresses.

"My bad, *Jada*, I didn't mean to insult you. It's a figure of speech," Antoine said in a flippant tone before raising his hand, signaling a pause. "All right, L.A. It's 8:48 a.m. and you're listening to 101.3 KTLM on your dial. I'm DJ Ant, the Prince of Romance, here to add a little spice to your morning. Next up—one of my favorites by Stevie Wonder—"As" from *Songs in the Key of Life.*

Spice? Calling me little lady didn't add a bit of spice to my morning. Jada briefly watched Antoine out the corners of her eyes, then diverted her attention before he noticed. She flipped through the log, made notes, then altered her stance. *Where did Denise dig up information about his attraction to me?*

Antoine removed his headset and swiveled his chair around to face Jada. He slumped in the chair and crossed one leg over the other. Their gazes met. Without a blink, his eyes ogled her inch-by-inch, from her face to her cleavage and down to her shapely bare legs where they stalled.

He licked his lips. "Can I ask you a question?"

"Depends on what it is." Although her white blouse, hot pink pencil skirt, and gold hoops kicked-butt, Antoine's attention didn't faze her. *If he doesn't stop staring...*

"Why're you so bitter?"

A frown splayed across Jada's face. "Excuse me. What do you mean bitter?"

"I'm just saying," he leaned back in his chair and paused. A bundle of dreadlocks tumbled around his peanut-butter brown face and shadow-beard. "You seem angry, easily agitated, like you're mad at the world."

Jada snapped her chin to her chest. "Sir, you don't know me well enough to make that judgment." *The nerve of him to make comments like that after his buffoonery, which was causing her heart to beat faster, and raising her anxiety level.*

"I don't have to. Your actions expose your feelings." His hazel eyes bored through hers and made her uncomfortable.

"That's your opinion. Bottom line. You don't know me. So, let's end this conversation now," she said, remembering to remain positive. "Have a good day." Jada forced a cheerful smile, placed an orange Post It Note on the log and laid it in his desk tray.

"Uh, huh. Can't stand hearing the truth." With a sly grin on his face, Antoine placed his headphones back on.

Jada maintained a smile and strutted to the door; she threw a palm up and walked out.

Who does he think he is? He has no idea what I've been through. His insensitive behavior will not interfere with me doing my job. I worked too hard to get this position. Just because I'm not stimulating his ego like the groupies who worship him, he's fuming. But that's the least of my worries right now. She rolled her shoulders, released Mr. Antoine's criticism from her mind and walked to the breakroom for coffee.

Chapter 3

JADA

Friday

The aroma of fresh percolating coffee triggered a craving that Jada would satisfy within minutes. She entered the breakroom, poured a cup and added French Vanilla creamer. After that little tit for tat with DJ Ant, she needed to recoup.

Thoughts of how much she and her mom loved coffee brought a pleasant smile on her face. Hazelnut, Caffe Latte, Folgers. Brands didn't matter if the label spelled coffee. Not a day had slipped by without fond memories of her parents, one of which was coffee chats with Momma before they left for work. Those chats varied. Some related to the seventeen debutante gowns her mom and Aunt Dee churned out in less than a month. Or Jada's Best Employee of the Year Award or more personal issues she'd discussed only with her mom. To this day, the void was still present—the pain hadn't ceased.

Two hairy arms clamped her waist, and she flinched. The familiar fragrance of Paco Rabanne cologne, warm breaths, and a kiss on her neck sent clues. She twirled around to Gordan's laughter.

"Guess who?" he asked.

"You scared me." As always, his presence rehashed old memories, and the energy used to avoid the dark-skinned, pretty-boy was ludicrous. At thirty-nine, Gordan was clean-shaven; his physique was impeccable; and he'd devoted the effort to maintain a youthful appearance.

"Sorry, bae. How you doing?"

"I'm okay. But you know what? Stop doing this. We don't want to stir up gossip around this place."

"J, our relationship is old news. Who doesn't know about us dating? Or previously dating?"

"That was then. This is my job, and nobody should see you doing what you just did," Jada pinched his arm. "Why are you here this early anyway?"

"I have a meeting with Griff and Simon at 10:00. My company's buying some spots, and I thought I'd check on you."

"Great. You're giving that deal to Denise, right?"

"Yep, I know she's your buddy. I'm meeting with her first. We're still on for lunch, right?"

Jada sighed. She lifted the coffee pot and refilled the half cup that she'd drank, then added cream and sugar. "I'm not sure. Listen, let's go to my office."

"Word? What's up now? We already agreed on this."

Jada glanced around and pressed an index finger against her mouth. She did a hand gesture toward her office. They walked the long-carpeted hallway lined with framed albums, awards, photographs of famous singers, and disc jockeys, including DJ Ant. They entered her office and closed the door.

She placed the coffee mug on a coaster and sat down. "Give me a minute," she said, while she opened her computer.

Although she'd reached ninety percent of 'relationship breakup' recovery mode, she still cared for the man. Jada often saw Gordan at the station after she was hired full-time. They became friends, and then dated years later. He popped into her life at a dismal time and helped expedite the help she required for generalized anxiety disorder. Smart, mature, fast-talking Gordan Pierce, who worked promotions in the music industry for sixteen years, became the man close to her heart.

Despite the self-promise to move forward, she

missed Gordan's soft lips, the way he touched her body... She shook her head. Their relationship shouldn't have happened, and they both knew better. He had too many ties to the station, too many women he called "just friends."

She jotted notes while fumbling with the silver locket on her chain. Jada glanced up at Gordan who was still standing and now staring in her eyes. "Take a seat. I forgot to ask if you wanted coffee."

"No, I had coffee."

He set his briefcase on top of her desk. "You know... if you break our lunch date, you'll miss out."

Jada paused and pressed a hand against her face. "Miss out on what?"

"Oh, no. I'll wait and ask my question at lunch. Are you going?"

"You must have forgotten our agreement," she slanted her head and looked at Gordan.

He leaned forward. "What agreement?"

"No more dating, Gordan. I'm thirty-two; I don't have time to waste. I plan to start dating other men."

"Bae, I understand, but we talked about lunch two weeks ago and you said yes. It's kinda like you and Denise going out to lunch sometimes."

"Uh, huh, and kinda like you and Evette in Sales going out to dinner?"

Gordan shook his head. "That was all business.

And I still think somebody told you we'd be there. The point is we said no exclusive dating. You know how I feel about you, and what's wrong with us kickin' it occasionally. We're still cool, right?"

Jada opened a window on her computer and started typing. "We'll always be cool. And I said *maybe* to lunch. FYI — this will be our last one. I need to wrap up here first. How long is your meeting?"

"Approximately an hour and a half. You know Griff is a talker; Simon never says much, though. My meeting with Denise shouldn't take long."

"We'll see. Between you and Griff, that meeting might last for hours."

"Not today. I'm going back to the office later."

The station sales manager, Griff was a fast-talking slickster who could strike up a sales deal with his eyes closed, and Gordan wasn't far behind. He'd climbed the corporate ladder fast at his job. Air Mist Record Company delivered on a promise after Gordan's gift of gab won favor with Griff, and Simon, the program director. Free batches of concert tickets as on-air giveaways were fresh honey on the buns for Griff. And a vast raise for Gordan lived at the top of his discussion list for weeks.

After their breakup, Jada decided the short period of friendship and casual dating was not emotionally healthy for her. Nearly a year had flown by when Gordan stopped by her office with concert tickets and an offer for dinner. His impromptu speech on being 'just friends' made sense at that time. She wasn't dating, neither was he, and she missed him. They should have companionship.

But companionship wasn't enough. Casual dating morphed into twice, sometimes three times a month, and then her guilt piled high. She wanted to let go and move on. Now, he was back again, and those old feelings were starting to surge. The ones she'd fought so hard to defeat — healing one day at a time —were all in vain.

The phone rang. Jada noticed the studio red line blinking and buzzing, a signal that Antoine likely had another trick in his shoe. She checked her watch. "He'll have to wait."

"You're not answering?"

"Not now. I must finish what I'm doing before we leave. Text me when your meeting is over. I'll be ready around noon."

"Fine with me. We're going to Roscoe's Chicken and Waffles. Will that work for you?"

Several minutes later, the door flew open. Antoine barreled in with a log in hand and a distorted facial expression.

"I didn't hear you knock," Jada slanted her head.

"I called you." He shifted his gaze to Gordan, then back to Jada before dropping a copy of the log on her desk. "There's a new spot on the log. Why is it there? I'm off shortly, so it should be on Lina's show."

She opened a window on the computer. Using her finger, she scrolled the log against his paper copy. "Confirmed. It's yours." She reached over and dropped it on the edge of the desk. "Address that with Denise, okay? It's her account."

Antoine waved his hand before folding those beautiful tattooed arms that Jada tried her best to ignore. "No, it's not okay. I'm off soon. Can we talk in private, please?"

Jada's eyes bounced back and forth from his face to his arms, back to his face faster than a ping pong match. "Shouldn't you be in the studio?" She asked.

"Don't worry about that. We need to address this issue now."

"Sure, but I can't change anything this late without approval. Try to catch Denise or Griff."

"I tried already. Neither are available," Antoine said.

Thoughts circled in every direction; she'd had enough of him. Jada picked up a pen and pad and scurried toward the door. "Excuse me, Gordan."

She and Antoine walked down the hall; Jada

paused a few feet away from her office. This situation didn't look favorable, and if she needed to sprint away from this fool, she would.

"Okay, explain why this happened," Antoine looked down at Jada.

"Because the client bought an extra spot and that's the time it airs. Look, you know this can happen any time," Jada stared in his eyes. *Don't pretend you don't know that.*

"Well, hip-hip-hoorah for the client, but you should've told me. It's unacceptable to add extra commercials this late."

"Since when? I thought you knew. Denise told you. I added it on the log. Did you check?"

"Yes, when I came in this morning. It wasn't there. Explain why it's there now." He threw his arms up in despair, forming a 'T' with both hands. "Time out, forget it. I don't care to hear your overinflated excuses for not mentioning this in the studio." He moved closer and glared down at her, pointing his finger in her face. "You're trying to sabotage my show."

The fury in Antoine's voice caused a tremor in her small stature. She tried to remain calm but gazing up at a man taller than the sky intensified her fear and anxiety. Jada backed up.

"That's ridiculous. I'm just doing my job." She

wiggled a pen in between her fingers, attempting to simmer down. If she didn't, a fireball would surely escape, and it would be on. He would not disrespect her.

"Well, you *flunk* at your job!" he said through clenched jaws. "This is wrong, and I'm taking it up with the GM." He stormed down the hallway.

He's lucky he walked away. "Yeah, well, go ahead. You should've taken it up with the account exec or Griff, not me," she shouted. Thankful no one overheard their spat, she was more confident now that he'd stepped out of her personal space and added, "and I'm not trying to sabotage your show. I put an orange Post It Note on that log." With one hand on her forehead, she leaned against the wall, inhaling and exhaling to decrease her anxiety until she felt refreshed by the seed of courage in her spirit.

She had to find a better way to deal with that man, but he or no one else would disrespect her.

Chapter 4

ANTOINE

Friday

Taking giant steps with the velocity of a hurricane, Antoine stormed down the hallway. Jada's perpetual defiance caused resentment that festered in his soul, and he didn't like her attitude. This time, her job title wouldn't make a difference, and he would report her to management. This maneuvering of spots, and always on his shift, had to stop.

Antoine paused at Griff's closed door. He knocked, but there was no answer. A few steps down, Kiley was at her desk; he lightly tapped the door and walked in.

"Hey. You know what time Griff or Toni will be in?"

Kiley glanced at him with her usual flirtatious

smile. "Griff won't be in until after 11:00 today. Not sure about Toni, but I'll check," she reached for the phone. "Marisol's probably in by now."

Antoine threw up a hand. "No, no... Forget it. I'm going back to the studio." He did a light jog to make sure he'd be in the studio before Will's newscast ended.

To Antoine's surprise, Lina was sitting in his chair.

She swiveled the chair around and stood. "I didn't think you'd left but figured something came up."

He sat in the chair and grabbed his headset. "I was down the hall. Our traffic director has a stick up her rump again," he said with a frown.

"You and Jada. What happened this time?"

"Nothing. I don't feel like discussing it." He prepared for the commercial breaks and spun his chair around while they ran. "What's crackin', DJ Lina RaShawn? You're here early."

"Yeah, to do studio work." Lina removed her compact and applied hot pink lipstick brighter than the pink glittery blouse she'd worn. She fingered her short red highlighted cut.

"You doing voice overs?"

"Yeah, and a few other things."

"Cool," Antoine gave her a thumbs up.

"I'll be back. Oh...are you busy next Saturday?" She said with a flat expression.

"I'm not sure. What's going on?"

"Some friends of mine are barbequing Saturday. Thought you might wanna tag along."

Shocked by her request, he didn't know how to answer. Lina barely said two words to him at work, now she was asking him to hang out? "Um...I think that's the weekend I go to San Francisco. I'll let you know, though."

"Okay. No worries."

She exited, and Antoine watched until she was out of sight. *Tag along with her? That can't be the Lina I know.* He heard a tap on the door, and Kiley walked in. Dang! Lina forgot to lock the door.

"Uh, I'll be on the air in one minute."

"I know," Kiley tossed her long hair behind her shoulders. "Here's today's schedules for Griff and Toni." She handed him a sheet of white paper with notes and quickly exited the studio.

Why Kiley catered to him so much was puzzling. He was used to the little 'DJ crushes' from time-to-time, which were normal in the business. Those tended to pass with time, but Kiley's seemed to linger. One time, he accepted what she claimed was Starbucks' error of giving her an extra coffee; afterward, she brought in breakfast, fruit, and other snacks until he kindly rejected them, making it clear that he couldn't accept anything from her or drop her off at home when she attended his events. For some reason, she continued to do certain unrequested favors, and he wished she would stop. He laid the paper down next to the mic, placed his headset on, and adjusted the mixing board.

"This is D.J. Ant, the Prince of Romance, and you're listening to 101.3 KTLM radio station. Up next is a special request from Dahlia. ""It's Yours" by Tamia." The paper was missing from the desk. He searched the desk, then the floor. Spotting it near his chair, he bent down, picked up the paper and an orange Post It note was underneath. Jada's note about the log change. "Ah, man!"

Chapter 5

JADA

Jada's office door opened, and Gordan's head popped from behind the door. With the cell to his ear, he said, "I understand. Let me call you back." He scanned the hallway and walked toward the breakroom.

Jada walked out carrying a coffee cup. "I'm on my way," she said, walking toward the office. "A sales exec stopped me in the hall."

"I heard you shouting, but I was talking to my boss. What happened?"

"Sorry about my outburst. It's nothing. Nothing at all," Jada marched inside the office. Gordan followed; he shut and locked the door. She flopped down in the chair. Pressing both hands to her face, she looked at Gordan who stared at her as if he was waiting for an explanation.

"I know that look," Jada said. "I'm okay."

Gordan's involvement in work issues — most definitely the ones concerning Antoine—could not happen. Knowing him, he'd wait outside the studio and approach Antoine about the situation.

Gordan walked over and dropped a hand on Jada's shoulder. "You're upset. Talk to me."

"I said I'm fine. You better go to your meeting. Me and Antoine had a misunderstanding. He's reporting me to Toni. I'm ready to defend myself because I'm right." She picked up her coffee cup and drank some.

"Word?" Gordan frowned, taking a seat in the chair next to Jada's desk. "The general manager. Why is he involving her?"

"Protocol is to meet with Griff first, so I'm sure Toni will inform him of station policies. I know my job."

"Yeah, you work hard." Gordan rolled his wrist and checked the time. "I have some time left; I'll hang around for a minute."

Jada inhaled and exhaled a few more times; the edginess gradually started to subside. She'd learned relaxation techniques and other activities to manage stress and anxiety from her therapy sessions. "I told you I'm okay." She scrolled the log and punched information into the computer. "I wouldn't move the spot; he's angry."

"And you didn't tell him off?"

Jada faced Gordan with a blank look. "Remember, I've changed. I don't do that anymore." She really wished Gordan would leave so she could rejuvenate and finish her work.

"Don't sweat it; forget him. He's new and has some growing up to do."

"Antoine, or *DJ Ant*, is not new. He's been here over a year. Everything was great until they changed his shift to days." She pulled some files from a drawer and sorted through them.

"So that's DJ Ant. I've left him a few promos but never met him. They moved him from nights?"

"Unfortunately, yes." She had worked too hard to restructure her methods of dealing with stress to allow an indignant DJ to ruin her career. Antoine was a tough one.

Gordan walked behind the desk and massaged her shoulders. "Don't forget to practice what you've learned. You can't allow people to upset you. Is that the necklace I bought you?"

"Sure is. The necklace and earrings." She pulled her hair back to give him a full view of the silver earrings. "I still wear them."

Gordan removed his black-framed scripts from his pocket and put them on. He stared at the locket and smiled. Gently lifting it from her chest, he opened and read the engravement out loud, "Locking up my heart. Love, GP." His smile slowly faded as he gazed at Jada. "Memories. We had a really cool thing going on."

He let the locket go and planted kisses on her neck. She paused and closed her eyes. *I should make him stop.* He slipped both hands down the back of her blouse, massaging the tension from her shoulders and back. "I better not hear of him giving you a hard time. I'ma make a quick call, and I'll text you later, okay?" He whispered.

She raised a finger, acknowledging his comments while taking a swig of bottled water to reduce her internal thermostat. *He gives the best massages.* One of the main reasons why she shouldn't go to lunch with him. Gordan knew her strengths and weaknesses quite well; he also knew that his touchy-feely, kissing-the-neck actions never failed to arouse burning desires that sent her prancing straight to his bed. *I need to stop allowing him to do this.* He finished the call, winked at Jada, and stuck the cell in his briefcase before he left.

Several hours later, Jada's phone buzzed and Gordan's message popped up. "Darn." His text would come in the middle of a task. She picked up the phone and texted that she'd walk to the corner shortly. Jada called Kiley, the sales secretary, and left a message on her voicemail. She hustled to the corner to avoid running into any employees who might be going in or leaving the building.

"Don't know about you, but I'm ready to chow down on some Roscoe's," Gordan said after Jada climbed into his gray Nissan Maxima.

"Me, too. I'm taking an early lunch, but the timing is great. I'm starved."

"I forgot you take late lunches. That is if you take one."

"If I take one is right." She fastened her seat belt and put on her sunglasses.

Gordan seemed preoccupied while driving and didn't say much. *Maybe the meeting didn't go well. Maybe... Could that be it?* Their dating anniversary was coming up, and he hadn't mentioned it. Maybe he wanted to. *No, surely, he's not thinking of us getting back together.* Their relationship had been close to perfect — friends for years, a two-year committed relationship, then back to a friendship.

Jada touched his hand. "You okay?"

He nodded.

She glanced at him as he drove, admiring his naturally black wavy hair slicked back in a ponytail. Gordan claimed people swore he was sporting a Jheri curl back in the day. Jada thought about the men in her family who dropped their afros for Jheri curls and tried not to laugh aloud. Long or short, you could have sworn their heads had been dipped in deep fryers, and no one was exempt from the stained shirt collars and jackets.

They arrived at Roscoe's before the heavy lunch traffic streamed in. The environment appeared quiet as the waitress seated them in a booth. They browsed the menu, but Jada already knew what she was going to order—the Obama's Special, one waffle and three wings. Gordan ordered the same.

"So, how's your fast tail sister?" Gordan rubbed his hands together.

"Humph," Jada turned up her nose. "Charmaine can't get her act together. The latest news is Char's job cut her hours, and she's not concerned. Between that and the different boyfriends every two to three months, it's nerve-racking."

"What? She still dating the basketball team?"

"Excuse me, that girl is not dating a team. She dated *two* players from different teams at different times. That's it."

"Yeah, the ones *you* know about. You sure those dudes are not paying her bills?" He chuckled at his own square joke while Jada dismissed him with a hand wave.

"I doubt that, and it's not funny. What I'm trying

to get through to Char is don't depend on anybody for help."

"Yeah, I hear you. Maybe she'll change some day. How's Celine?"

"Celine? She's finishing her bachelor's next year. Still working as an R.N. in the E.R. and dating Darius."

The waiter came over to the table with water, and they ordered meals and drinks.

"We all miss our parents, but Char... I don't know. I think she's still suffering. She was a hardcore daddy's girl."

"I remember you telling me. What's she gonna do when you get married?" he asked with a glow on his face.

Jada paused and stared at Gordan. "To be honest... I don't know. I've never thought about that."

"Why don't you consider selling or renting the house? Then split the profit."

She shook her head. "Why would I? The house will be paid off in a few years."

"Start talking to them about options. You won't be single forever, and the ladies have to get out on their own."

Jada stared at the lemonade. *Sell my parents' house? What is he trying to say?*

"You got them through school; it's your time to live. Am I right or wrong?"

"I guess so." She clamped her face between her hands and pondered. "It's just... you know

living in California is tough. Rent is unaffordable for many people, finding jobs is challenging. With that administration in the White House, who knows what's next? The house is our mainstay."

Jada smiled, "Celine doesn't know this, but I overheard her and Darius talking. I don't know when, but I think they're planning to get married."

"I get it. You're looking out for your sisters. Eavesdropping on your sister's conversation is not cool, though. What if she'd caught you?" Gordan's dreamboat eyes captured her attention, she wished he would hurry up with the question. He could sit here and give advice all day.

"Please. I didn't listen that long. Just needed to know they're moving in the right direction. Momma always said no shacking, and Celine wouldn't do that anyway. Now Char... I'm not sure what she'd do."

"Yeah, your Aunt Dee would cut that off quick."

That was Gordan. His caring and kindness attracted her to him from the day they met. If he could have only focused on work more than women, maybe they're relationship would have lasted.

"How did your meetings go?" Jada asked.

"Very productive. Your girl, Denise hooked us up with good drive-time rates. The Air Mist Record execs are happy." Gordan opened a packet of sugar and added it to his coffee. "This is off topic. Close your eyes and give me your hand."

"For what?" Jada clasped the glass and sipped her lemonade. *This man is always up to something.*

"My question. Remember? Bae, just let me know what you think." His eyes beamed on Jada. "I'm thirty-nine and it's time to dive into this before I change my mind. I'd like your opinion."

Giving him a cautious stare before squeezing her eyelids shut, Jada reached across the table. She fought an urge to sneak a peek before Gordan dropped a small box in her palm. When she viewed the round yellow-gold diamond ring, she clapped a hand to her mouth and gasped.

"Oh, wow!" she said louder than she'd intended.

"So, what's your opinion?"

"It's beautiful!" Jada slipped the ring on her left ring finger, leaped from the booth and hugged his neck. "Why didn't you tell me?" She sat down, extended her hand and stared at the ring. "Good thing I got my manicure this week. And leave it to you to propose in Roscoe's," she rambled on, giggling.

Excited about the proposal, yet ambivalent, Jada had not focused on the sudden change in Gordan's behavior. He kept rubbing his hands together more than usual. He wiped his sweaty face with a napkin. "Bae, can I —"

An older woman turned around from the booth behind them. "Scuse me, did I hear you say he proposed?"

"Yes, ma'am," Jada bent her wrist for the woman to see her ring.

"Young lady, your parents know you gettin' married?" she asked, looking over the rims of her glasses.

Jada sighed. "Mam, I'm thirty-two- years-old." Being 5' 1" and petite, she was often mistaken for a teenager and always asked for I.D. when she entered certain places.

"Thirty-two? I'll say. Chile, I thought you was about sixteen." She smiled, "Congratulations. Hey, y'all, we got a couple over here who got engaged!" She waved a hand toward Jada and Gordan.

The people in the restaurant applauded, some shouted "congratulations" and "woot-woots." A male customer rushed to the table and gave Gordan a high-five and congratulated them. Jada's mocha brown face blushed over all the public attention. Stunned over the sudden proposal, she and Gordan would have to discuss a few issues. They had not been dating exclusively for a year, and now he's ready to walk down the aisle. What happened, and why the rush to get married?

That waitress returned to the table. "Your order should be ready soon."

"Can you please cancel it? We need to leave," Gordan said.

"Sure can. Do you want take out?" the waitress asked Gordan.

"Uh, I don't." Jada gave Gordan a quizzical stare.

"No, thank you."

After the waitress walked away, Jada said, "Why'd you cancel?"

"Listen, we gotta talk. But not here." Gordan reached across the table for Jada's hand. "Come on. Let's take a ride," he glanced around the restaurant. "I changed my mind about Roscoe's."

Chapter 6

ANTOINE

Friday Afternoon

"Man, what do you mean you got into it with the Traffic Director? You've been on your job a split second, now you arguing with employees? You wanna lose your job?" Derrick asked in his best Mickey Mouse vibrato.

"That's what I said." Antoine propped his feet up on the coffee table. "And losing my job won't happen."

"You're gonna lose your head if you don't keep your feet off my table, bro'."

"Sorry, my head is messed up right now." Antoine's feet swung to the floor and he slouched on the couch.

"Mine would be too if I got out of line with a co-worker. But then again..." Derrick swung his head around to face Antoine, "we know that wouldn't happen. Have you slept with her yet?"

"No. Why'd you ask me that crazy question? I barely knew her before they moved my show. Attractive woman, pissy attitude. Like some of the other women I've met in L.A. That's unless they're star-struck on *DJ Ant*."

"I shouldn't have asked. Watch your mouth about L.A. women. They're probably three-fourths of your fans." Derrick rolled his eyes. "I'm talking sex, you're complaining about the woman being pissy. Get Fiona out your system, man." He added mixtures to his blender and turned it on. "You want a margarita?"

Antoine gave him a pointed glare. "No thanks. Where are you digging up these assumptions? Fiona is history."

"Don't get me started. Most straight guys need to keep their zippers closed. You need a little help with unzipping yours. Can't you see what's happening? You're plain cranky 'cause you haven't had a piece lately."

Antoine shook his head. "Would you stop? I don't need a woman to fuel my physical or psychological well-being. I have a boss career and I'm straight."

Derrick's large eyes fluttered faster than a

butterfly's wings, and he continued staring at Antoine.

Antoine clasped his hands behind his head and stared back. "Anyway, how would you know about my sex life?"

"It's not hard to figure out."

Antoine could almost read Derrick's mind. "Believe me, it's not like that. I'm not interested in Jada. I swear on a stack of my favorite books, when the right lady shows up, I'll start dating again. And you'll be the first to know." He paused and crossed his arms. "Okay, she's gorgeous, doesn't wear a ton of makeup either, has a head full of beautiful hair. A bit shorter than I prefer..." *But Jada's finer than fine, and it was hard to take my eyes off her face and shapely legs.*

"And? You're over six feet, and what's her height, three feet?" Derrick opened the dishwasher and began stacking dishes in the cabinets.

Running a hand through his dreads, Antoine sighed. "No, she's not that short; she's not my type. Let's just say we mix like dynamite and a torch lighter." He regretted spilling his guts to Derrick. This was personal. He didn't want Derrick hounding him for more information.

"What can I say? People are different. Ask her out

to dinner. If you two get to know each other, your work relationship should get better."

"That's not possible. The problem is I messed up." Antoine bent forward with both elbows on his knees. "We argued fiercely. I mean we took bow and arrow shots that hurt, and I was hella mad. She didn't mention adding an extra commercial. I later found the orange Post It note she wrote on the floor."

"Uh, huh. That's why you're stressed out. Well, admit it and apologize."

"Heck no. And get my head blown off? I mean, it wasn't all my fault. I was on the air, and she should've talked to me."

His cousin could be brazen at times, and Antoine didn't have qualms about setting him straight. Derrick's nitpicking about orderliness in the house wore him out. With the money he received monthly out of his trust fund, and the added cherry of his wages from the station, he could lease an apartment or buy a home by the beach, but he wasn't ready to own a home in the Bay area and in L.A. It was also too risky. He didn't want anyone to know about his wealth.

"Again, you admitted being wrong. Now tell her. A nice candlelight dinner, glass of wine... Antoine, you've got swag. She'll forget about that argument."

Antoine wagged his finger at Derrick. "Not that simple. And like I said, she's not my type. So, why ask her on a date?"

"Yes, but you have to work with her, and you're not dating. Take my advice. By the way, Uncle Roland left a message for you on my cell. Said he couldn't reach you." Derrick opened a bag of chips and dumped them in a bowl. "I'm getting hungry."

"What's the message about?"

Derrick bit into a chip, crunching and smacking like always. But that was one life-long habit Antoine wouldn't try to correct.

"It's about your townhouse. What else? You don't go up there enough." Derrick licked the salt from his fingertips. "I don't understand you. The Bay Area is still your first home and you love it up there. If you're not working weekends, you're in that stuffy room. Why don't you fly home more often, get with your friends? Have you stopped writing and doing spoken word?"

Derrick's rambling without taking a breath was getting to him. "Other than taking Rashad out to play ball, or hanging with Ellis, hitting the Power of Words Lounge is all I do in Oakland. Pacific Heights is boring, and I'm tired of not seeing black people in my neighborhood. Oh, and FYI, I'm doing a spoken word performance in Fillmore soon."

"That's great. So, if Uncle Roland calls again, I'm saying I spoke with you. He said Aunt Faye's the same."

"I'll call Pop. I have to call Nikki and Joy soon, too."

Derrick lifted his glass and shook his head. "Nikki don't give me crap when I call about Aunt Faye."

Antoine rubbed his shoulders. "You know me. All I want is to hear is Mom's voice and I'm straight." He watched his cousin dip chips in salsa, smack, and sip his margarita.

When his cousin Derrick, a certified public accountant, offered to share his spacious three-bedroom home in Baldwin Hills after his relocation, Antoine gladly accepted. Then the bombshell hit, and he discovered his cousin's affiliation with the LGBTQ community. Not that Derrick being gay bothered him, but that axed plans to hang out with him and meet new women other than groupies.

Derrick's phone rang; he picked it up and hurried to his bedroom. No doubt, it was likely Romero on the phone. Antoine pulled up his father's number on his cell but couldn't bring himself to dial.

An occasional dark mood overshadowed Antoine's quintessential lifestyle when he thought of his mother. The fact that Faye Bailey, the smart, witty music teacher and socialite, battled

Alzheimer's Disease affected him like nothing else in life. After his father's real estate company experienced booming growth, he moved his family from East Oakland to the Oakland Hills. Antoine's fondest memory was his mom's warm hugs when she reassured her kids they'd be okay after the move. At thirteen, all he cared about was missing his school and friends, mainly Ellis Taylor.

When it came to cooking, his mother's couldn't be matched—nor could her eloquent voice—a blend of wisdom and affection. He missed the cherished mother-son discussions about poetry, artwork, and music. Her slow deteriorating memory and health issues changed the family dynamics. Though they vowed to stay by her side, their lives were forever changed, and family no longer had the same meaning.

Derrick walked back in the room and sipped his drink. "Yep, Nikki can be a flip chick-a-dee." He flapped his arms like a chicken and let out a chortle. "I have nothing more to say about her, though. She's my cuz."

"Yes, well, I wish you'd tell your *cuz* to step off me. I can't run back and forth to the east coast very often."

"Uh, I'm out in that situation. Talk to Nikki. Back to Ms. Traffic Director, jump on that before it's too late, and I'm expecting Romero in a couple of hours." He looked at Antoine with a familiar stupefied gaze whenever he mentioned his boyfriend's visits. *Weird.*

A couple of margaritas, and the haughtiness of Mr. Derrick Bailey broke out in full swing. Despite Antoine's disagreement over not being visible when Romero visited, he still loved and respected his cousin like a big brother. Two years his senior, he'd given Antoine some valuable advice over the years.

Antoine picked up the remote from the coffee table and changed the television channel. "Sometimes you're worse than a horny old man," he joked with his cousin.

Derrick lifted the glass to his mouth and slurped like a thirsty animal before chuckling and smacking his lips. "Horny old man? You're the one with no lover."

Antoine chewed his bottom lip and glanced at his giddy-acting cousin. "Right. Well, Romero's not here yet, so I'll chill, then I'm out of here."

"Yeah, and don't pop up until I text you," Derrick winked as he walked to his bedroom with a bowl of chips and the margarita in hand.

Antoine knew what that meant, and Derrick never gave a rational explanation. Seldom was there a variance from the norm, and Derrick's text to his cell chimed at the same time if Antoine wasn't at home in his bedroom. Staring at his watch, it was almost 12:00 p.m. This is when he longed to return to the nightshift. There would be no interferences with Derrick's dates, no dealing with the traffic director, only the sheer enjoyment of entertaining fans. *It's time to buy a television for my room.*

Chapter 7

ANTOINE

Friday

Antoine's transition to rising at 4:00 a.m. for a 6:00 a.m. show required more discipline than he'd expected. Morning runs to the gym decreased from seven days a week to five, and early afternoon naps at times were unavoidable. He rested his head back on the sofa, thinking he'd go to the station and work on several voice overs later.

He watched CNN news, pondering politics and the American government. Derrick popped into his head; his cousin loved to discuss politics. Derrick's ridiculous suggestion that he take more trips to San Francisco seemed irrational. Most of his friends, including Ellis, were married and mingling with them was awkward since he didn't have a girlfriend.

The job opportunity at KTLM came at the perfect

time, so he'd packed up and moved to L.A. That was a chance to break free, start over, and get past the trauma that constantly nagged him. He was over Fiona, but he had an inkling that she may not be over him. His main desire was to cope with the memories of the tumultuous end to their three-year love connection and move forward.

SAN FRANCISCO, CA – 2016

After arriving at Washington-Dulles International Airport, Antoine walked through the security check and removed his tennis shoes, watch, and iPad from the conveyor belt. He glanced at the flight information display system. Great. He would arrive in Los Angeles in time to surprise Fiona and celebrate the last hours of her birthday. He purchased a caramel latte at Starbucks and found Gate 1712.

He unzipped the inner lining of his coat and removed the gray velvet box. A brief concealed view of the two-carat custom made heart-shaped diamond solitaire made his chest swell. Antoine spent more than he'd intended but buying a special ring for the angel in his life meant a lot. His cell chimed. Fiona. He put his Bluetooth on and answered.

"Hey, sweetie. What's happening?"

"Not much. Just waiting for you to come home."

"I know. I'm sorry I couldn't be there earlier. Promise I'll make it up. Do you miss me?"

A moment of silence drifted by.

"Fiona, did you hear me?" He placed the gray box back in his jacket and scanned the area before taking a seat next to a lady with two talkative kids.

"I heard you. You could've called earlier. Where are you? I hear kids in the background."

"Uh, I'm picking up take-out," he turned his back to the woman and her kids. "I asked if you miss me?"

"I always miss you. I just wish you'd cancelled your trip. Weekends alone are no fun."

Visiting his mother was hard, and Antoine could not fathom why Fiona continued to ask to accompany him. The answer was always the same; she was too sick for visitors outside the family. His mother had deteriorated significantly, and each visit created a downward spiral emotionally. And the epitome of evil? His father had the audacity to divorce the sick mother of his children to be with a younger woman.

"Don't worry. I won't be leaving again any time soon. I'll be there tomorrow."

"You're not with another woman, I hope."

He frowned. "Of course not. You know better, plus you reap the rewards from those weekends that I work."

"Babe, you do that by choice. All that family wealth, and you work harder than a poor man."

"Because I love what I do. And you keep recycling old issues. I'm wealthy, but I don't flaunt it. I live a simple life; you know that. I prefer to use some of my money to give back."

Fiona's deep breath seeped into his ear. "Skip it," she said. "I'm not going there, and I'm tired of hearing it. How much you think your people care about you? What they care about is your money."

"No, seriously. Why'd you bring that up again? I want to know."

"Because your mom is ill. I hate that you and your family are on opposite ends. My belief is peace in broken families can happen with effort."

Antoine sighed and stood to see if another seat was available. "Maybe so, but I'm not bending to pacify my family," he twisted his mouth. "I'll keep doing what I want. Listen, I've gotta go. I'll call when I land in LAX tomorrow."

"Yeah, bye."

Clearly, Fiona spoke partial truth, and he could not dispute her practical opinion, but he hated conversations about his family. The once close bond between the Bailey family withered after his mom's health started to decline. He learned the importance of giving back when his mom retained her teaching job in East Oakland after the Bailey Real Estate Group exploded. Antoine's relationship with his father and older sister changed, and if he could figure out how to resolve their conflicts, he would. But the situation was too complicated.

The plane landed in LAX on schedule, Antoine exited the plane and scurried to baggage claim, excited about what was to come. This evening, he would propose to his best friend, lover, and beautiful partner. He picked up a dozen red roses on the way home, but when he pulled into the carport, his brows furrowed. *Why is there another car parked in my slot? Wait... that can't be. I'd know that red Mitsubishi SUV anywhere.*

He pressed a fist against his mouth. "What is Kelvin doing here?"

Antoine parked behind Fiona's Infiniti Q70L and cut off the ignition. With both hands on the steering wheel, his body stiffened as his thinking muddled like scrambled pieces of a jigsaw puzzle. He picked up the bouquet, strutted up the walkway to the elevator, and exited on the third floor. Pausing at the front door, an eerie feeling in his soul said leave. Instead, he slipped the key in the lock and walked in. The pungent odor of incense and sex attacked his gut, then nausea set in. The bedroom door was ajar. He heard the loud moans of a man. A woman's moans. And then a man's voice echoed from the bedroom. Fiona's voice echoed from the bedroom. Antoine kicked the door all the way open and balled up his fist so tight his nails dug into his palms.

Fiona screamed and pulled the covers to her chin; his

friend Kelvin jumped out of bed. "What are you doing here?" Fiona asked.

Antoine flared his nostrils. "I live here. Or did you forget? So, you missed me, huh?" He threw the flowers at her. "Happy Birthday, Liar."

Kelvin searched beneath the covers for his underwear. "Bro, I'm sorry. I swear I am," he hastily put on his clothes.

"Yeah, bro', you're sorry all right. Both of you are scum," Antoine shouted. "If you value your lives, leave. And be quick about it."

"No, Antoine, listen to me. I was lonely. This was a mistake, I swear. I love you," Fiona slipped on a sundress and fingered her long hair in place. "This was the first time; it won't happen again."

While Kelvin scuttled out the door, Fiona ran to Antoine and threw her arms around his neck. He shoved her against the wall.

"Don't touch me," he shouted. "You slept with my friend. You think I'm gonna fall for your crooked lies?"

"Antoine... Honey," Fiona cried out, "let's talk about this please. I'm so sorry."

He squinted, "Talk about what? It's over. I want you out of here."

"All right, you're angry," Fiona flipped her hair over her shoulders. "I... I thought you had another woman. You're gone a lot. What else was I supposed to think?"

Antoine frowned. "Oh, so you're trying to accuse me of cheating?"

"I, uh... no." She pushed her fingers to her temples. "But—"

"You're wrong. And why my friend Kelvin? I wasn't good enough for you? Or was he a better lover than me?"

"Stop! Antoine, it just happened."

He bum-rushed Fiona and shoved her on the bed. "You think he's a better lover? I'll show you better."

With his feet spread apart, he glared at Fiona. "Take off your dress," he said in a calm voice.

"What for?"

"I said take it off," he yelled.

"No."

He grabbed the front of her dress.

"No, stop it," she slapped his hand away. Antoine ripped the dress down the front and tousled to get it off. Kicking, she screamed, "You're hurting me."

Antoine froze. He realized he'd lost control and let go of her arm. He jumped from the bed and looked up at the ceiling, uttering a prayer. "Dear God, please forgive me." Returning his gaze to Fiona, he paused before he spoke. "You're not worth it."

Fiona wrapped a throw blanket around her shoulders. "I said I'm sorry. What more do you want?" She asked in a steel tone.

"A woman who'll be loyal. Not one time have I ever

slept with another woman during our relationship." He unzipped his coat pocket and pulled out the gray box and opened it. "You see, this is how serious I was about us. Did my love mean anything to you?"

Fiona's head dropped to her chest as a flood of tears streamed down her face. Her nonchalance about cheating ticked him off, and Antoine was afraid the boiling rage would return. He paced back and forth, feverishly contemplating his options. Kick her out or leave and cool down. Ellis. He had to talk to his friend. Removing his cell from his pocket, he said, "Siri, call Ellis."

Ellis answered, "Hey, Champ, what you been up to?"

"Man, I need you. Now." Still pacing, he said, "Get over here pronto before I hurt somebody. I'll explain later." He tossed Fiona a funky glare before punching the wall, and then rushed out of the apartment.

"Ant. Ant, wake up," Derrick shook Antoine's shoulder.

"Hey, hey." He sat up and rubbed his eyes. "I passed out. What time is it?"

"It's time for you to leave. Romero is on his way."

Somewhat annoyed, Antoine was relieved the dream had ended. He put on his jacket and grabbed his car keys from the table. Before he could get to the door, the doorbell rang.

Antoine opened the door to Romero's permanent smiley face.

"Well, hello! Long time no see," Romero said.

"Yeah, talk to Derrick about that. I'm out."

Chapter 8

JADA

Friday – Santa Monica, CA

Gordan parked near the Santa Monica Beach pier. Before they left the car, he licked his thick lips and pulled Jada to his chest. They kissed for what seemed like forever. After the kiss, he hugged her so tight she could hardly breathe. The engagement. This moment was truly amazing, but her uneasiness had not subsided. And kissing in the car like two puppy love high-school teenagers? *This is so not Gordan.* He was a private person. There had to be something on his mind that he needed to discuss.

They held hands and went into one of their favorite restaurants on the pier. Jada enjoyed the ocean view while they immersed in a 'free-the-mind' conversation during lunch. Strange. At one point, Gordan stopped talking, but she re-engaged further with other topics to keep their communication going. During the conversation, Gordan kept losing focus and forgetting what he intended to say. Jada doubted work or personal problems was the reason for his change in behavior.

A waitress with a slight limp balanced a tray on one shoulder, delivering luscious Cajun shrimp, a salmon salad and corn on the cob to their table. The food smelled and looked tasty. Having polished off a half glass of raspberry iced tea, Jada could only eat a few bites of the meal. After their meal, they strolled the deck gazing at boats as they sailed. The blue waves rippled along the edge of the sand and fizzled down to foam offering a romantic atmosphere and profound relaxation. Jada glanced at Gordan. This was the perfect time to dig into his head.

She ran her hands through her hair and leaned against Gordan's arm. "Baby, you know what? This proposal caught me off guard. I think it's best to have an extended engagement. What are your thoughts?"

"Yeah, bae, I know," he said with a dry voice before shifting his attention to the sea. His gloomy mood continued to baffle her. *This man proposed to me. He should be in sheer bliss, ready to jump over the moon.*

Throughout their time together, she sensed Gordan had the kind of tension she'd experienced after stressful events in the past. The difference was Gordan would always be open to discussing his concerns, and he managed stress effectively. He referred her to a family friend who was a therapist to help her learn to do the same. After counseling, she'd adapted to utilizing better coping skills.

They sat down on a bench, and she placed her hand on Gordan's. He didn't move or speak. "All right. I'm asking again. Are you okay? If not, it's time to ante up and throw the dice," she joked, hoping he would laugh or smile. He didn't.

He rubbed his hands together. "I'm not okay. I've got something important to say and it's embarrassing and crazy."

She looked into his eyes. "Honey, talk to me," she squeezed his hand. "What is it?"

"I should've told you at Roscoe's, but the good ol' Cheer Team revved up." He licked his lips. "Bae, I'm sorry. The ring is Kiley's. I plan to ask her to marry me. I wanted your opinion of the ring."

The bottom dropped out of her world, and Jada's forehead crinkled. Her mouth twisted. It felt like she'd been kicked in the chest. The heat in her body started rising as her eyes widened. "Kiley? Not Kiley Henson at KTLM?"

"Yeah, that Kiley."

Before his lips parted, she whacked his face with a palm and jumped to her feet.

"So, you've been taking me out and seeing Kiley, too?"

Appearing dazed, he frowned and pushed a hand against his face. "Was that necessary? We need to talk."

"No!" Jada waved her hands. "I don't wanna hear it." She twisted the ring off and threw it at him. "Take your ring," she said with tight jaws. He tried to catch the ring as it bounced off his chest and hit the ground. "How could you do this to me?"

"Do what? You got this twisted. I didn't ask you to marry me. Just your opinion of the ring." He picked up the ring and placed it inside his jacket pocket.

"My opinion?" she screamed. "You brought me out here for lunch, smooches in the car, and now you wanna ask my opinion of another woman's ring? You must've lost your dang mind."

Gordan looked around before standing up, then he stepped in front of her face. "It's not what you think," he said in a calm tone. "Would you calm down? Listen...instead of putting our business in the street, let's go to the car."

"I'm not going anywhere with you!" Jada shouted. "For all I care, the whole freakin' world should know.

Now leave me alone. I'm calling for a ride." She pulled out her cell and started dialing.

Multiple people walked past, turned their heads and started whispering. Several others stopped, watching the action like they were Jay Z and Beyoncé – center stage attractions.

"Don't do this, J. Let's go somewhere and talk." Gordan tried to grab her phone.

Jada jerked her hand away. "No."

"You ended our relationship last year. Why would you expect a ring?"

Jada popped a fist to one hip. "I didn't. You dropped the ring in my hand. You wouldn't leave me alone. All that talk about companionship, missing me, and remember our last date? We made love in your bed. But you know what? I wouldn't have married you anyway," she snapped.

"Whoa, that's cold," a young man laughed, covering his mouth. Additional people with curious stares delayed their walks, lingering nearby. The whispers started to grow, but Jada didn't care. In her mind, the more who listened, the better.

Gordan gave the young man an evil eye and glanced over the small crowd. "And what is everybody looking at? Mind your own business and keep it pushin'," he said with an irritated voice.

Jada narrowed her eyes, "Kiley should be here; not me."

"I was wrong, okay? You're my confidante, J, my best friend. This is about more than just the ring. Give me a chance to explain what's going on."

"That's unacceptable."

"Word?" he extended his hands. "You won't give me five minutes?"

"Can't you understand?" Jada pressed a hand against her face. "I don't owe you five minutes."

Gordan had no idea how she felt. If she could only make him feel a piece of her pain. She used deep breathing to try to keep it together, but her conscious mind said no. She needed to leave. She placed her Bluetooth in her ear and started walking down the pier. What had she done to deserve this kind of treatment? She was such a fool.

Gordan ran after her and clutched her from behind, lifting her off the ground. "J, I still love you."

"Stop it. Let me go," she yelled.

He held on to her. "Give me a chance to explain."

"Take your hands off me." She attempted to pry his arms from her waist and dropped her purse and cell phone. They wrestled as she struggled to get away, until Gordan let go.

Wiping away tears, Jada squatted to pick up her cell and threw several items back in her purse. She scurried down the pier. "Go on. Be stubborn," Gordan yelled at her. "I had your back, stuck by your side to get you past this kinda behavior. No matter what, I'll always love you."

"Bull! Love's not supposed to hurt," she shouted back, walking even faster.

"You lost control. All that counseling for nothing. Be reasonable, J," he pleaded.

Keeping her pace, Jada didn't answer. No matter how much he begged and attempted to rationalize at this point, it didn't matter. Jada's mind was full of conflict and unanswered questions. Not the right place to be. Although she'd exploded with just cause, she knew walking away would've been a better solution. Sure, she wanted marriage and kids, but not with Gordan. The gall of him to do what he did was what hurt. She'd conquered old weak points, but violence wasn't one. This time, her 'act first, think later' action overpowered sound judgment.

Jada tried Celine's cell twice. Why she hadn't answered or texted back was a concern. This was her day off, and she never failed to get back to her immediately unless she was on duty in the Emergency Room. Desperate to quickly escape Gordan, Jada initially hadn't given a thought to how she'd get back to the radio station. Now, she'd have to call Uber, which meant a chunk of money she couldn't afford or call her last resort, Charmaine. She texted Griff that she'd gone to lunch and would be back in an hour, and then looked back. Gordan had stopped following but stood in one place watching her from afar.

Walking until she could no longer bear the discomfort of her aching feet, Jada stopped and kicked off her heels. She carried them in her hands, and after a few minutes, she glanced behind. No Gordan. But in her distraught state, she had forgotten to check her text messages and her phone was on silent. Charmaine had texted saying she'd be here in twenty minutes. Knowing her sister, she hoped that was true. Jada responded to Charmaine, found a bench and sat to rub her feet. She laid her black heels on the bench. "This really sucks. Our relationship was over. Why did I believe this friendship would work?"

Dating after their breakup was the biggest mistake she'd ever made, but Gordan should have confessed about Kiley long before today. There was no way she'd give him the benefit of explaining this catastrophe.

Chapter 9

JADA

Friday Afternoon

Jada tugged the collar of her blouse up to her chin attempting to block a spritz of ocean air that grazed her face. The weather had cooled down, but she had not. *Huh. Accidently giving me a ring that was Kiley's. What was he thinking?* Not in the mood for Gordan's pitiful excuses, she ignored his barrage of calls and texts while waiting for Charmaine. What was taking her so long when she claimed to be twenty minutes away? Jada heard a car horn and stood, quickly strutting in the direction of her sister's white Kia.

She opened the door and climbed inside. "It's about time."

"Aww dry up! I told you I'd be here."

"Yes, in twenty minutes. Not an hour later. I could've called an Uber."

"Traffic jam. Why'd you let Gordan bring you here, anyway? Thought you were over that loser. He's nothing but a playa." Charmaine tossed her honey-blond weave over her shoulder.

"I can't talk about him now. Drive and be quiet."

"Look. You called me to drive wa-a-a-y over here. Do yourself a favor and listen to me. Gordan is scum."

Jada dismissed her sister with a wave. "Yeah, yeah. You giving me advice about men is a joke. I called you because I couldn't reach Celine."

Charmaine dug her foot in the pedal, swerved around the corner and slammed on the brakes.

"What the heck are you doing? Trying to kill us?" Jada's heart raced; she started wagging her foot. *Remember, cool down. She wants to agitate you; don't act like the fool she is.*

"No. I did it to make a point. You should be grateful I'm here."

"Grateful? Is that what you think after you took your sweet time? It's cold out here, and

I was in severe distress. You know I can still call an Uber." Jada sighed, rummaging through her bag for her phone.

"Sissy, throw the cell back in your bag. I'm here now."

Charmaine opened a pack of Doublemint and removed a stick of gum. She tossed the wrapper out the window, and then rolled the window all the way down before resting her arm on the door. "Where you wanna go?"

Jada agonized over the pop, pop of Charmaine's bad gum cracking habit. It was so ghetto. "I'll tell you what... take me to the station."

Charmaine gunned the engine. "Why'd he leave you stranded? That was stupid. And taking an Uber home? You'll be broke."

"I said I'm going back to work," Jada raised her brow.

"Huh, you're not going to the station with those red-bull eyes. If you know what's best, stay your behind in this car. I wouldn't wanna hear about some crazy dude snatchin' you up while you're waiting on an Uber."

Jada twisted her lips and tried to avoid laughing. She rested her head against the headrest, "Girl, shut up! I'm not in the mood for laughing."

"What?" Charmaine shot a glance at Jada. "Do it. You wanna laugh; let it roll, 'cause you won't be laughing when that Charles Manson looking guy is after you."

Jada covered her mouth to stifle the laughter but let out a holler, and Charmaine did the same. One thing her baby sister had was the gift of humor. Like their father, Charmaine had a plethora of humor underneath her steel armor that could bring cheer to anybody's bad day. After all they'd been through with losing their parents, Jada understood her sister's pain. But she wished that she could get through to her sister and help her see what to expect in the real world when she's on her own. Charmaine would need to grow up and be responsible someday. Jada blew out a huge sigh and told Charmaine about her argument with Gordan.

"Sis, I'm sorry. I know you're hurting right now. Oooh...he's a dog. I would've slapped him so—"

Jada waved her hand. "Don't say that."

Charmaine stopped at a red light, cracking gum so loud, it would've been hard to hear an ambulance or a police siren. She tipped her head to the side and glanced at Jada.

"What?" Jada asked.

"What'd you do?"

"Shush! I can't talk about it."

"You got pissed and told that brother off, I bet. I know that look."

"I–I didn't mean to. It's just..." Jada rubbed the back of her neck. "Kiley and marriage in the same sentence made me snap. Before I knew it, I'd slapped him, but it wasn't intentional."

"You hit him? Girl, are you nuts? I was just joking when I said slap him."

She gazed at her sister, then shifted her eyes to the streets, pondering on the mess she'd made of the whole situation.

"No, I'm not nuts. I made a mistake."

"Yeah, you sure did." Charmaine rolled her eyes. "Wasn't therapy about change? You can't hit people. What if he'd hit you back?"

"I get heated at times, but therapy really helped. I've never hit *anybody* until today. And that's bothering me."

"How're you gonna move on? You said he's at the station a lot, and that wacky Kiley is there."

"Don't remind me. This was my fault because I started going out with him again. When we broke up, that should've been the end. No communication, no friendship. Let me tell Celine about this, okay?"

"I'm not saying a word. You sure you wanna go back to work? Tell your boss you need to leave."

"Nope, work is calling my name. I have to finish my day."

Charmaine parked in front of the station, and Jada gave her a hug before reaching for her purse. "Thanks, Sis." She opened the door, and a letter fell from the side pocket on the passenger side. Jada picked up the envelope and frowned. "What's this doing in the car?"

"What is it?"

"Mail for me from some real estate company. Probably advertisement."

"Oh, I'm sorry. I was on my way out one day and picked up the mail. Checked through it and stuck yours in there."

Jada stuffed the envelope inside her purse. "Be careful about that. If bill notices are missed, it could mean utilities get cut off. See you later."

As much as Jada hated returning to work, she did. She eased in the lobby door of the radio station and glanced around before powerwalking to the bathroom with a bottle of Visine in hand. Maybe she should've given Gordan a chance to explain. But Kiley and Gordan? Jada could swear that half the time that woman's head was on backward.

She exited the restroom and headed to her office. She shoved her purse inside the desk drawer and sat still for a moment, trying to clear her head. After that catastrophe, she was hopeful she'd be able to finish out the day.

Rosa, one of the account executives, entered her office. "All right, missy, do you mind informing Kiley when you leave for lunch? I've been hunting you down about the O'Connor account. They want additional air time."

If she only knew what I feel like telling Kiley. "I left Kiley a message. You know I don't go out much. Too *bogged* down here. Why didn't you text me?"

Rosa shrugged. "No biggie, but please save them a slot in prime time. I'm leaving to get contracts signed now."

"Call me after they're signed. You know I can't save slots."

"I can't even get a favor, Chica?" Rosa smiled.

"I'm doing my job and being fair," she said to Rosa's back as the woman jetted out as fast as she'd entered the office.

Griff walked in with a harried expression. "Oh, you're back! Can we meet briefly? In say...ten minutes."

"Will do."

"Uh, I need you to print up a log and bring it with you."

Not waiting for a reply, he swarmed out of the room faster than a scared rabbit. Between him and Rosa, anybody would swear they drank energy drinks all day. Before she could walk to his office, two more account executives popped in back-to-back with new commercials and changes. This was not the best day for the mad rushes. Charmaine was right. She should've called Griff and said she was leaving early today, but Jada was too dedicated to leave her boss in a rut. Hopefully, this meeting would be short.

After her meeting with Griff, Jada had three more hours, and she would call it a day. She walked past the sales office and noticed two account executives at their desks. With most of the sales execs out of the office, she should wrap up on time. She went to the lounge to get water before returning to her office, and rammed into Antoine as she walked in.

He caught Jada in his arms and broke her fall. "Ooops! I'm sorry. You okay?"

"Yeah, thank you. I guess I was walking too fast." Jada pushed her hair away from her face.

"Actually, it was my fault. I wasn't paying attention," he said with a glistening smile.

"No, really, it's not a problem."

Antoine looked around. "Are you busy?"

Okay what does he want now? "Yes, I am. Can I help you with something?"

He pulled his earlobe. "No, but can I stop by your office? Uh, it doesn't have to be now. But before you leave."

Jada filled a paper cup with Sparkletts water. "Sure, but listen... I'm off at five o'clock. So, if it's about work, can it wait until tomorrow morning?"

"I wouldn't say it's directly related to work, and it'll only take a few minutes. I promise."

Jada was surprised by his request after the squabble they'd had earlier.

He pointed at the Sparkletts bottle. "You drink that water?"

Jada lifted her brows and shrugged. "Occasionally, if I forget my own. Why?"

Antoine let out a chuckle and crossed his arms. His striking tattoos seized her attention again. "Hey, I'm sorry. I guess it's just me. Drinking from that bottle is like drinking from a public fountain. You know... people touching the spout. Potential bacteria."

"What?" Jada giggled as she poured the water down the sink and threw the cup in the trash. "I hadn't thought about that. I'll finish up in a few hours. It's okay to stop by around 4:30."

He nodded, and Jada watched him walk away. *What's up with D.J. Ant? This certainly isn't the same man I clashed with earlier. He must've consumed a magical drink or stopped by an early Happy Hour for lunch.*

Later, she placed a stack of papers in a folder on her office desk and prepared to leave. After a light knock at the door, Antoine opened it. "Am I too late?"

"No, come on in."

"I was afraid I'd missed you." He closed the door.

"I'm leaving soon, what's up?"

He walked over to the desk and handed her a Dasani bottled water and a manila envelope. "This is for you. I apologize for the way I acted earlier. That's not who I am." He rubbed the side of his face. "I've been tired lately, but that's no excuse for my behavior. I found your note, so that was my oversight."

"Apology accepted. We all make mistakes, and I should've confirmed that you saw the note." She opened the envelope and pulled out an eight by ten card with purple flowers on the front and a handwritten poem inside. Jada pushed her fingers to her jaw. "Did you write this?"

"Yes. I create poetry when time permits. I thought about an apology letter. Changed my mind."

"Nah. This is way better. It's the most beautiful poem I've ever read. Thanks for this and the water. How long you been writing?"

Antoine sat across from her. "Forever. I have a niche for creative arts, so that's where my time goes. Well... not entirely," he laughed. "I volunteer for Big Brothers too."

"Volunteer work? That's interesting," she opened

the water and sipped. "How long have you done that?"

"Six and a half years. My bond with the kid I mentor is awesome. Relocating here was hard, he didn't want a new mentor. I told him I'd try to get up to Oakland about once a month so we could hang out."

"Oakland. Is that your hometown?"

He folded one leg over the other. "Yes, it is."

"Mentoring kids can really make a difference. I used to be a reading tutor for elementary school kids. Between my job and personal life, it was too much."

"What counts is you tried. That's why I volunteer for Big Brothers. I believe in giving back. So many kids need role models to look up to, especially in our communities. Listen, have you eaten dinner yet?"

"Not yet."

"Why don't we go somewhere to eat...talk...chill?"

She looked at him with a wary expression. "You asking me out?"

"Unofficially, I guess so. I'm hungry, and I'm sure by now, you're hungry, too. Correct?"

She nodded. "Starved."

"You like seafood?" He pushed his dreads back and bit his lower lip.

"Seafood is one of my favorites."

"Well, let's bounce."

Jada touched her jaw with an index finger. This wasn't a good idea. How could she go out with this man? They couldn't stand each other, had come close to blows this morning, and now they were going out for dinner. This was insane.

"I–I'm sorry...I can't. I need to go home."

Antoine's smile faded. "We're just going to eat. Come on, I feel bad about what happened. I owe you."

Jada pondered his offer as she shut down her computer and gathered her belongings.

"Two hours. I know you're tired, and I have to be in the studio by 5:00 a.m. What do you say?"

Jada gazed into his hazel eyes, recognizing sincerity and kindness in a man who truly wanted forgiveness. Honestly, Antoine and Gordan had crushed her spirit, and she didn't feel up to dinner, talking, or anything else after two eventful altercations, but maybe this might officially end their feuds.

"I must say... you're sharp at persuasion. I'm going to the bathroom to freshen up, then I'll be ready."

Chapter 10

JADA

Jada entered her car and waited for Antoine to reach the end of the block. They had agreed that driving their own vehicles would avoid rumors in case someone saw them together. The time interval gave her a chance to rethink their date. Maybe she should call and cancel. She picked up her phone and remembered she didn't have his number, and then texted Celine to cancel the return call. She threw the phone on the seat and pondered over barely knowing this man. Did she really want to go out with Antoine?

At Harold & Belle's, Antoine paid the valet for both cars. *Impressive.* They walked into a jovial crowd of people who were laughing and socializing. Thank God. This was far from a romantic setting, and the presence of other people would provide a haven.

After being seated at a table, the waiter handed them menus.

"Have you eaten here before?" Antoine asked.

"A few times. The food is tasty. I live close by, and I've had dinner here, or picked up takeout."

"Well, that's convenient. How about a glass of wine or whatever you prefer?"

Jada shook her head. "I'm fine with water. A drink might spoil my appetite."

After placing their orders, Jada scanned the restaurant. People poured in either coupled up or in groups. A little on edge, she mulled over what to say. Within seconds, the waitress broke their awkward silence, bringing a glass of water for Jada and red wine for Antoine.

"Should we do cheers to a new friendship?" He asked lifting his glass.

Jada lifted her glass. "Sure, no more feuding."

Antoine sipped his wine. "So, tell me something about Jada."

She shrugged. "What do you wanna know?"

"Whatever you feel like sharing." He removed a windbreaker, exposing his tattooed arms.

Jada fought hard to prevent her wandering eyes from focusing on those gorgeous arms and his dimpled smile. "Uh, I'm from L.A., graduated from Dorsey High School..." She went on to tell him about losing her parents in an airplane crash and how she'd cared for her teen sisters while finishing college. She also told him she'd started her internship with the radio station while she was doing her undergrad degree in Communications at Pepperdine University, and from that experience, she was hired full-time.

"Back then, I wanted a job as a newscaster. After the internship at KTLM, I knew the radio station was where I belonged."

Antoine listened attentively. "Yes, radio broadcasting is boss. Our station reaches so many people in urban communities, that's the main reason I love my career. It's powerful." He pressed a finger to his temple. "I'm sorry to hear about your parents. Seems like you've been through a lot, finishing college must've been a challenge."

"It was, but I survived, and a year ago, I broke up a bad relationship." Jada pushed a strand of hair behind her ear. "I'm stronger, and that's what survival is about." *Survival is also getting past the catastrophe with Gordan today.*

"True. I haven't been through trauma like yours, but I have experienced a few hard knocks here and there. My philosophy is we've got to keep on living. I'm writing a book about healing and survival. Up until I was thirteen, my family lived in East Bay,

Oakland. I grew up in a two-parent home with two sisters and one inherited older brother."

"Inherited older brother?" She chuckled and cupped her chin.

"He's actually my cousin, but more like a brother. My parents adopted him after my aunt passed away."

"That was kind of your parents. Where did you go to college?"

"UC Berkeley. And guess what? My major was Communications and Media studies, then I attended Columbia for a Master's in Journalism. But...that didn't settle well with my father, though." He tapped his fingers on the table. "Pops went from selling insurance to real estate; after his business prospered, we moved out the hood, and he made it clear that all the kids should work for his business. Only one of us did. My mom is...uh, I mean *was* a music teacher. She's retired."

"Mmm...Columbia and Berkeley. Impressive," Jada took a sip of her water. "No desire to follow your father's footsteps? Take part in his business?"

His shoulders dipped slightly; he gazed at his wine glass for a second and then at Jada. "Selling real estate wasn't my niche. Fresh out of Columbia, I stayed in New York, worked in the corporate world a couple of years until the right break came along. When an opportunity at a radio station popped up, my career took off." He picked up his wine glass and sipped. "I guess I can say I'm fortunate. What I do for a living is cool and I love it. I'm a spoken word poet and I play music. I've written six poetry books, and I'm out in the community giving back. Oh, and I told you about Big Brothers."

"Yes, you did. Kudos on Big Brothers." She leaned forward. "Six poetry books?" What kind of poetry do you write?"

"Mostly spoken word," he pushed a finger to his temple. "It flows naturally. I use a few notes, sometimes none, when I speak. I write page poetry for publications, and this year, I was offered a book deal for a nonfiction book. But I need to finish it before they cancel my contract." He laughed.

"Wow. Your memory bank must be vast. Which poetry is your preference?"

"Well...think about it this way. Many people are great listeners but reading and writing doesn't stimulate everybody in the world. To me...spoken word bridges the gap between written poetry and storytelling. I love seeing people's reactions at my spoken word sessions. It's priceless."

"Makes sense. I'm a music lover, and I love reading fiction books."

"What a coincidence," Antoine sucked his

bottom lip and pointed at Jada. "We share too much in common to be battling like wild animals."

A smile crossed Jada's face. "Those days are over. Do you agree?" She lifted her glass, and he lifted his, and they clinked them together once more.

"I agree. And no more poking your tongue at me."

Jada's mouth dropped open; her face flushed. "You saw me do that?"

"Yep," he chuckled. "Watch what you do behind people's backs."

She cast her gaze at her glass and back at him. "I'm sorry. I was wrong," Jada sipped her water. That smile on his flawless face, the dimples, those arms... Spellbinding. How her opinion of him had switched so rapidly carved a question mark in her mind. Maybe it was the experience of his mellow side or the offer to end their silly quarrels.

"No. Seriously, I was on a gripey binge for a minute, so I deserved the hits. I'm glad we had this opportunity to get to know each other better."

She didn't know whether this date would just tie up the ripped cords or lead to something extra special. After dinner and several hours of sharing information, laughing, and enjoying each other's company, Jada had a feeling this wouldn't be their last date.

She pulled up in her driveway much later than

planned and parked her black Honda Civic behind a yellow Corvette. *Now, whose car is this?*

"Wait, don't get out yet." Charmaine yelled from the porch. "We're leaving." Standing behind her was a tall lanky man Jada had never seen before.

"Well, come on," she huffed. "I'm ready to go inside and please park on the street next time."

"Yes, ma'am," the young man opened the door for Charmaine.

Charmaine waved to Jada. "Be back later."

Jada started her car and backed out of the driveway until Charmaine and her guest pulled away. She drove back into her spot. Once inside, she entered the living room and threw her purse on the couch and headed for the kitchen. "So, who's the new guy and where are they going at this hour?" she asked Celine.

"Maybe out to eat... they didn't eat here," Celine poured French dressing on a salad.

"That girl dates too many new men. I told her once and I'll tell her again, I don't want guys running in and out of here like we're running a brothel." Jada uncovered a steamy pan of sizzling hot chicken. "Mmm...Chicken Marsala. Thanks for cooking. You're eating late."

"Yeah, I got some studying done and decided to cook later. Who'd you go out with, Gordan?" Celine sat her food on the table and poured a glass of apple juice.

"Nope. I went out with DJ Ant. AKA Antoine Bailey."

"What?" Celine jutted her chin. "After all the chaos with him?"

Jada sat next to her sister. "Girl, that's what I told myself. He apologized from the heart, then asked me to dinner, so I accepted. This evening was unbelievable," she shook her head. "I couldn't believe he was the same man. We talked nonstop. I still don't know where the time went. Oh, and I also went to lunch with Gordan earlier. You didn't call me back"

"My classmate picked me up for a study group, and I left my phone at home." Celine dropped her fork in the plate and wiped her mouth. "Sissy, don't tell me you two are together again."

"Nothing like that. You won't believe this; he gave me an engagement ring." Jada informed Celine about what happened. As she explained, a frown spread across Celine's face.

"He finally said the ring wasn't yours? That man is simple and outrageous. Why did he leave Roscoe's and not tell you?"

Jada flipped her hand. "Who knows. He said he was sorry, but I'm done. Char picked me up and took me to the station. I haven't answered his calls. I sent him a text and told him to skip my office whenever he's at the station."

Celine clapped Jada's palm. "Way to go, girl. I would've done the same. Shoot. Don't you dare renege either. Sorry I didn't get your call earlier," she scooped up another forkful of food. "How could he date you and another woman at your job? That's shoddy."

"Yeah, it is. This takes me back to Momma's old saying of when you call it quits, it's over, and no second helpings." They both laughed.

"Momma and her catchy words," Celine said.

"I'm going to bed. Goodnight." Jada went back to the living room, picked up her purse, removed the letter and read it. "What the... Oh, no. Celine, come here." She flopped on the couch.

Celine walked from the kitchen holding her plate and glass. "What is it?"

Shaking her head, Jada held out the letter to Celine. Celine placed her plate and glass on the coffee table and reached for the letter. She eased down on the edge of the sofa as she read it. "This can't be true. They're evicting us in six months. Why?"

"I can't say. We're paying the rent on time. And the letter is dated over thirty days ago." Jada paused and touched her forehead. "You know what...that letter was in Char's car all this time."

Celine handed the letter back to Jada, exhaled an exasperated breath and dropped her head. "Over twenty-one years as a tenant and they're kickin' us out the dress shop? We can't afford to move. How will we find another reasonable location?"

"No, this is unfair. We're not moving," Jada threw the letter on the table. "Overhill Drive is a prime area. If we lose our site, we lose clients. I don't know how, but we'll fight this." She turned to Celine, "Let's not say anything to Aunt Dee until later."

Celine nodded. "I agree. She'll get all stressed, and that shouldn't happen."

Chapter 11

JADA

Saturday Morning

Loud Reggae music forced Jada from the sofa. She had dozed off while watching the news or attempting to watch the news, while mulling over the eviction notice. She tied her robe and trudged to the window to see who was disturbing the peace at almost 1:00 a.m. Charmaine exited the yellow Corvette that she'd left in earlier.

Jada opened the door, and Charmaine walked in. "Was that you at the window spying on me again?"

"Why would I spy? I met the strange guy you left with earlier. I assumed you'd come home with him."

"Funny." Charmaine flipped her long weave over her shoulders. "So funny I'm not even laughin'. Where's Celine?"

"She's in her room. We need to talk."

"Only a minute 'cause tomorrow's my workday, and I'm tired." Charmaine slithered onto the couch and pulled off her large gold hoops, dropping them on the coffee table.

Jada sat at the end of the couch and shot Charmaine a stare that should've made her duck for cover. "You don't leave for work until late afternoon. We're talking right now. First, please tell your dates to keep the music down. We don't want the neighbors calling the police."

"Okay. Anything else?"

"Yes, a lot more. That mail you forgot to give me a month ago? It was related to the dress shop. We may lose the lease, and now we have less time to settle this."

"Well dang, calm down, Sissy," Charmaine lifted her hand. "I'm sorry, okay? It's not the end of the world."

"Really?" Jada snapped. Then she paused, reminding herself to think before saying something that would cause a backlash. "Sorry won't get it. That was irresponsible and inconsiderate of you to hold my mail, which now has Touch of Class dress shop in jeopardy. No, you know what?" She shook her head. "I'm not saying another word because I'm not sure you care."

"I do care. But the way you comin' at me is wrong."

"Like I said, I'm done. That wasn't what I wanted to discuss anyway. What new plans do you have for a better job?"

"And what's wrong with Huckabee's? I make good tips, especially on weekends."

"You told me that before. We said you'd try to find another part-time job for more income or full-time work. Have you tried?"

Jada pulled her legs up on the couch and watched her little sister twirl strands of hair around her fingers. Charmaine had become the Queen of Hair Weaves. When Jada asked why she didn't go to cosmetology school, Charmaine said working on nappy heads all day wasn't her thing. *Like her own natural hair wasn't nappy.*

"Where am I supposed to look? I don't have any experience."

"There's other jobs out there."

Charmaine pointed at Jada. "*You* always say that, but I don't have the skills you and Celine have."

"You're talented. We've discussed potential career goals, and Aunt Dee said you're rarely helping at the shop lately."

"Here you go again. Much as I loved Momma and appreciate what she and Aunt Dee taught me, makin' clothes is not my style." Charmaine crossed her legs.

"Yes, but you're good at it. Lots of people dislike their money makers. Those jobs keep food on the table. Many people work full-time and part-time jobs before they get their dream jobs. You can do that until you figure out yours."

Conversations about career goals and better job opportunities had been endless. Charmaine hadn't grasped the importance of finding a real career, and Jada would not back off on encouraging her to do better. Charmaine had relied on her sisters for too long. She was no longer a child; she was a grown woman with responsibilities.

"Since you got all the answers, tell me where I should work. Just 'cause you have a degree and Celine's working on another one—"

"Lower your voice and stop comparing yourself to me and Celine. This is about you."

"I'm fine. Aunt Dee knows I'm pickin' up extra shifts at Huckabee's this month. I've gotta make my car note."

"You're not fine. Now that we have a situation with the shop, I may have to hire an attorney, so all of us need to contribute. I'll let you know when. This home belongs to all of us, but now we stand to lose Momma's dress shop location."

Charmaine's pouty red glossed lips made Jada want to cancel handling this topic with class and get straight up ghetto, but she didn't.

"I get tired of hearin' what I'm not doing. And you know this house is *really* yours. A few more years and it'll be paid off. Then what?" she batted her false eyelashes.

"What are you insinuating?"

"You already know."

"I don't get it. Why are you always at odds with whatever Celine and I ask you to do? Start seeking additional work. End of conversation."

"Yeah, yeah." Charmaine picked up her earrings and bag. "I'm goin' to bed."

"Take my advice. You can always call Aunt Dee and pick up a couple of days at the shop." Jada ended the conversation and sang, "You don't want an eviction notice from your sisters."

Charmaine cut her eyes at Jada and walked to her room.

Chapter 12

JADA

Monday

Jada turned over in bed, her head throbbed as if two giant hydraulic clamps had squeezed her temples to the max. The weekend seemed too short. A headache was the perfect excuse to stay home and not deal with Gordan on a Monday morning. Without a doubt, he'd drop in and slide into her office, and she would not listen to his sorry lies. She'd switched her cell to silent after receiving six texts from him. *Why is it so important to speak with me when he has Kiley?*

Sleep drifted in a few hours before daybreak, somewhere after 3:00 a.m. Three hours of rest would hardly suffice for a productive eight-hour day. A day at home to unwind, read a book, and listen to music could be in her favor. That meant either Doreen or

Shamika would handle her work today, and Griff would be upset. After dismissing the thought, Jada sat up and stretched. *Impossible.* The crew would be lost, and Griff would be calling throughout the day. She showered, ate a bowl of cereal and popped two Motrins before she left for work.

She pulled into the parking lot and cut off the ignition. Not ready to face the chaos of Monday morning or seeing Kiley, she closed her eyes, took a deep breath and rubbed her temples.

As she walked to her office, she saw Kiley at her door with a stack of paperwork.

Jada brushed past her and unlocked the door.

Kiley followed her inside and cleared her throat. "Not speaking this morning?"

"What do you need?" Uninterested in Kiley or the paperwork she was holding, Jada turned on her computer and flipped through some paperwork on her desk.

Kiley dropped the paperwork in Jada's inbox and started toward the door.

"Wait a minute," Jada said.

Kiley paused and turned around with a frown on her face.

"What's this?" Jada extended her hand toward the pile.

"Well, you talking to me or not?" She inspected extra-long purple acrylic nails.

How she managed to type or get any work done was a pure guess.

"Yes, if you'd give me time to get in the office. I asked what you dropped in my box."

"It's from Griff. He said give it to you when you got in. Which should've been..." she glanced at the wall clock, "twelve minutes ago."

"Forget it. I'll talk to Griff."

Kiley smirked and tossed her long straight weave over her shoulders. Jada pressed her lips together when she saw Gordan's engagement ring on Kiley's left ring finger. *He didn't waste any time delivering the ring.*

What in the world did Gordan possibly see in her? Everything on her is fake. Miffed about her boss sending Kiley to drop off work, Jada closed her eyes for a moment of quietness. *This day will not start with chaos.* Thinking before speaking or reacting, reframing negative thoughts into positive ones came to mind. And she'd faithfully followed her therapist's advice. With steepled fingers pushed to her chin, she smiled. *I will not let anybody upset me today. Kiley can have Gordan.* She calmly picked up the paperwork and walked to Griff's office.

Jada waited at Griff's door while he continued a

phone conversation. He waved her in and pointed to a seat in front of his desk.

"I see," Griff said. "Well, tell Adkins his spots ran on time. If he didn't like what he heard...oh, well. His rep and sales exec said they were fine. Tell you what. Let's give him two free spots, one in drive time and one on Saturday – midday. Run that by him and get back to me. Later." He hung up and scratched his head.

Jada lifted her brows. "Unhappy client?"

"Adkins Limo Service. He's a bizarre dude, but he's a long-term client." He got up and closed the door. "What's going on with you and Kiley?"

Jada shrugged her shoulders, "Nothing that I know of. Why'd you ask?"

Griff rolled up his long-sleeved white shirt and took a seat behind his desk. He ran a hand over his salt and pepper goatee before removing his black-rimmed glasses. After nine years of working with Griffey Brown, Jada knew when he was concerned. Following her internship and graduation, Griff offered Jada a sales secretary job. Two years later, she received a promotion to traffic director.

Jada crossed her legs. "What did I do wrong?"

"No, nothing's wrong," Griff shook his head. "I'm trying to figure out why some folks don't like Kiley.

She's still learning her way around. Is there a way that you can help her out?"

"She's been here almost a year. Isn't that enough time to learn her job?"

"Yes, that's true. Everybody doesn't learn at the same pace."

"If this is about our interaction this morning, I can explain. I was a little late because I woke up with a headache. I walked in and she was standing outside my door..." Jada went on to explain what transpired. When she finished, she pressed her hand to her chest. "Griff...you know me well."

Griff nodded. "I see your point. I'm trying to avoid riffraff in the office, if you know what I mean. Minimizing distractions helps to maintain a cohesive work environment."

"And I agree. We have a great team, and everyone works hard." She could say that now, but yesterday she'd planned to talk to Griff about Antoine's behavior. Like Aunt Dee always said, God works in mysterious ways. He worked it out right on time.

Griff picked up a pen and jotted down some notes. "Kiley has bad days. Overall, she's done a decent job since she's been here. I wish I could squash a few rumors about her. Uh, you know anything about those?" His dark eyes locked with hers.

"No, I don't," she handed him some reports from

yesterday. "I haven't checked the ones Kiley delivered, but I think you should mention two things — improving her attitude and communication skills."

"Yeah, sure. A couple of sales execs mentioned that, too. I'll speak with Kiley. Uh, those documents she dropped off are for your files."

Jada was sure if Griff had knowledge of Kiley's dating history, there would be a cold storm that would decimate the station's atmosphere. Although she didn't elaborate, Denise had mentioned Kiley's colorful dating entourage that included one of the DJs and several other men at the station. Something neither Griff nor Gordan obviously knew anything about. And her lips were zipped tight. Nevertheless, she was relieved that Griff had moved past his concerns about her and Kiley.

After she left Griff's office, she headed toward the studio to say hello to Antoine. He'd sign off the air shortly. He and Lina were chatting, their backs to the door. Jada didn't want to intrude, so she walked down the hall and stopped in the lounge for coffee. When she entered her office, Antoine was standing near her desk.

"Oh, I didn't expect to see you." Jada smiled.

"Good morning." He skimmed her up and down

and smiled. "I caught a glimpse of you in the hallway. How's your day going?"

"I'm well. I'll feel much better after I have my coffee."

"Well, I stopped by to say I enjoyed our time together last night. I'm hoping I can see you again."

She sat down, sipping her coffee. "Possibly."

"Possibly? What does that mean?"

"Um...I have one condition. Keep our dating a secret and I'm all for it."

"That might be hard, but if undercover works for you, cool." Folding his arms, Antoine's eyes stayed on Jada. "Say, how do you feel about oldies but goodies music?"

"My mom and dad played it when I was growing up. I love oldies but goodies."

"Well, if you're free this Thursday evening, how about accompanying me to a Frankie Beverly and Maze concert?"

"Yes, yes! I'd love to." Excited, Jada waved her hand. "They're one of my all-time favorites. What time?"

"The show starts at 7:00. One catch... I'm the M.C., and I can't sit with you during the whole event. I'll be back and forth. After the concert, there's an after party. Those are boss, and they'll have plenty of food and drinks. Is that cool?"

"Hey, I'm all for it. I'll even leave work a little earlier."

"Awesome. I'll swing by your place early. We can chill and talk before the concert. I'm going in the studio, so let's exchange numbers."

He gave Jada his number, and she dialed his phone.

"Got it," he said and added her number to his phone. Can I call you later?"

"Uh, yes. I'm available around 7:00."

"Talk to you then," he said and left.

She was really digging her feet into wet sand. Another date so soon? Well, it was only a concert, and he would probably be backstage for most of the show. She thought of last night, their conversation, and how much she enjoyed his company.

Chapter 13

JADA

Thursday

After receiving Antoine's text, Jada hurried out the door. He jumped out and opened the passenger side of a super clean blue Range Rover. As Jada walked to the car, she saw sparks in his warm eyes. The gaze and smile that never strayed, also made her smile. Just what she'd hoped for. The paisley patterned black, pink and white off the shoulder dress she'd worn with black wedges caught his attention.

"You are gorgeous."

"Thank you." She checked out his copper-colored leather Big Apple cap, brown shirt and jacket that he had worn. *That outfit must've cost him a whole paycheck.*

"You look fly, too. Will we make it on time?" Jada

looked at the time on his dashboard. He was running behind on their arrival time.

"Yes, we'll be okay. I'll just push my foot to the pedal a bit."

They arrived at the Greek Theatre, where a valet waited ready to open their doors. Antoine led the way through the VIP entry and escorted her to the front row.

"So, this is my plan. After I introduce the entertainers, I'll join you until they break."

"Sounds good."

Antoine leaned over, kissed her cheek and disappeared backstage. When the spotlight hit the stage minutes later, he walked out with a mic in hand; sparks and satellites from that kiss were still orbiting around her head. *All right, Jada, get it together.*

"Good evening, LA.! I'm Antoine Bailey, AKA DJ Ant from 101.3 KTLM radio station. Are you ready for a grand slam performance by Frankie Beverly and Maze?"

The crowd shouted and applauded as Antoine introduced the group. When the lights shifted and the group started performing, Jada rocked back and forth, waving her hands to the music. Antoine returned and gave her a hug. Hearing Frankie Beverly and Maze sing their songs from the past brought back sweet memories of her parents. They loved to play albums on a record player with an arm and needle. As a child, she never understood how music came from a needle that touched a large record and spun around until the songs ended. Her parents did the hop, electric slide, cabbage patch and other dances, and she and her sisters would mimic their steps.

It was the first time she'd ever seen Frankie Beverly in person and his performance was epic, but what impressed her the most that evening was Antoine. Even though he was working, he made sure to return and chat as time permitted throughout the show.

After the show, they went to a large studio nearby for the after party. Jazz music blasted the room as Jada entered the studio on Antoine's arm, elated that she'd accepted his offer to attend. As expected, he was bombarded with greetings and side-eyed glares from the chicks, but she didn't care one bit. Jada smiled and waved as if she were Queen for a Day, and then she froze. Gordan was at the bar talking to another man.

"Hey, you all right?" Antoine asked with a concerned look.

"Yes. Uh, I need to use the restroom. You know where it is?"

"Make a right and it's at the end of the hall. I'll be at the bar," he pointed in Gordan's direction.

The bar. Can't go anywhere near the bar. "Great. Could you get me a glass of red wine or champagne?"

"No problem."

She quickly walked to the restroom and stared at herself in the mirror. *Am I ready to face Gordan tonight?* Closing her eyes, she inhaled a deep breath to regain composure. She couldn't leave the restroom right away, so she touched up her lipstick and rechecked her curly ponytail. After checking her watch, she opened the door and searched the room for Antoine, hoping that either he or Gordan had moved away from the bar.

Taking small steps, Jada scanned the studio for Antoine as she walked toward the center of the room. Then she heard, "What's happening, J?"

She twirled around, and Gordan stood almost in front of her face. "Hey," she took a quick step back. *He must've followed me after I walked out the restroom.*

"I thought I saw you come in." He pushed his glasses up on his nose. "So, you here with DJ Ant?" He asked with a glare.

"I am. If you'll excuse me," she stepped around Gordan. "I'm on my way to find him."

"Why you not answering my calls?" Gordan's tone was edgy.

She stopped and faced him. No, he would not take her to a place where she didn't want to go. There were too many people in here for him to act a fool. "I'm not discussing this here or anywhere. I told you our relationship is over. No friendship. Nothing."

"Just like that. You won't let me explain my side?"

Without answering, Jada avoided eye contact.

He tipped his head. "No answer. Well, I guess not since you're here with *DJ Ant*. Tell me something...what you doing here with him anyway? The way he treated you, now you're dating the brotha?" He huffed out a curt laugh and gazed at Jada. "You're a fool."

"I was a fool for dating you," she snapped. "This conversation's over." Jada walked away and circled the room, surveying the crowded room before she walked toward the bar. She kept her eye on Gordan to ensure he didn't follow her to the bar or anywhere near Antoine. Chit-chatting with him this evening would not happen, and his inquiry about Antoine? That was none of his business.

"Jada," Antoine said.

"Oh, there you are," she rushed to his side.

"I found a table close to the buffet." He handed her a glass of wine, and she followed him without glancing back. When Gordan passed their table, his gaze landed on Jada along with a crooked smile. Jada's heart leaped, hoping he wouldn't make a scene. Gordan's personality was mellow, but he didn't like when someone disrespected him, and she knew that would make him go off. But her actions were justified, and life went on.

After they finished their meal, Antoine reached for Jada's hand. "You ready to hit the dance floor?" Jada nodded and placed her hand in his. They strolled to the dance floor and danced to "Endless Love" by Kenny G.

"DJ Ant," a man in a brown suit moved toward them.

"Hey, what's going on, Stan? Long time no see," Antoine stopped dancing long enough to shake his hand.

"Yeah, they changed my region. Say, when can we get together?" The man responded.

"Soon. Give me a call. Uh, this is my lady, Jada. Babe, this is Stan. He works for Motown."

His lady? "Nice to meet you." Jada extended her hand.

Stan stared at Jada and shook her hand. "Same here. Beautiful lady, man."

"Thank you," Antoine said.

Hey, I'll catch up with you soon," Stan said, before he walked off.

Jada lost count of the artists, record industry, and radio station executives she met throughout the evening. But when Frankie Beverly and his entourage strolled through, she clutched her chest to subdue the stream of excitement from breaking out.

"Come on," Antoine grabbed her hand. "I'll introduce you to Frankie."

Even though her heart was doing a drum roll as they did a run-walk across the room, Jada forced herself not to appear nervous. Antoine must've sensed her feelings.

"Frankie. What's up, brother?"

"DJ Ant. Good to see you. It's been a few years." They gripped hands and hugged.

"I'm at KTLM Radio Station in L.A. now. Hey, this is my girl, Jada. She's one of your biggest fans."

His girl?

"Hi, I'm Frankie," he gave Jada a hug.

"I love your music, and the concert was awesome," Jada said, feeling the blush on her face.

"That's awesome and thank you, I'm glad you enjoyed it."

It didn't take long for others to bombard him, so their meeting was brief. Frankie Beverly was delightful. Holding her hand, Antoine maneuvered through the crowded studio, introducing Jada to several more former co-workers from the Bay area.

She'd been to a few parties over the years, but nothing like this one. What really surprised her was Antoine's popularity with so many people. Jada wasn't bothered by the number of female executives and artists he knew. He made a point to introduce her as "his girl or lady" to everyone. She kind of understood why. A lot of the guys laid eyes on her, and several approached her whenever he left their table.

At 7:00 every night, Antoine had called Jada and they chatted. And being at the after party with him was mind-boggling. They danced and talked for hours. She reveled in the pleasure of his courtesy, attention, and the way he made her feel. The party ended at midnight, and he drove up to Baldwin Hills, parking at the top of the steep hills. A view of the city, weather, and conversation with Antoine was relaxing.

"I won't ask why we're up here this late. We have to work tomorrow," Jada said, watching Antoine.

"True. I want to unwind, and I'd like to talk to you. I'm glad my shift was changed to days. We'd still be going for each other's throats if I was still working nights."

Jada laughed. "Please don't say that. Now that we're acquainted, I don't think we'd do that."

"No, we wouldn't. I'm straight now. I can be a little fierce at times, but I'm a gentle lion." He chewed his bottom lip and glanced at Jada. "Thank you for coming with me tonight."

"No, thank you. I loved the show and the after party. And meeting Frankie Beverly was a treat."

Antoine smiled. "I'm glad you had a good time. I can't believe this is real. I mean, you're beautiful." He rubbed his chin. "Uh, I do have a question though. Are you dating the record company exec from Air Mist?"

Surprised by his question, Jada sighed. "I was. How'd you know?"

"Mmm...that wasn't too hard to figure out. I mean, I've seen him in your office a few times, and I noticed him talking to you tonight."

"Our relationship is over. We went out a few times after we broke up, but I'm not seeing him anymore."

Antoine nodded. "When did your relationship end?"

"A year, maybe a little over that time."

"That's what I wanted to know." There was excitement in his voice. "It's no secret that hiding certain personal info in this business is hard. Like who I'm dating. Being in the limelight a lot, I haven't dated exclusively for a few years."

Jada smiled and kept her eyes on him, waiting to see exactly where he was going with this conversation.

He bit his lower lip again; his eyes on Jada. "I'll be honest, and this might be too soon, but I have to ask. Lady, I'm smitten with you." He lifted Jada's hand and kissed it, interlocking their fingers. "Are you cool with being my lady?"

She wasn't too surprised with his question, but her thoughts stopped midstream. They were moving rapidly, and was she ready to commit to another man?

"If you need time, I understand. I usually move slow when it comes to women. It's just...I have this gut feeling that we should be together."

If she told Antoine the truth, he would probably laugh. Out of all the guys she'd dated, only one became her boyfriend before the three-month trial ended. This brother here... was like a cold glass of lemonade after a long hike in the desert.

Squeezing his hand, Jada said, "Yes, I'd love to be your lady. And I have that gut feeling, too. It's not like we just met. It's cool that we're learning more about each other. But, uh, we'll take it slow. No announcements about this right away."

"We don't have to make announcements. Sooner or later, everyone will figure it out. I have another question," Antoine held both hands up. "Can I kiss you?"

She smiled and nodded. "You didn't have to ask." A breath caught in her throat as he bent down and slipped his arms around her shoulders. His soft lips against hers sent tremors through her body. Kisses on her face, neck, and back to her mouth, and then a moan signaled his enjoyment.

"Should I stop?" he whispered, touching her cheek with a finger. She pressed her hands to his face. "Don't you dare," she said, kissing him back. The thrill of being with this man stimulated every part of her body. *What a night.*

Chapter 14

ANTOINE

Friday, Three months later

An echo of the captain's voice woke Antoine from a short, peaceful snooze. He raised his seat and buckled his seatbelt. Glancing at the empty seat next to his, the seat he'd purchased for Jada, he missed her already. Strange how life could shift quicker than a snap of the finger. Three months had passed since they'd started dating, and he still couldn't get her on a plane to San Francisco. She canceled the first time, and understandably so since their relationship was so new. That weekend, he'd rescheduled his trip and stayed in L.A. to be with her.

As the plane glided across the runway, Antoine let out a sigh of relief for a safe landing at the San Francisco International Airport. Not having Jada with him was a huge disappointment. This was the weekend he was supposed to expose his inner soul. He'd reveal parts of his life that he learned to cope with by staying busy and volunteering with Big Brothers.

Antoine grabbed his iPad case from underneath the seat before opening the overhead bin to remove his duffle bag. He exited the plane and walked through the airport. The minute he reached the curbside, he busted out laughing. *That boy is a nut.* His friend Ellis was making crazy hand signals like a traffic police. Antoine thought of their longtime friendship that had started in elementary school after their moms met at an open house. They had remained friends throughout their early school years and college. Uber or Lyft were foreign words to his friend, who always insisted on picking him up, even if he called at the last minute.

"Hey, Champ." Ellis shouted the nickname he'd often called Antoine after he made a three-point shot and won a basketball championship for their high school team.

"Thanks for coming," Antoine said. They clapped hands and hugged. Antoine placed his duffle bag and computer in the trunk.

"You know that's no problem. Glad to see you, bro'."

"How's Sherrie doing?"

"Sherrie's better. I don't know if I told you, we thought she was pregnant last month. False alarm. We're not pregnant yet, but..." he shook his head. "Still not giving up. I've got to keep my chin up on this one. The positive news is I got a promotion."

"Sorry to hear about the pregnancy. Congrats on the promotion, man. When do you start?"

"I started right before you came up last. Forgot to mention it." He peered over at Antoine. "Bro' I was out of sync for a minute after that situation with the pregnancy. I'm now a senior quality assurance engineer, and I'm happy. I'd be happier if I was a daddy, though."

"Hang in there, dude. It'll happen one day." Antoine glanced at his friend, remembering the disappointment in his voice after he'd called and announced Fiona's unplanned pregnancy. Despite his friends' attempts to conceive and their physician's inability to determine reasons why they weren't successful, they'd been plagued with infertility problems for more than four years. Antoine tugged his earlobe trying to forget about the unborn child Fiona had lost in her second trimester while his best friend yearned for the special gift of a child.

"You wanna grab some food or go home?" Ellis said.

"I thought you'd want to get home to Sherrie. Don't you two normally dine out on Fridays?"

"I meant I'd take you to get food. It's 7:45, bro. Me and Sherrie ate. She was off today so she baked some tilapia."

"Oh, my bad. I forgot about the time. I'm not hungry, but we can stop at Starbucks."

Ellis parked, and they went inside, ordered coffee, and found a table.

Taking a sip of black coffee, Ellis said, "Tell me what's new?"

"Honestly? A lot is new. Number one, I'm in a new relationship." He grinned, nodding his head. "My girl's name is Jada."

"Whoa, it's about time," Ellis said with an excited tone. He pushed his fist out to bump Antoine's. "Man, I was worried about you after that breakup with Fiona."

"Yeah, I went through a lot. But that's behind me. I'm happy with Jada. We have a lot in common."

"Where did you meet?"

"You won't believe me," Antoine smiled and stirred his coffee. "But... it was at the radio station."

"Oh. Is she a DJ?"

"Nope. Remember the woman who gave me a hard time over the logs? The one I thought was out to sabotage me?"

"What?" Ellis turned his head to the side, "Not the one you said was coo-coo."

Antoine broke out in laughter and slapped his leg. "Man, cut it out. I never said that. We had a few disagreements, but that's over." He blew into his cup to cool the coffee before taking a sip. "For real, she's the best thing that ever happened to me."

Rubbing his bald head, Ellis gave Antoine that turned up lip, head nod, and they slapped hands. That was their routine action in college whenever one of them first hooked up with a new girlfriend. Ellis raised his brows. "Okay, did you hit it or not?"

"You had to go there, huh? I'm not saying."

"That's right, I went there. We're brothers for life, right?"

A little embarrassed, Antoine shook his head. "Not yet. Jada's not ready. So, I'm cool with waiting. For a little while, anyway."

"How long you two been together?"

Antoine shifted a blank gaze at his friend. "Now that I'm not disclosing."

"Dude. What's up with you? We always share." Ellis picked up his cup

"It'll be three months this coming Monday."

His friend almost choked on a cup of coffee. "What? Who you think you kiddin'? Dawg, you didn't mention her when you came up before."

Antoine looked around Starbucks. "Man, cool it. I don't want the world knowing my business." His friend had supported him through ongoing family disputes and with moving past the trauma of Fiona, which nearly wiped him out. But some things in life should be private.

"Uh huh. I bet you don't."

"We're not rushing. You know me. I'm into a woman's intellect, personal and ethical values." Antoine wasn't lying; these things were important. But he also couldn't wait to make smoking hot love to his woman.

"Ant, I'm not trying to be funny. Honestly, you've been dating that girl three months and ain't tapped that bud yet?" Ellis lifted his cup in a salute.

Antoine sipped his coffee. "The answer is *no*, Mr. Derrick number two. You and my cuz need to stay out my love life. Aren't you interested in her personality, where she went to college, her hobbies?"

"No," Ellis chuckled. "Just joking, Ant. Tell me about her."

Dedicated students, both Ellis and Antoine attended UC Berkeley. Their college days were filled with attending classes and studying, but as members of Alpha Phi Alpha Fraternity – Alpha Epsilon Chapter, they also made plenty of time for frat parties and tracking how many fine sisters they could bed. In Antoine's freshman year, he was a devoted follow the leader rookie. By the second year, relationships had become more meaningful, and he learned to date and treat women with respect.

He and Ellis talked for another hour, and Antoine told him about Jada and how they'd made peace and grown closer the past three months.

"Yeah, dude, I was surprised how fast things moved along for us. After our second date, I realized I wanted a relationship with that fine woman."

"I'm happy for you, bro. I can tell you really care about her." He removed a pack of Tic-Tacs from his shirt and popped a few in his mouth. He held the box out to Antoine.

"No, I'm straight. I won't be kissing anybody this weekend." Antoine twisted his mouth and stroked his dreadlocks. "I'm hanging out with Rashad. I'll pick him up at Big Brothers and take him to his basketball game tomorrow. After that, I'm off to Poet's Night Out."

"Me and Sherrie might check you out at the lounge. And I forgot he played ball. That's cool that you're still mentoring him. When does he graduate?"

"Next year. In fact, he got a scholarship to Prairie View A & M."

"All right. So, he's going to school out of state?"

"Yeah, he won't be that far away. I'm proud of him and so is his mom. She was hoping he'd get into an HBCU and stay on campus."

"Cool. Now back to Jada...she told you about her family. Did you talk to her about yours?"

"Man, I will." Antoine placed his hands on the table. "I don't have a choice. She poured everything out to me. My obligation is to be upfront."

"Better now than later. Man, go on and make her day. Tell her she hooked up with a rich D.J." Ellis said, laughing.

"You're real funny. After I told Fiona, that turned into a serious problem."

"Yeah, but glamour girl was a trip."

"I know, but I brought it on myself. I gave her everything, but I was out of town too much."

"It wasn't you, and see there? You're still blaming yourself. You did what any man would've done if he'd caught his woman in bed with another man. And of all people, our boy, Kelvin." Ellis cracked his knuckles. "I'd still be in jail today if she'd been my woman."

Antoine leaned back. "Yeah, well, Fiona's old baggage, and I don't hang with Kelvin anymore. My life is renewed. I have Jada, and she met Derrick. Eventually I'll get her up here to meet everybody else."

"Awesome. My man Derrick is cool. Say," Ellis raised his brows. "What happened to that other girl you dated at the station? Kellie or...what's her name?"

"Kellie?" Antoine frowned; he snapped his finger. "Oh, you mean Kiley. I never dated her. She attended a few events where I was the MC. Tried to get my attention, but that didn't happen."

Ellis cupped his chin. "And?"

"Nothing happened." Antoine watched a super-sized grin overtake Ellis's face. He lifted his hands in defense. "Let me get this straight. You know I'm thirty-five. Kiley is, I think she said twenty-three. Believe me, I don't date women that young."

And that was a fact, although not all of them.

After one of his MC events, Kiley had asked him to take her home and help her connect a new sound system. At first, he declined, saying it was too late. After thinking it over, he finally agreed. Setting up her sound system shouldn't take very long. Kiley served him iced tea and lemon cake, and by the time he'd finished setting up the equipment, grogginess had overwhelmed him. A couple of glasses of wine at the event shouldn't have made him feel that way, and he was nauseous and too dizzy to leave. Thinking he had eaten bad food, he staggered to Kiley's couch and woke up hours later at 4:13 a.m.

Initially, he didn't even remember falling asleep, but he got up and left. From that day forward, he hadn't said much to Kiley and refused to do anymore favors or take her home.

Chapter 15

ANTOINE

Saturday

Waking up in the comfort of his four-bedroom townhouse in Pacific Heights brought on a mellow mood. Antoine loved his townhouse but hated the location. He could walk a few blocks to a plethora of outdoor activities, but rarely did. He opened the sliding glass door, walked out on the sun deck, stretched his arms upward and inhaled. The Bay area lived in his pores. Even when he was away, he'd visualize this moment of peace that freed his spirit and mind. There was nothing more relaxing than a view of the water, bay, marina, San Francisco, and the Twin Peaks hills.

He walked back into his living room and glanced around at the high ceilings, hardwood floors, and wood burning fireplace. His home was everything most single or married people would cherish.

Living in an upscale, predominantly white neighborhood was his father's choice. The clashes he'd had with his father came to mind. Antoine blew out a long breath and thought of his mother. She'd convinced him to accept the gift his father had given to all his kids — their own mortgage-free properties. He desperately wanted to introduce Jada to the other side of his world, but when was the question.

Antoine sat at the table and opened his briefcase. He spread out his paperwork, browsing through a catalogue of poetry. With his brain fixed on Jada, he smiled. They had talked last night for hours. He missed that fine woman, her voice and everything that related to her. He scribbled a new poem, thinking it was better than the one he'd originally written for tonight. *This one is for my lady, and someday I'll present it to her.* He had no intention of hiding his true feelings. Poetry instilled a greater appreciation for love, peace, hope, social justice, and other controversial topics. That's why he enjoyed spoken word.

His cell blasted with one of his spoken word poems, "Engulf Love."

"Hey, Nikki, what's up?"

"Mom's asking about you. Here. Talk to her."

"I'm fine, and how are *you* doing?" Antoine said to his sister.

"I'll talk with you shortly," she snapped in her usual irritated voice.

Before he could answer, his mother said, "How's my baby boy? I miss you."

"I miss you, too, Mom." Antoine dropped his head. This was always tough, and his sister knew it. He and his younger sister, Joy had all but pleaded with Nikki to notify them in advance before calling. This would give them time to prep for conversations with their mother, who had trouble recalling previous conversations and information.

"Come soon, please and bring a pound cake."

A smile tugged at Antoine's lips. "I'll try to remember. Listen, I won't be in D.C. until Thanksgiving. Okay?"

"Thanksgiving? Why? You live close by."

Rarely at a loss for words, he stroked his head and mulled over how to make his mother understand. "No, Mom. I'm in California, and that's a long way from where you are. Remember, you live in Washington, D.C. with Nicole."

"Who?"

"Nicole. Nikki, your oldest daughter, your grandchildren's mother."

"Oh, yeah, Nikki. Well..." She paused for a few seconds.

"Mom?"

"I hear you."

"Do you remember Joy, your youngest daughter?"

"Joy. Of course, I do. She's the flight attendant."

Antoine pulled his earlobe. "Joy is an attorney."

"Okay, Roland. I'm tired."

At times, hearing his mother's weak voice stirred up raw emotions. Conversations with a vibrant, intellectual woman had withered down to senseless, short phrases. He loved his mom but hated talking to her; it felt as though he was talking to a stranger. Every conversation drained a well of energy and hurt so bad.

"Mom, this is Antoine."

"Bye, honey."

"Mom. Mom!" He blew out a heavy breath.

"All right, that'll satisfy her for another two weeks," Nikki said sarcastically.

"She won't remember talking to me in two weeks. That's part of her illness. Would you consider not catching me off guard? A text or email would give me time to prepare. We discussed this previously."

"Do I need permission to call about your mother?"

Antoine ran his hands through his dreads and sighed. "You know that's not the case."

"Then what is?"

His lips parted to respond, but Nikki cut him off. "I don't understand you, Joy, or your greedy father. Money is his priority. You all live on the other side of the world, enjoying your lives while me and Ryan are caring for Mom. Why should I call you, anyway? Next time you want to speak with Mom, call me."

She hung up in his face. His mouth twisted, he sprung from the chair, pacing as he called back. Hanging up in his face was totally unacceptable. He paused, then disconnected the call. *Why waste time?* He'd pass this problem on to Joy. She knew how to deal with Nikki better than he did. And as for his father, he hadn't spoken with him in months.

He tapped out a text message to Joy.

Just talked to Mom. Nikki hung up in my face. Call and handle her before I cuss her out!

Joy answered in less than a minute.

No! You're better than that. I'll call her.

Joy was right; he couldn't do something that cold. He loved Nikki. It's just that he'd had enough of her rude, disrespectful behavior. Yes, she and her husband cared for Mom, and he empathized with Nikki and Ryan and their two kids. But it wasn't as bad as Nikki claimed. Mom had around the clock professional care during the week. That was one responsibility their father had promised to keep, along with mortgage-free homes for each of his children, including Derrick.

Antoine called Rashad to let him know he'd pick him up at 9:00 for breakfast. When Antoine pulled up at Big Brothers, Rashad was standing in front with a backpack on his shoulder wearing a pair of Air Jordans for the game. Antoine had cautioned him about wearing his Air Jordans only during basketball games. There was so much crime in certain areas of the inner city, Antoine often reminded Rashad to think first about safety. The teen rushed to the car and opened the door.

"What's up?" Rashad fastened his seatbelt. "What happened to your G-Wagon?"

"I decided to start driving this one to the games. G-Wagon means too much attention." He glanced at Rashad, patting the dashboard of the Jeep Cherokee SUV. "Dude, you don't like this ride?"

Rashad scanned the car. "Uh, I like the G-Wagon better. But this beats riding my bike to my basketball game." Rashad laughed.

"I agree. Where we going for breakfast?"

"McDonald's is cool."

With his eyes on the road, Antoine turned his nose up. "Yuck. You sure you want fast food?"

"Yep. It's quick, and I've gotta be there on time."

Antoine tapped his GPS for the nearest

McDonald's close to the school. Throughout their meal, Rashad chatted about school and about his new part-time job at a supermarket. They arrived at Oakland High School ten minutes earlier than Rashad's expected arrival time. He jumped out the car and sprinted toward the building.

During the game, Antoine watched Rashad, the team's point guard, dribble the ball across the court and leap high to make a shot. The boy gloated with pride. That shot reminded Antoine of his high school basketball games. Especially the night he made a three-point shot and helped his team win the championship. And education meant more than playing basketball to Antoine. He had plans for college. Funny thing was... Rashad's first career choice wasn't professional basketball either. His goal was to become an engineer, and Antoine encouraged him to maintain that mindset.

Chapter 16

ANTOINE

Saturday Evening

Antoine strolled into the Power of Words lounge to warm greetings from friends and acquaintances that made him feel at home. This was his night of leisure, a night to bring the house down with spoken word poetry.

He made his way over to Ellis, Sherrie and two other couples. After greeting Ellis with a fist bump, he hugged Sherrie and shook hands with everyone else at the table. "Hello, everybody."

"You look well," Sherrie smiled.

Antoine nodded. "I'm living. Working, enjoying life as much as possible."

"Ant, you know Jared, and this is his wife Natalie. That's Matthew, my co-worker and his wife Lucinda."

"Nice meeting all of you and thank you for coming out. I wish you could've met my girl as well, but she couldn't make it this time." With everyone paired up, Antoine felt awkward without a date. "Maybe next time," he said, rubbing his hands together.

"Man, we've been hearing about your spoken word poetry. We can't wait to hear you speak. You planning to publish your work?" Matthew said.

Antoine reached into his bag for a few promo cards and passed them around the table. "I appreciate your support. I've published six poetry books with over forty poems, and I'm working on a nonfiction book."

"That's cool," Matthew read the card. "What's your book about?"

"It's a self-help book about healing and survival."

Matthew nodded. "Interesting. I'd like to read it after it's published."

"Awesome. Check my website from time to time for updates. Hey, I'm buying tonight — wine or your choice of drinks." Antoine summoned the waitress, and everybody gave her their orders. "Oh, Ellis," he said, "Rashad's team killed it today. They beat the other team by fifteen points."

"Aww, bro', that's cool," Ellis said. "Text me his game schedule. I wanna go to his next game."

Antoine's phone vibrated in his jacket pocket.

"Excuse me, I need to answer this." He walked outside, hoping the call was from Jada. He pulled his phone out but didn't recognize the number. He was going to ignore the call but changed his mind. *Maybe she's calling from a different number.* Antoine put his Bluetooth on and hit redial. A familiar voice answered.

"Hello, sweetie pie. What are you doing?"

His brows furrowed. "You must have the wrong number."

"You don't know the voice of your baby's mama? It's Kiley," the woman on the other end cackled with laughter.

He scanned the area to ensure no one could hear his conversation. Patrons walking by in groups and as couples meant the lounge was filling quickly. His session was coming up soon.

"Is this some kind of joke?" He placed his hand on his forehead. "You know we never had sex."

"You sound irritated. This baby growing in my belly sure wasn't black magic. Why don't you come by so we can talk?"

"Look, I'm not in L.A. We'll talk, and it'll be a long one."

"When will that be?"

"Expect my call one day this week. Okay? And

143

don't approach me at work; this situation is between me and you. I'm out."

His heart raced as anger climbed higher than Mount Everest. This was not the time to discuss a pregnancy that he wasn't responsible for, but he blamed himself for not meeting with Kiley after she'd told him about the positive pregnancy test. She'd obviously mixed up the guys she'd been dating, and he wasn't one of them. The baby couldn't be his. Avoidance would not result in a resolution, so he would deal with Kiley when he got back to LA.

Antoine closed his eyes for a moment of silent prayer, then walked back inside in time to hear his name announced. He drank a few sips of wine and decided not to let the "baby-mama-drama" affect his session. After a sprint to the stage, the applause generated a burst of energy. At the podium, he shaded his eyes with one hand and checked out the audience.

"All right, everybody in the house. What's up? I'm Antoine Bailey. Welcome and thank you for being here." He waved to a group who had taken seats at the table next to Ellis and Sherrie. "Wow! I see a lot of familiar faces in the audience. *Poet's Night Out* holds a special place in my heart. My Spoken Word Poetry is provocative storytelling. Its curative properties have healing powers that can be therapeutic, spiritual, and most of all...romantic."

He licked his lips as his eyes journeyed around the room, captivating the attention of the audience, most of whom were women. He leaned toward the microphone and deepened his voice. "My poetry is sumptuous foretastes of romantic escapades." Oohs and aahs echoed through the room.

"Can poetry heal being broke?" a young man said. Laughter filtered through the lounge.

Antoine grinned and pointed at the man. "Good question, my brother. In my opinion, if you add spirituality and positivity to romance, poetry can heal a broken heart and being broke. It's your call. For those of you who don't know me, I'm originally from the Bay area, but I'm currently in L.A. working for KTLM radio station, 101.3 FM.

Tonight, I present to you a poem that I wrote today, and I'm dedicating it to my lady, Jada. By the way, she's not here tonight, but that's okay." A few chuckles from the crowd caused Antoine to laugh. "I'll start with a song to get you in the groove. My poem is called "My Heartbeat, My Love." He cued the DJ, and with closed eyes, arms raised, Antoine swayed back and forth to "Would You Mind" by Earth, Wind, and Fire while snapping his fingers. The audience clapped and many sang along with the recording. The music gradually faded in the background as his poetry enthralled the audience.

"My heartbeat, my love, a sweet, sweet dove. Your beautiful skin, a waist so slim..." As he continued to speak, a stunning woman with long dark, silky hair, wearing a red low-cut top sauntered in and sat at a table up front. The moment he placed the woman as Fiona, he inhaled a deep breath and almost forgot to exhale. He straightened the collar of his jacket and continued his performance.

The woman he'd planned to marry — the woman who was supposed to birth his babies— focused on him for an hour. But her starry-eyed gaze did little except trigger a few droplets of sweat on his forehead. He pulled out a hanky and swiped the sweat away. Their past had moments of beauty, but her behavior toward the end of their relationship was more bizarre than a Picasso painting. *Why is she here?*

Antoine ended his session and pressed his hands together. "So again, I thank you for coming out tonight. Enjoy your evening and God bless you. Ciao!" A rousing applause polished his night; he saluted his audience and walked off the stage. He preferred to return to his friends' table, but rudeness wasn't his style. He strutted over to Fiona, and she arose and accepted his warm hug.

"Thanks for coming out."

"I heard you'd be here tonight, and I was in the area." She touched his hair. "I love the locks; they're longer.

He dispensed a slight smile. "They've grown since you've last seen them. Why don't you join me and my friends? Their table is over there." He pointed in the direction of his friends and immediately noticed the disappointment on her face when she glanced at his friends engaged in social conversation. *Exactly what I thought.*

"No. Well, I-I...have another engagement." She ran her fingers through her straight hair. "I had a craving for your poetry, and I must say...you're still the master of coining words. How long will you be in town?"

"Not long. I'm flying back to L.A. tomorrow."

She removed a business card from her wallet and handed it to him. "Call me sometimes. We're not strangers. Maybe we can hook up for coffee or lunch when you come back."

He stuffed her card in his shirt pocket and whispered in her ear, "I'll keep that in the back of my mind. I have a girlfriend now." He pecked her cheek. "Take care of yourself."

A quick exit from that conversation was the best pathway out. He strolled over to his friends' table.

He'd tell Jada soon enough about his ex-girlfriend and the history of that relationship. What he didn't desire was any part of Fiona's reunion attempts — friendship or otherwise. No one or anything would be a hindrance in his relationship with Jada.

Chapter 17

JADA

Twelve thirty-seven, and not a hint of sleep. After hours of changing positions multiple times, Jada rolled over again and stared at the alarm clock, wishing a mystical hand would touch her fatigued body. She sat up and pushed her back against two pillows. How would she sit through Sunday service if she didn't rest? Jada would have to start taking the Melatonin again if she continued having sleepless nights. Two issues whirled around in her mind —Aunt Dee and Antoine. What surprise had he planned for her? Where were they going this afternoon? And why, oh why, had she turned down a trip to San Francisco?

Jada tossed the layers of cover to the side and swung her feet to the floor. She wrapped the robe around her shoulders and went to check the hall thermostat. The house felt chilly for late spring.

Celine must have cut the heater off again to save a few dollars on the gas bill. She turned on the heat before they all froze like icicles. A beam of light shone in the hall, and Jada followed it into the kitchen where Celine stood. A bonnet covered braids, and a thick pull-over sweater covered her pajama top.

"Hey, there," Jada said.

Celine jumped; the knife she was holding fell to the floor. "Oh! You scared me. Why're you up so late?" She rinsed the knife and stuck it in the Miracle Whip jar.

"Can't sleep. I don't have to ask why you're up." Jada leaned against the counter.

"Well, it's not that I can't sleep. I took a nap after I studied earlier, so now I'm not sleepy. I'll read or watch TV and doze off in an hour or two." Celine spread mayonnaise and mustard on French bread and added slices of tomato and turkey. "You want a sandwich?"

"No thanks. Food will keep me up longer, and if you don't stop eating so late, your hips are gonna spread wider than the Hoover Dam." Jada giggled.

"Not hardly. Running around that E.R. for twelve hours keeps me slim."

Jada slipped her arms inside her robe. "About the

meeting with Aunt Dee, you think she'll be upset with us?"

"Yeah, she'll be bummed after we mention the eviction. We've got to think smart, though. Get her full of sausage, eggs and grits, then she might calm down." Celine placed the meat and mayonnaise in the refrigerator.

Jada lifted her hand. "You do the talking since she seems to listen to you." Aunt Dee was crazy about Celine. Jada knew her aunt loved all her nieces, but there was something about Celine that apparently made her the favorite out of the three. Jada believed Celine's commitment to the church was part of the reason she and Aunt Dee were close.

"I'll be ready. We don't have a new location, but we've made progress and that's what counts. I wanna know why they're evicting us when we've never missed a payment." Celine placed her food and a glass of cranberry juice on the table. "I'm still figuring out the scoop on the owner."

"What progress? That property management company is getting over on us. We deserve more time to find another location and notify our clients." Jada smacked her lips. "In all those files Momma kept, I didn't see anything on the owner."

"Don't get discouraged. We've got a little time left, and God can do the impossible. Some company called R and B Real Estate responded to my email today. I sent my information and yours."

"Okay. I'll keep an eye out for it."

"Did you talk to Antoine today?"

"Last night before he left for a poetry session. I didn't mention this to Aunt Dee, but Antoine might be at church tomorrow. He was checking for early flights while we talked. Jada opened the refrigerator and retrieved a bottled water.

"All right now. I was wondering why you hadn't brought him to church. You know Aunt Dee got to meet him. And I met him only one time."

"You know how that is. I didn't want to bring him around family right away. And he's at work Monday through Friday at 5:00 a.m. We do a lot of texting and phone talk, then get together on the weekends."

"Girl, that's the reason you should've gone with him. You could be up there enjoying time with your man in the Bay Area. Why'd you turn down a free trip, anyway?

"Yeah, Yeah. That was the plan. He was excited about me seeing Oakland and meeting his friends and family." Jada pushed the water bottle to her mouth and swigged. She hated to let him down at the last minute, but she wasn't ready for that. "What if Darius offered you an out of town trip after only three months of dating?"

Celine sat at the table. "Simple. If it was free, that would've been a yes."

Jada sat down and pressed her hand against her face. "I just hope I don't wake up one morning and find out this is a dream."

"You're not dreaming. Relax and enjoy the ride. You two are okay, right?" Celine bit into the sandwich and wiped her mouth.

"For sure. Antoine is magnetic. Thinking about how we didn't get along at work is hilarious." Jada laughed. "Well, now it is. Our relationship jumped off fast, but I'm not sure about out-of-town trips yet."

"I bet I know why." Celine squeezed Jada's arm and smiled.

"What do you mean?"

"Why you didn't go with him. You're not ready for sex 'til that ring is on your finger. Am I right?" A wide smile spread across Celine's face.

Unable to believe what she'd heard, Jada turned to Celine and stared hard. The best she could do was press her lips together and say nothing. *My sister is asking about my sex life?*

"Aha, that's the reason," Celine laughed. "I've been in that pit hole before."

Jada picked up the water bottle and gulped the rest of it while considering how to answer Celine's question. She and Antoine hadn't slept together, and she appreciated his understanding her desire to wait.

"Well, is it?" Celine asked with a gleam in her eyes.

"Yeah...I mean no. Or close... Ugh, girl, that's too much for me to think about. I'm going back to bed." She leaped from the chair and dashed to the bedroom. *How can I ever tell Celine that my rose was snipped by my first boyfriend in college?* She sprawled across the foot of the bed, turned on her side and closed her eyes. Fifteen minutes later, she heard a knock; Celine peeked in.

"You up?"

"I am. What's going on?"

Celine walked over to the bed and sat down. "I kinda thought that was it. You know...your reason for not traveling with Antoine. That's a tough subject, and temptation is a sniper that will wipe you out. If he asks you for a little sumptin' sumptin,' tell him no."

With her back to Celine, Jada placed a hand against her mouth and fought the urge to laugh. "Sis, I gotcha."

Celine crossed her arms. "Darius knows he ain't getting nothin' until we're married."

"Right, I understand." Jada sat up and stretched.

"Uh, I'm getting sleepy." She threw the robe at the foot of the bed and slipped under the covers. "Can you turn the light off?"

"Okay, but think about what I said. Update me after you talk to Antoine."

"Sure will," Jada turned on her side. "Goodnight."

After she heard the squeaky door close, Jada rolled on her back and slapped her forehead. *Mercy. She's a virgin. I can't believe I didn't pick up on that. But...twenty-six and never had sex?* Her eyes stretched to the size of dinner plates as she tried to absorb a dictionary of advice from her sister.

Jada hadn't talked much to her sisters about premarital sex. She didn't have to. Long before their parents passed, Momma, but mostly Aunt Dee, had preached from sunrise to sunset, and then sunset to dawn about marriage first, sex afterward. No options. *This part of my life will be a well-kept secret.*

Chapter 18

JADA

Sunday Morning

Jada managed to get five hours of rest and hoped that would suffice. After waking up three times, it really didn't add up to a whole five hours, she showered and dressed. Then she and Celine were on their way to pick-up Aunt Dee. Greater Saints Church of Christ held two services every Sunday. Why they preferred the first service at 8:00 a.m. instead of 11:00 was her question? Their breakfast meeting with Aunt Dee following the service would work. Then she'd have time to rest before seeing Antoine this afternoon.

Celine surprised Jada with the best Sunday morning blessing ever and volunteered to drive. Usually, she was too tired, and Jada understood. Working three twelve-hour shifts in a row in the emergency room and attending school had to be exhausting. Aunt Dee strolled to the car while putting on her glasses.

"Mornin', ladies. How's the world treatin' you?" Aunt Dee pinned loose strands of salt and pepper hair with a bobby pin. Healthy and active, she didn't look like a sixty-seven-year-old woman. She'd maintained a trim figure from years of daily morning walks and strict eating habits.

"I'm well," Celine said.

"I'm mediocre," Jada said.

Aunt Dee frowned. "Uh oh! What's that Charmaine up to now? I bet this meeting is about her," she turned to face Jada, who sat in the back seat.

"Her problems are ongoing. It's not Char this time, though. We'll talk later," Jada attempted a weak smile.

Aunt Dee tilted her head. "I know y'all ain't holdin' nothin' back from me."

"We'll tell you at breakfast. Okay?" Celine quickly added, "I'm sure church comes before business."

Aunt Dee grunted, "Huh," and mumbled under her breath while gazing out of the window.

Celine turned on the Bluetooth player, and Brian Courtney Wilson's song, "Increase My Faith" filled the car. She stopped at a red light, humming and clapping to the song.

After Aunt Dee regained her composure, she turned around again. "Jada, I understand you're datin' one of the DJs at the station."

Celine glanced at Jada through the rearview mirror and shrugged. "I didn't tell her."

"No, you didn't," Aunt Dee said. "I ran into Gordan at church a few weeks ago. I think you worked that weekend, Celine. Now, you girls are grown women, and I don't get in your business," she clutched her black Bible, "but if you need guidance, I'm always available for a chat or to pray with you."

Jada caught Celine's gaze in the rearview mirror before covering her mouth to stifle her giggles. Celine let out a brief laugh.

Aunt Dee furrowed her brows. "What's so funny?"

"Don't mind us. It's something we talked about earlier," Celine said.

Not only was Aunt Dee in their business, she was in *all* their business, personal as well. With no children of her own, their aunt had played a huge role in helping their parents with the girls, before and after their deaths.

Gordan had mentioned joining a church several months ago, but never mentioned he was considering her aunt's. "So, who told you about Antoine?" Jada asked.

"I'm not givin' up my sources," Aunt Dee waved her hand. "I asked Gordan about you. After he said you two broke up, I was so embarrassed. You girls oughta keep me in the loop," she pressed her hand to her chest.

"Aunt Dee, our relationship is still new...and, well, I needed time to know him better. I wanted to tell you at the right time. That would've been today."

"Sooner would've been appropriate," Aunt Dee said with a blank expression.

"I totally forgot to mention my breakup with Gordan. Our relationship ended a little over a year ago. We still hung out sometimes, but I'm not seeing him anymore."

"Well, I hope not. What a shame you couldn't stay together. You don't find many men like Gordan these days. He was such a gentleman, treated you well, helped you at a bad time in your life." She turned and looked at Jada. Then came the bonus question — the one Jada was certain her aunt would ask. "Which Sunday you bringin' your boyfriend to church? I'll cook a special dinner that day."

Jada sighed. "Soon. Real soon."

Aunt Dee liked and respected Gordan, and in her aunt's eyes, he deserved an accolade for the Best

Man in the World. What her aunt didn't know was the truth, but Jada refused to elaborate on her complicated relationship with Gordan.

Antoine's presence in her life opened a new journey of light and joy that no one she'd ever dated could unequivocally match. Not even Gordan. Although Jada and Antoine's three-month relationship was new, she and her man were like two fresh balls of clay in the sculptured pottery class they'd taken. They'd placed the balls of clay on a potter's wheel, massaged, structured, and molded their pieces of clay in place. Then came the glazing of their finished products to produce beautiful pieces of artwork that would last forever. That was the shape of their love.

They arrived at church on time, and upon entering the sanctuary, a sweet fragrance from several multicolored flower arrangements flowed through the air. The atmosphere was set for praise and worship. The head of the Usher Board, Sister Robbins, greeted them with a pleasant disposition. The woman rarely smiled, but her professionalism and kindness were impeccable.

"Good morning, Sister Burns, I see you've got your nieces accompanying you."

"Yes, Charmaine couldn't make it. But we're prayin' for her. You remember Jada?"

"I sure do. We've missed you, Lady." She offered Jada a hug, and then Celine and Aunt Dee. "I'll be right with you, so don't move." She hand-gestured another usher, who rushed to Sister Robbins' side, listening to her instructions. "Sister Davis will take you to your seats. Have a blessed Sunday."

As the usher walked them down the aisle, Jada's eyes roamed the church. Two months seemed like forever. She took a deep breath to release the uneasy tension, which typically occurred after her absence from worship service. Nothing had changed, and it never would. The same wooden pews, same podium, and the same Bishop Riley, who preached the kind of Sunday morning sermons that had members dancing in the aisles. When they reached Aunt Dee's favorite section — middle aisle, three rows from the front, the usher extended a white-gloved hand to their seats. Celine whispered something to the usher, and left a seat open by sitting her purse in the seat. Jada almost forgot that Antoine might show up but doubted that he would since he had not called or texted.

Sitting in the pew where her family worshipped every Sunday — memories of Momma fanning her face, Daddy frequently shouting 'amen'— made Jada's heart ache. It always did. There was so much about the church that she'd enthusiastically embraced, yet after her parents' demise, dark patches in life mounted. Despite the hardships, she tried to avoid questioning her faith, but the loss of both parents left her angry. *Why them?* She closed her eyes and bowed her head.

A short time later, she looked up and saw an usher guiding Antoine to their row. Thankfully, she had told him where they sat each week, and thankfully he'd worn a suit, which he hated wearing. Celine got up; Antoine hugged, sat next to Jada and kissed her cheek. The look on Aunt Dee's face was hysterical.

"Aunt Dee, this is Antoine," Jada said.

"Nice to meet you, Aunt Dee, and nice to see you again, Celine." He rose and hugged Aunt Dee.

"God bless you and welcome to Greater Saints," Aunt Dee said with a broad smile.

"We're glad you made it. Did your flight just get in?" Celine asked.

"Yes, not long ago. I was hoping I wouldn't be late."

Praise and worship started. After an inspirational message and altar call, Bishop Riley ended the benediction precisely at ten. Celine led the way down the crowded aisle to prevent Aunt Dee's pauses for long chats with the church sisters.

After they exited the sanctuary, the first question

Aunt Dee asked was, "Antoine, are you comin' to breakfast with us?"

Antoine extended his hand to her aunt and said, "Aunt Dee, I appreciate the invite. Maybe next time. I have some work at the studio this morning."

"Okay. I'll invite you to dinner one Sunday," Aunt Dee said.

"I look forward to that. You all have a great breakfast."

He and Jada walked a few feet away. "Baby, thank you for coming," Jada told Antoine.

"I wanted to keep my promise. Look, we're still on for this afternoon, okay?"

"Sure. We're going to breakfast and then have a business meeting with my aunt. Call or text me later."

He kissed her cheek and said, "I'll do that. I'm heading to the station."

Jada caught up with her aunt and Celine as they walked to the lot.

"Hey, family!" Gordan called out as they walked. Jada twirled around. He waved her his way. "J, can I speak with you for a moment?"

Jada searched to see if Antoine was close by, then blew air from her lips. "We're on our way to breakfast."

"Uh, nice to see you, Gordan," Aunt Dee said.

She whispered in Jada's ear, "Don't be rude. We'll meet you at the car."

Celine shot Gordan a brief stare and turned to Jada. "Keep in mind, I'm ready to go."

"Y'all know we're in front of the Lord's house." Aunt Dee looked at Jada, and then Celine. Jada didn't move, and Aunt Dee shooed her away. "Go see what he wants. Might be important."

"Aunt Dee, what he has to say doesn't matter. Jada's with Antoine now."

"Give me five minutes. I'll be right there." Out of respect for Aunt Dee's wishes, Jada didn't want to seem arrogant or rude. Forgiveness came fast, but any unrealistic beliefs her aunt had of a happy reunion were zero. He was with Kiley; she was with Antoine.

Jada walked toward Gordan. "Hey, pretty girl. How you been doing?"

"I'm well. I told Celine I wouldn't be long. We're riding with her."

"I got it. Your sister doesn't look happy to see me," he glanced at Celine and Aunt Dee. "We can't talk out here. Why don't we walk to my car, and I'll drive you to the lot?"

Jada smirked, shifting her weight. "To your car? Uh, I'm not sure I should do that."

"I arrived early, and I'm not far away. I won't hold you up long."

They walked to his car, exchanging remarks about how they enjoyed the church service. Jada kept an eye out for Antoine's truck. Once they were seated inside Gordan's car, he retrieved a tan bag from the glove compartment and unzipped it. He removed the small box and showed Jada the engagement ring he'd given Kiley.

"That's Kiley's ring. What happened, she canceled the wedding?" Jada said with tongue in cheek.

"Me and Kiley are through, and I have to get this off my chest." He placed the ring box back inside the bag, and then straightened the starched collar of his aqua-blue shirt before placing a hand on the steering wheel.

Jada eyed him warily. Gordan appeared rested, he looked and smelled good.

"I've hit some rough spots. And when you cut me outta your life that hurt."

Jada threw up a palm. "Stop right there. I'm not discussing our relationship. That's in a closed file."

"Would you please listen? It's not what you think. I lost you, and I finally accepted that. You should know my dating Kiley was not to get even or to hurt you."

"I never assumed that."

"Well, I need to get things right with you. We, uh, clicked...started kickin' it together, and I admit I was wrong for not telling you." Gordan touched her hand. "I apologize from my heart for any pain I caused you. I joined the church, and I'm trying to change. I'm asking if you'd forgive me."

Gordan begging for her forgiveness was something she'd never expected.

Jada glanced at him. "I've already forgiven you. But had you told me about Kiley, that funky drama at the beach — my misunderstanding — never would've gone down."

"I get that now." He huffed out a breath. "J, me and you had parted ways, and I don't know what came over me. I had some fairy-tale infatuation with Kiley." He paused. "Didn't take long to realize that proposal shouldn't have happened. She lied and told me she was twenty-nine. Turned out, she's twenty-three and has a lot of serious issues."

Jada leaned back in the seat and stared at Gordan. This could be the leverage she needed to validate the issues she'd encountered with Kiley. She wouldn't ask, but she still didn't understand what he saw in her. "So, what happened between you two?"

Gordan rubbed his hands together. "Let me put it like this, Kiley is moody. I'm outta that situation, and I have nothing else to say about that sista. My reputation is important."

"Oh, your reputation, huh?" She wondered why he hadn't given his reputation a thought while he was dating a zoo full of women. Some while they were together.

"You know what I mean. My business reputation."

"I know, I know. Just kidding. She can be difficult, and I try to keep my distance to stay calm." Jada shook her head. "The problem is, you men pay too much attention to what's on the outside when it comes to women. Glam don't always get it."

"Yeah, you're right."

"Seriously, if you believe she might bring harm to the station or any of our employees, tap Griff or Simon on the shoulder. I'm sure they'd keep any information confidential. My apologies to you for my behavior. I slapped you, and that was wrong." She didn't have the heart to tell Gordan that Denise had informed her of Kiley's dating habits.

Gordan licked his lips and looked down. "No, I'm not saying a word. And you didn't have to apologize. I deserved that punch a long time ago. How's everything going with you and Antoine?"

"Why do you ask?"

"Don't go there. Everybody knows you're his woman. Just like they knew about us."

Jada folded her arms. "The key is privacy. Just because people are seen together, shouldn't automatically be an assumption that they're dating." She smiled. "We're very close, and I'm happy. That's it."

Gordan swiped her cheek with his finger. "Bae, I still love you. But it's okay, he's a blessed dude. I wish you two well. You and me? We had a good thang."

"There's no more *we*; hasn't been in a while. I refused to admit it and had a hard time letting go." Feeling slightly uncomfortable, Jada cast her gaze out the window. "I better go before Celine leaves."

Gordan drove Jada to the first floor of the parking structure.

"Thank you for allowing me to express myself," Gordan said.

"You're welcome."

"If there's anything you ever need, don't hesitate to call me."

"I appreciate that." She kissed his jaw. "Take care." She opened the car door and fast walked to Celine's car.

Before Jada could fasten her seatbelt, Aunt Dee glanced back and asked, "How'd your talk with Gordan go?"

"Everything went fine." Jada shifted her gaze out the window to avoid Aunt Dee's long stare.

Celine drove to M'Dears Bakery and Bistro in Carson. The Sunday morning crowd hadn't drifted in yet, and Jada was happy they'd gone to the 8:00 a.m. service. After the waitress handed them menus, Aunt Dee dived on Jada again about her conversation with Gordan. Jada shared a little, but anything more would have turned into a long back and forth question and answer session, and they were supposed to be focusing on the dress shop.

After their food arrived, Celine initiated the conversation about the eviction notice. Aunt Dee didn't take the information very well. She wiped tears from the corners of her eyes with a handkerchief. "Three months, and I'm findin' out now? Doggone it. Why'd y'all wait so long? This is totally unfair to me."

"We know, Aunt Dee," Celine said. "It's just...we didn't want to burden you."

"Right, and we rely on you to run the shop. So, we tried to handle this with the hope of finding a new location," Jada said.

"That's ridiculous. Findin' out this late is what burdens me." Aunt Dee pushed a balled fist to her temple. "Your momma worked hard to keep that business. And I was right by her side when work slowed down at the first shop on Central Avenue. God blessed us with a break." Aunt Dee smiled. "An opportunity came to move to the west side." She glanced at Jada and Celine with sad eyes. "We gotta save the business." Aunt Dee rocked back and forth, "Lord, please help us."

"Now, don't get your hopes up on this. I found a potential place in Inglewood and made an early appointment with the owner. Sissy, we can meet him before you go to work. If it works out okay, we'll take you over there, Aunt Dee."

"Oh, bless the Lord," Aunt Dee said.

"That's positive news. Where in Inglewood?" Jada asked, sipping coffee.

"On West Boulevard, close to Word of Life Bookstore. It's pricey, but maybe we can barter."

"Girls, do your best."

"We will." Celine rubbed her aunt's back, and Jada reached across the table and squeezed Aunt Dee's hand. "We got this, Aunt Dee. You taught us to hold on to faith and never let go. We'll work together and get it done."

Celine and Jada discussed the information they'd managed to compile about the property management company that handled the lease for their dress shop. Aunt Dee offered suggestions, and they made plans to follow-up. Aunt Dee's primary concern was hiring an attorney immediately if the location in Inglewood did not work out. Celine had spoken with the property management company for their current location. They confirmed the eviction was still in effect, but they would not disclose the owner's name or contact information. Jada and her sisters had ninety days left to move.

Chapter 19

ANTOINE

Sunday Evening

As Antoine drove to the station, his mind trailed to Jada. *Why was she in Gordan's car?* He wasn't a jealous person, but something about seeing his girl talking to her former boyfriend brought in negative vibes. After church, he had made a call to his mother before he left the lot and noticed Jada riding in the passenger side of Gordan's vehicle. He assumed she got a lift to her car since they were in the church parking lot.

Antoine turned into the Starbucks drive-thru for coffee and a sandwich. After he'd eaten, he pushed those negative vibes aside. Jada was his woman, and he trusted her, so he shrugged that off his shoulders and drove to the radio station to work on some voice-overs.

After he finished his work, he went home for some rest, changed clothes, and called Jada.

"Hello."

"Hey, Love. What's up?" He squeezed lemon into a cup of Chai tea latte.

"I apologize for not calling you back. I was tired after our meeting with Aunt Dee."

"Babe, it's all right. What time can I pick you up?"

"How about dinner tomorrow?"

"What? Lady, we have a date set for this afternoon."

"Right. We said afternoon. It's evening," she said with a soft laugh.

"Please?" He bit his bottom lip. "I intended to call sooner, but I was at the station longer than expected. I've missed you." She didn't know how much he'd missed her, nor would she ever guess his surprise plans for this evening.

"I missed you, too. Okay, where we going? Not to your cousin's I hope."

"For real? I've been waiting to have you all to myself, and you think I'm taking you to the house? Besides, you know how nosy Derrick is. He'd probably have his ear to my bedroom door all night." They laughed simultaneously.

"Hmm...your bedroom door? Exactly what do you have in mind?"

"You'll see. It's a surprise."

"Uh, huh...that sounds like an expensive outing."

"This is our night. What time will you be ready?"

"I'll drive so you won't have to drop me off. Just give me the address and time to get ready."

Antoine had reserved a room at the Montage Hotel – Beverly Hills two weeks prior but chose to surprise Jada. He arrived before she did, checked in and had the bellhop bring her gifts to the room. *Everything is ready. She should love this spacious suite.* He walked through each room in the suite. The walls had loads of colorful pictures and a big screen television. Best of all, the suite boasted a large private balcony.

Antoine scanned the suite one more time before he left the room. He exited the hotel elevator at the same time Jada strolled into the lobby, wearing a lime green blouse, short brown skirt, and brown high heels. As she walked toward him, his spirit wasn't the only thing that lifted. *Those shapely legs are gorgeous!*

"Hey, beautiful." Antoine planted a kiss on her lips.

"Hi."

They embraced for several seconds; he closed his eyes, enjoying the lavender scent of her skin and the smell of freshly washed hair.

He reached for her small overnight bag, and they walked together to the restaurant for drinks and dinner.

After dinner, they took the elevator to the eleventh floor. When they walked into the suite, Jada yelled, "Oh, my gosh! What is this?" She lifted both arms above her head, then pointed to the bouquet of red roses in a large white vase on the table. She glanced up at the massive red and white balloons floating in the air and started laughing. A small card and box sat in front of the flower vase. "This room is larger than an apartment. A big screen TV?" Jada walked through the large suite. "You must've paid a fortune for this."

"Stop worrying about the cost and open your gift." Antoine grinned.

She placed her purse on the table and sniffed the bouquet.

He folded his arms, watching her read the card. She opened the box and removed a gold diamond ring. Kissing her hand, he bowed on one knee, "This is a unique ring. In the future, there will be another one. Happy three-month anniversary! I love you, babe."

"Oh, my! It's beautiful." He watched her admire the cluster-diamond, yellow-gold ring. "Thank you," she smiled and leaned down to puckered lips. After the kiss, her head dropped. "I feel bad about not buying you anything. I'll make it up to you."

Antoine rose to his feet. "You don't have to. I know we haven't been together that long, but our ebb and flow is so cool. Love has no time limits; for me, this is real."

Jada rubbed her finger down his nose and smiled. "You make me happy, too, baby. I love you."

He lifted her chin and kissed her; she succumbed to his strong arms. He hadn't been able to eat or sleep much while he was out of town. He'd missed her laugh, fresh scent, the close bond that made their relationship special. Antoine held her hand and led her out on the private balcony. A full moon and a million bright stars twinkled in the sky while two small pole lamps brightened the dark night. He treasured every moment of having Jada by his side, it was surreal.

Their conversation led to Antoine's trip and Rashad's game. He wrapped his arm around Jada and kissed her forehead. The night had gone smoothly as he had hoped, and most important, she liked the ring. This woman changed his life; he loved her. He had fought the urge to buy an engagement ring.

"You seem a little preoccupied. What's wrong?" He gazed into her eyes.

"Yeah, I am. I feel bad. Me and Celine...well, we

talked to Aunt Dee today, and I didn't expect her to get so upset. I haven't talked much about my family's business because it's in a rut."

"What's going on?" he asked, hoping it was nothing serious.

"My mom owned a dress shop. After she passed, we kept it going in a building we're leasing." She clasped her hands. "We've been in the same location for over twenty-one years."

When she paused, he sensed a bundle of raw emotions that she couldn't express.

"Babe, what's wrong?"

"Months ago, we got an eviction notice. And we, uh, haven't found another location." She gazed up at him. "Either the buildings are not in good areas or rent is too high."

"Oh, no." He placed both hands on her shoulders. "Okay, who owns the building?"

"That's the problem. We pay rent to a property management company, and they won't release the owner's name. Our hopes were high about a building in Inglewood. The owner canceled this morning."

"Sorry to hear that. Do you have a lawyer?"

"We've contacted one. To keep the cost down, me and Celine tried to find more information before we hire him." She clapped her palms together, "We kept it from our aunt who runs the shop. Now, Aunt Dee is upset, and we're running out of time."

Antoine's back stiffened as Jada shared the discussion between her aunt and sister. The worry that scribbled her face signaled it was time to step up and find a resolution. "Babe," he tipped her chin up. "Calm down. I'll take care of the attorney fees and I'll help you. Just give me a few days to reach out to my contacts, okay?"

She stepped back and shook her head. "No. See...that's why I didn't say anything. You, Mr. DJ Ant..." she pressed an index finger to his chest, "... have your own expenses. You live with your cousin. And how can you afford this expensive suite, jewelry, flowers—"

He clamped her tiny waist and brought her closer. "Don't worry about that. I said I'll take care of it. Believe me, I have multiple streams of income."

Antoine considered disclosing his wealth to Jada, and then his conscious mind kicked in with rationalizations like *that's crazy. Do you want to lose her?* Jada's trust meant a lot, and he'd met part of her family. Nowhere in the equation would the Bailey family squabbles, backbiting, or his wealth fit into the framework of supporting Jada. He'd gone down that road of exposing his wealth to Fiona, and it became disastrous. No way would he make that same mistake. He'd call Joy for advice. She'd be in town next week, and it was time for them to get together.

Antoine and Jada cuddled. Her warm breath made the hair on his chest rise as the blood in his veins sizzled. Spellbound, his primary thought revolved around his love for this woman. He pulled off his shirt and pants and carefully lifted her green blouse over her head. She tossed her bra onto the velvet burgundy ottoman as Antoine ran the tip of his tongue along the lateral parts of her neck. He pulled her down onto the oversized chaise.

"Uh, excuse me," Jada said in between kisses. "We're not doing anything out here. It's cooler tonight."

Antoine picked up the throw blanket at the foot of the chair and wrapped it around her shoulders. "There. You won't be cold for long." The softness of her lips ignited the kind of excitement children have when they walk inside a candy store. Hoisting Jada on his lap, their lips locked, and Antoine deepened the kiss with a fervent desire to make sweet love. Brushing his moist mouth around her nipples, he tasted the sweetness of soft brown skin. He helped Jada to her feet and watched her wiggle out of her skirt and panties.

She sat on the chaise, crossed her legs and posed like she was modeling for *Ebony Magazine*. Antoine grinned and grabbed his cell from the ottoman. "Don't move." The phone clicked.

She flinched. "No, you didn't take a naked picture of me," Jada hopped off the chair and bolted over to Antoine. "Gimme that phone." She jumped and stretched to get the phone from his hand, but she would need a ladder to reach his long arm lifted high above his head.

"Nope, this is mine," he laughed, jogging away.

Jada chased him; they tussled playfully back and forth for the phone until he gave it to her. She deleted the photo. "Promise me. No more nude photos." Jada handed him back the cell.

Forget the phone. He rubbed her back, planting kisses on her neck. She pushed his hand away. Had he messed up? Was Jada upset? She couldn't be. "Babe, are you okay?"

She pouted her lips. "No, you need to promise you won't take another nude photo."

"I promise, and I'm sorry if I offended you," Antoine lifted both hands in defense. "I was going to delete it." He touched her face. "Do you accept my apology?"

"No!" she stormed toward the glass door. "I'm leaving."

His faced dropped at the shock of her comments. "But what did I—"

A few feet away from the door, Jada whipped around and pointed her finger at him. "Gotcha!" She laughed, and then ran back to the chaise. "Now come here and give me some of that sweet brown sugar."

His eyes roamed her nude body, his heart pumped so fast he could hardly contain himself. *Be cool and take it slow.* Antoine's face broke into a wide grin. "Okay, you got me this time," he scratched his head. "Leaving with no clothes on? I should've caught that prank from the start."

He scuttled to the chaise and crawled from the bottom upward like a tiger on the prowl. On his knees, he planted a kiss on her lips. "Mmm...you're real funny, but I'll get you back."

Raising her arms overhead, Jada arched her back and giggled. "That's what you think."

"Watch me." He planted kisses from her luscious lips to her breasts, swirling his tongue around full nipples then down to her navel, tenderly scattering kisses in a trail back to her mouth. He caught her lips in between his, kissing her deeply. His fingers moved in between her soft legs. His rod stood erect as the Queen's guard at Buckingham Palace as he entered her damp canal. They rocked slowly in seesaw motion, fast then faster. His excitement soared higher. He moaned; she moaned. Their bodies shuddered, and an immense explosion like fireworks released. Then they started over again.

Antoine kissed Jada's forehead before he rolled over and threaded his arms around her shoulders. Neither said a word nor moved for a while.

"Baby, hand me that throw blanket. I'm getting cold," Jada said.

"Cold? With all this heat between us?" He picked up the blanket that she had pitched on the floor and handed it to her. Jada got up, sheathed her body and tied a knot before walking inside the room.

"Uh! We're not done yet." Antoine followed her. His plan — was to make love all night with his beautiful woman.

"What are you saying?" Jada laughed.

"I can't get enough of you, girl."

"You're being greedy."

"That's right. And I'm going to be greedy a little while longer. Remember how long I waited?" He unwrapped the blanket and gently placed her face in between his palms. "Gorgeous lady, I love you. You're mine."

Jada squeezed Antoine's waist and laid against his chest. "I love you, too, honey."

Chapter 20

JADA

Monday

The foreign sound of an alarm clock that wasn't hers woke Jada from a deep sleep. Wiping her eyes, she sat up slowly remembering that she had stayed at the Montage after an enchanting night with Antoine. She rarely stayed out all night, but Antoine's generosity and suite reservation for date night made her second think this one. She'd texted Celine and informed her she would not be home.

Jada noticed a small pad with a handwritten note on the nightstand. She picked it up. GM, *babe. I left early for work. Room Service will bring breakfast. Call them when you're ready. Thank you for last night. Love you, Ant.* Jada smiled. Last night, now room service? This was way overboard. Honestly, she wasn't sure if she was ready for the Queen Bee treatment. A vision of Antoine's fine face on his knees, the ring, thwarted doubts that occasionally crept into her head. Jada walked to the closet and removed one of the white terrycloth robes and the spare outfit she'd brought up from the car last night.

After exiting the shower, she wrapped her body in a towel. A quick glance at her hair in the mirror was a reminder that she'd left her hair products at home. She added body lotion to her skin, smoothed her hair back and pulled it up into a curly-kinky afro puff before slipping on a two-piece orange and brown wide-legged palazzo pants outfit and beige open-toe wedges. Perfect for the weather prediction of another warm day. She heard a knock at the door.

"Who's there?"

"Room Service," a male voice said.

Jada swung the door open to a friendly middle-aged man who rolled in a cart.

"Thank you. Oooh...this smells delicious," Jada said, handing him a tip.

"You're welcome, ma'am, and thank you for the tip."

He left the pleasant smell of bacon, eggs, and coffee lingering in the air. Jada moved the plate and coffee to a round table, lifted the silver lid covering on the plate and clicked on the big screen. Adding a little hot sauce to the eggs, she wished Antoine could've joined her for this meal that was suitable for royalty. Her phone chimed. It was Denise.

"Hey, lady. What's going on this early?" Jada asked.

"Nothing. Just checkin' in on you. We didn't talk this weekend."

"Well, that's because I was busy."

"I see. Busy doin' what?"

"I'll tell you later. I gotta leave in a minute. Hit me up when you get to the office."

"Okay, bye."

As Jada prepared to leave, she noticed a slip of paper gliding underneath the door. She placed the flowers and her overnight bag on a chair and bent down to pick up what appeared to be the hotel bill. "What?" She gasped, covering her mouth. The bill nearly knocked her over. This was way too much to spend for one night in a hotel. She and Antoine would have to talk.

The station was quiet when Jada arrived for work. She unlocked her office, placed her flowers on the desk, and opened her desktop before she tipped back to the studio. Antoine was on the air and seemed busy, but when he saw her peering in the window, he pressed a finger to his lips and blew her a kiss. She scribbled a note with a smiley face on a piece of paper and pressed it to the window.

TALK TO YOU LATER.

She stopped by the employee mailbox section where a small envelope that she hadn't seen on Friday was the single item present. She opened it and smiled after viewing two photos. One of Antoine on a couch with his eyes closed and shirt unbuttoned and another showing a television and furniture in someone's living room. Jada frowned. *This couch is not the same as the one at Derrick's place. Maybe he was visiting someone, and they shot this photo. Or it could've been taken at his place in San Francisco.* She returned to her office and propped the door open. As the morning progressed, she would close it to stay focused. The phone chimed. It was Charmaine.

"Hi, Char."

"Morning. I'm checkin' in. Celine said you didn't make it home last night."

"Um, I texted her about that. I went out with Denise. It was late, so I, uh...I bunked at her place."

"Okay. If you say so. I'll tell Celine."

"Hey. You know I would've called if something was wrong."

"Sissy, I know. Now you see how I feel. I'll tell Celine we talked."

She would go there. At least I'm dating one man.

"Yeah, well, I'll be home this evening. I'm at work,

so talk to you later." Jada rotated her head in a circle, stretched, and opened her computer. Kiley walked in the door. She stared at the bouquet on Jada's desk and frowned. It was the funkiest expression Jada had ever seen. Without a good morning, Kiley handed her a stack of paperwork.

"Griff wants you at a sales meeting today." Kiley fanned her face with a sheet of paper.

"Those meetings are usually on Thursdays. What time is the meeting?"

She rolled her eyes at Jada. "I don't know. Call and ask him," she snapped.

Jada glanced up with a 'no you didn't say that to me' look. "I take it Griff asked *you* to deliver the message. And since *you* don't have all the details, *you* should call him."

"He's not in yet, and I'm leaving early for an appointment."

"Well, please text him and send me the info before you leave."

"Why should I?" Kiley scrunched her face.

Jada tilted her head and stared at Kiley. *This woman is not normal.* "For the time and location of the meeting."

"It's your meeting. I might not be here when he gets in." Kiley shifted her focus to the bouquet on Jada's desk.

Jada stopped typing, crossed her arms and looked at Kiley who wore a blanket of red-burgundy weave that trailed to the middle of her back.

"You know what? It's your responsibility to do what your boss asked. What's the problem?"

With pursed lips, Kiley squinted at Jada. "That's what you think, and I don't have a problem."

That was the end of what she'd say to Kiley. She had the nerve to refuse to follow-up with Griff's request. What was up with this woman? Her attitude had never been this nasty, and Jada intended to let Griff know. Denise likely had information if the meeting concerned the Sales Department. She picked up her phone and called her friend.

"Hey," Denise said in a sluggish voice.

"Girl, did you go back to sleep?"

"I'm woke but in bed. What's goin' on?"

"Kiley mentioned a sales meeting Griff's having today. You know what time it starts?"

"No. Our meetings are not until Thursday. Same time. Where'd she get that info?"

"Never mind. That dizzy woman didn't give me any information. I asked her to check with Griff, and she refused."

"Okay, but text me if there's a sales meeting."

Time seemed to drag by during the quarterly management team meeting. For some reason, Kiley didn't add the meeting date to Jada's Outlook calendar, which she was supposed to do for her and Griff. Jada wasn't a manager, but they felt she should be present since the agenda involved covering some of her responsibilities.

Jada left the conference room and glanced at her watch; she looked down the hallway. Antoine's shift ended over an hour ago, and he hadn't stopped by her office before the meeting. Not even to creep through for a two-minute chat during the newscasts or while the music played. Fighting off a strong urge to go look for him, she turned and strutted back to her office. He was likely in the studio doing voice overs or working on another project.

She sat at her desk and swiveled her chair around to the computer. She tried to remember if he'd mentioned an appointment that she'd forgotten. Nothing popped up on the calendar in her cell. She picked up her cell and texted Antoine.

Hey, baby. I missed you. Did you leave the station?

As the seconds ticked into minutes, Jada stared at the computer, doing her work in between worrying. It was unusual for him not to text or call back immediately if he wasn't on the air or in the studio. When her cell chimed, she picked it up.

In a business meeting. We'll talk tomorrow. Love you!

A slow breath escaped her lungs, relaxing every tense muscle in her body. At least it was nothing urgent. But why couldn't he call her this evening?

Chapter 21

ANTOINE

Monday

The drive to the LAX Airport Courthouse wouldn't take long. Not that Antoine cared, this meeting with Kiley was apparently a fraud or blackmail. His sad mood, a rarity from his upbeat, positive character, was the reason he didn't stop by Jada's office before he headed out to meet Kiley. He didn't want to give off any unintentional negative signs. Jada's intuition was sharp, and he'd already been under her radar.

He found a parking spot in the courthouse parking lot off LaCienega and parked in between two cars. Once he turned the music down, the turmoil that swarmed full force returned. How did he get caught up in a mess like this? What, and how, would he explain to Jada? There was no logical explanation for something that never happened. He leaned back on the headrest and waited. When he saw a woman, who resembled Kiley walking across the lot, his eyes followed her. She stopped at the entry and slipped her arms into a bulky black sweater as she strutted through the door.

He waited ten minutes, and then picked up his briefcase before climbing out the SUV and setting the alarm. Before he headed for the courthouse cafeteria, he remembered to text Joy an approximate time that he'd be available for lunch at the café across the street. Antoine set his iPhone on record and placed the cell and Bluetooth inside his briefcase.

From the time he walked in, Antoine discerned the sneaky smile that smeared Kiley's face. His suspicion heightened. He wanted to admonish her not to play games and thought hard for two seconds about threatening to report her to Griff. The issue with that — everybody at the station would know his business, including Jada.

He slid into a chair across from Kiley. "I don't have time to waste. This meeting will be brief. What's this about?" he placed his briefcase on the table.

"Like you don't know." Kiley narrowed her eyes. "You made me come here to a courthouse?" She sneered and glanced around. "This is so tacky."

"I didn't *make* you do nothing. This was your idea,

and what did you expect, lunch at Ruth's Chris Steakhouse?"

She rolled her eyes. "I don't even know where that place is. You coulda treated me to lunch at the Sizzler."

"For the record, I'm here strictly because you asked to meet face-to-face. Now, what do you want?" He scanned the cafeteria noting the small number of people talking and eating lunch. Others waited at the counter for their food. Antoine was relieved that none of the customers were close enough to hear their conversation.

"Knock off the denial. I'm sixteen weeks pregnant and this baby is yours."

He leaned forward. "Have you lost your mind? We talked about this before. I've never had sex with you."

"Wrong. Oh, we had sex." Kiley splayed her fingers, inspecting her long red fingernails. "Problem is," she wagged a finger, "you don't wanna remember. The night you gave me a lift home, got my sound system up. Sound familiar?" She gazed at Antoine. "It happened after a few shots of Chivas Regal, and it was so good." Her pink lips stretched from ear-to-ear.

Antoine stared at her. Kiley's antics smoldered the last bit of his kindness as his patience ran short.

"That's a lie, and I'm not going for it. I don't even drink Chivas Regal."

Kiley unbuttoned the sweater and placed her hands on a small bump in her stomach. "You drank it that night. And you did more than drink alcohol. Deny it if you wish, but...I wouldn't do that."

Antoine folded his arms and leaned back trying to wrap his mind around this calamity. He was bothered by his vague memory of that night. Why couldn't he remember everything? This woman was obviously trying to blackmail him for money, attention, or whatever. "You know what? You served me tea and lemon cake. Unless you spiked it, I don't recall drinking anything else. And I don't believe I had sex with you, so what's next?"

Her silly grin remained in place as she snickered. "You'll find out. Count on it."

Antoine kept his cool as Joy recommended. He rose and lifted his briefcase from the table. "Screw up my job or personal life and *you* can count on me suing you. This meeting is over."

Chapter 22

ANTOINE

Monday

Antoine jogged across the parking lot from the courthouse and entered the Bistro Town Café. He spotted Joy sitting in a corner tapping information into her cell. She pushed up from the seat when she saw Antoine, and they embraced.

"Hey, baby sis, you look fab." Antoine admired his sister. Joy graduated at the top of her class from Stanford Law School. She always dressed professionally and kept her shoulder-length hair looking as if she'd just left the salon.

"What's new with the job?" Joy asked. She removed the matching brown and beige jacket to her dress and placed it over the back of the chair.

"It's all cool. They switched my show to days; that was a surprise."

"Oh. No more driving home at 2:00 in the morning. But you prefer nights, how are days working for you?"

"I'm adjusting; still love my job."

"I ordered already; I was hungry. Are you eating?"

"No, I'm straight. Grabbed a bite on the way. How's the hubs and my niece?"

"Merlon's fine, busy as ever at the law firm. And Cheyenne celebrated her fourth birthday last week."

"What? You should've FaceTimed and let me wish her a Happy Birthday."

She rolled her eyes. "Like I would've caught up with you. I don't know how you find time to eat, sleep, or do anything with your schedule. And you have a new girlfriend, too? Cheyenne had a ball at her party. We invited a few friends from her daycare."

"That's boss. I'm busy, but I'll always find time for family and my girl." Antoine dug in his briefcase and removed his cell and wireless Bluetooth, pushing them across the table to Joy. "Here's the recording. The meeting wasn't long, so I don't know if this will help."

His sister placed the Bluetooth in her ear. "After I listen, we'll talk about this Kiley woman." A short time later, she handed the phone and Bluetooth back to Antoine.

"First, are you positive about not having sex with her?"

"Absolutely."

"Because nothing that I do will matter if you're the father of her child."

"As I've said before, we work at the station together. That's it."

"And that's ridiculous," Joy cocked her head to the side. "She says you're the father; you say no. You both have different opinions on whether you had sex?"

If Antoine could ax this conversation right now, he would. Kiley's insinuations were outrageous and embarrassing. How could he explain that to his sister?

He pulled his right earlobe. "I don't know what's up with that woman. She flirted a lot, but I wasn't interested. I never dated her."

Joy raised a brow, "I'm asking one more time."

He twisted his mouth. If he wanted his sister's help, he had to empty his crap on the table. "I'm about ninety-nine percent sure that nothing happened. I took her home, set up her stereo system. I don't remember anything else."

Joy's eyes bulged so wide they could have fallen out the sockets. "Ninety-nine percent sure, and you don't remember?"

Antoine nodded.

The waiter returned to the table and placed Joy's salmon salad and diet coke in front of her. "We may have a problem. You didn't tell me that part. What happened that night before and after you went to Kiley's? No, wait." After a bite of salmon, she dabbed her mouth with a napkin and handed Antoine a pen and tablet. "Brainstorm that question while I eat. When you're ready, start writing details. *Everything*."

He wrote notes for almost twenty minutes, stopped and read them, continuing until he finished. He slid the tablet across the table. "That's what I recall."

Joy pushed her plate aside and picked up the paper. At one point, she frowned and glanced at Antoine. "Iced tea and lemon cake at one in the morning?"

He hunched his shoulders. "Why not? I was working on her sound system. She offered it to me."

"Ant, clarify this part." Joy underlined a section of his notes and showed it to him.

Antoine went on to explain why he went up to Kiley's place. He also revealed the details that occurred at the event and at Kiley's, including the weird feeling that overpowered him before he fell asleep. Joy asked for one or two weeks to work on all the information that he'd provided, and she also volunteered to contact a private investigation firm to dig into Kiley's background.

"I won't make assumptions. What I know is she sounds like trouble, big brother." Joy tapped her nails on the table. "What do you believe is her motive for possibly framing you with this pregnancy? Money, notoriety, revenge because she can't have you. Mental illness should be a consideration, too." She placed the tablet in her briefcase.

"I wish I knew. You know I'm picky about the women I date, and this is a prime example of why." He rested his face against a palm and gazed at the table. "I mean...there was no relationship. At all. That's why this whole situation is beyond crazy."

"You're right. Did you see a doctor?"

"I did. The next day I went to a clinic, saw a doctor and he ordered labs. I felt better, so I never returned for the results."

Joy tilted her head and said, "Ant. You know that was important, right?"

"I get that. Just wanted to clear my head and move on. I'm dating a smart, beautiful woman now. I need a copy of those labs."

"I'll email you a release of authorization form. Sign it and send it back."

"Speaking of dating...when will Pop and I get to

meet this gem you've told me about? I'm sure you plan to bring her up north. Merlon can fire up the grill one weekend."

"Whenever she's ready." His cell chimed with a text notification. He lifted his phone off the table and smiled. "Jada," he glanced at his sister. "You know...Uh, I'd prefer you not tell Pop I'm dating. I'll get around to telling him."

A scant smile crossed Joy's lips. "You don't plan to, do you?"

"It's not a priority. I'm working on my problems down here first. Jada doesn't know about this Kiley dilemma. What do I say to her? Kiley said she's carrying my baby and we've never had sex?" He shook his head. "This is insane."

Joy frowned. "I can imagine. But the first chance you get, tell her. By the way, I've read the information you sent on the dress shop. Do you want to give Jada my number?"

"Not really. I promised her I'd handle this."

"You have issues of your own to handle, and I may need some additional information."

"Text me what you need, and I'll communicate with her. I need the owner's name. If you find that info, I'll take care of the rest."

"Okay. Be careful," Joy said.

Antoine recognized a familiar expression on her

face. The same one she had when she warned him about Fiona

"Jada's your lady and you care for her. I know you, so don't get in above your head."

"I've got this. She's stressing out."

Joy leaned forward. "And so are you."

Antoine chewed his bottom lip but remained silent. *She doesn't understand how close Jada and I are.* Their relationship had reached a profound level that neither had expected this soon.

Joy touched his hand. "I'm looking out for you. That's all."

He gazed into her eyes. "She's not like Fiona."

"Ant, I'm not implying that she is. I just think—"

"I know what you're thinking," he cut her off. He stared at his sister. "I appreciate your concern. I'm straight." He rubbed the side of his face. "In fact. I, uh, haven't told her about our family dynasty yet, either. She thinks I'm a DJ who lives with my cousin. I'll keep it that way for now."

Joy repositioned in her seat. "Ant, you can't keep hiding your family's wealth. Don't you think it's time to inform Jada?"

"It's way past time, but I haven't figured out how to do that yet."

"Pray about it, sit down and have that discussion with her soon."

Chapter 23

JADA

Tuesday

Is this way too good to be true? Jada's spirit felt something wasn't right with Antoine. Lately, a black cloud seemed to be hovering and hadn't lifted. Other than the one text from him, she'd received no messages or calls. She texted him last night and called this morning, but no answer.

The light turned red and she hit the brakes. Antoine had her so distracted, she'd nearly ran a red light. She pressed a hand to her chest. Why hadn't she called in today? Although Doreen could use some additional training, Shamika was sharp and capable of handling her job. Jada swerved into the radio station parking lot and spotted Antoine's blue truck. She pressed her lips together; she wasn't about to chase him down to find out why he hadn't called. "Hmph," she parked several slots down from his car, got out, and hit the alarm.

It was early; hopefully someone had made coffee because she needed some. She opened her office door and propped it open with a doorstop. After placing her purse in a side drawer, she removed her red mug and headed toward the break room. The smell of coffee in the hallway was a positive sign. Will, the News Director, and his staff came in early but rarely made coffee. She stopped by the Sales office and peeked in.

"You're here early. What's going on?" Jada asked.

"Hey, girl." Denise lifted her head from the computer. "Not much. Just thought I'd get here earlier to get some work done. How're you?"

"Pretty good. You make the coffee?"

"I sure did. You know I can't start my day without it."

"Yeah, me too," Jada kept looking down the hall, which led to the studios where the DJs work. She wanted to speak with Antoine so badly to clarify why he didn't call, and she wanted to ask about those doggone pictures. They'd talked every day for months, and now either he was upset, or something must have happened.

"Is something wrong?" Denise asked.

"No. Well, maybe." She crossed her arms. "You free for lunch today?"

Denise looked at her desk calendar. "I'm free 'til one-thirty. Then I've got to be at Belkin's Shoe Store. I need to catch up with the owner while business is good. Who knows when he'll advertise again?" She sipped from her coffee cup.

Jada chuckled and glanced down the hall again. "Funny. Is he still asking for discounts?"

"Huh, are you serious? Mr. Belkin won't advertise without a discount. When he's on vacation, his daughter orders extra spots. Is 11:30 okay for lunch?"

"Yeah, text me when you're ready. See you then."

As she passed the employee mailboxes, she stopped when she saw a small piece of mail inside her box. She walked in and removed the small envelope addressed to her at the station, slipped it inside her jacket, and went to get coffee. *Antoine must be at it again with these photos.* Besides the hotel bill, this was another issue they clearly had to discuss. Why the photos and who and where had they been taken?

Jada poured a cup of coffee and returned to her desk. Forgetting about the envelope in her jacket, she opened her computer and started working. A short time later, she dug in her pocket and opened the envelope. She gasped and covered her mouth to stifle a scream. There. Right in front of her eyes. Antoine lay asleep on the couch with a naked woman on his lap with her back to the camera. She ran to the door and locked it as she tried to keep it together. *What is this all about? I have to get out of here.* Her heart was beating rapidly, she inhaled and exhaled, fighting off tears that moistened her eyes. She snatched a tissue out the Kleenex box, picked up the phone, and dialed Denise's extension.

"Hi, Jada."

"Come to my office now."

"Girl, you all right?"

"No. Come now," Jada hung up the phone. She threw the envelope with the other two pictures on the desk. Someone twisted the doorknob; Jada ran to unlock the door and Denise walked in.

"Hey, Hon. What happened?" Denise frowned.

"I've gotta leave."

She handed Denise the pictures.

Within seconds, smoke sailed from Denise's nostrils. "What the freakin'... Where did you get these?"

Jada shook her head. "In my mailbox. This one today; two others yesterday."

"Did you show Antoine these pictures?"

"No, I haven't talked to him. I'm too upset. I can't

stay here because my anxiety is up. Who knows how many people got those pictures."

"Give me a minute. I'll check the mailroom to see if anybody else received mail today. Shamika lives close by, I'll text Griff and tell him you got sick and had to leave. He can contact Shamika to relieve you. Let me get my purse and iPad, and we're out."

"Good morning, ladies," Antoine strutted in with a smile.

Jada threw up a palm, wiped the corners of her eyes and rested her forehead over both arms. She was too upset to speak with Antoine.

A frown crossed his face. "What happened?" He looked at Denise. "What's wrong with her?"

Denise blocked his access to Jada. "She's leaving for the day."

"Hold up. That's my girl. Let me by," Antoine opened his palms as he tried to go around Denise.

"Stop!" Denise held up one hand.

"Jada, why're you crying?" He said louder.

"Antoine, listen to me, Hon," Denise said calmly. "She'll talk to you. Not now. Okay? Can we step outside for a minute?" She waved him to the door.

He cast a quizzical gaze at Jada before nodding his head to Denise. "Babe, be sure to call me later." He followed Denise out to the hallway, huffing out a sigh as he went.

Jada lifted her head. "What am I doing?" she said, sniffling. She thought about how foolish she felt and made a quick effort to clean up the tears. She should be trying to find out which idiot left those filthy photos in her box or tell Antoine to track down the fan or person who sent them. But she was too anxious.

She was thankful Denise had come in early and rapidly switched to superwoman mode. Girlfriend was on key; she'd stepped up and voluntarily worked out the potential malfunctions that could've occurred if Jada had to stay at work. The way Denise managed to calm Antoine down was brilliant. Jada knew Antoine had no filter when he got riled up; he would put anybody in their place. But she didn't care about that.

After Denise returned, Jada grabbed her purse and locked the door. The two of them skedaddled out of the radio station faster than a thief after robbing a bank. The rest of the office staff and administrators would be in soon, and the last thing Jada wanted to stir up was gossip related to tears and bloodshot eyes.

Chapter 24

JADA

Tuesday

"You're too upset, I'm driving." Denise told Jada as they walked to the parking lot.

"You saved me in there. I can drive, and you won't have to bring me back."

Peering over the rim of her shades, Denise shot Jada that familiar bulldog expression whenever she disagreed.

"Okay, okay. You drive." What would she do without her bossy friend?

"Now you're talking. Don't want you bawling in the car. You might have an accident, and you sure don't need another problem." Denise hit the car alarm, and they both entered the car. She drove to the exit and stopped. Jada froze when Griff zoomed into the parking lot like he was driving in the Indianapolis Speedway Race.

"Okay, did Griff see us?" Jada turned around and watched him park his car.

"Fast as he was driving? No. Even if he did, you're okay. Girl, I handled Griff." I figured we should go to The Coffee Company since that's not close to the station."

"I'm okay with that." Jada did a quick calculation in her head of everything that had happened. When she left yesterday, nothing was inside her mailbox. The pictures. That woman sitting on her man's lap was slowly eating away her trust.

Inside the restaurant, the hostess seated them at a booth near the window, which streamed comforting rays of sunshine. The waitress brought them water and menus.

"Now that I've considered this, all I can say is it's crazy," Denise said.

"I agree. And I don't have a clue of what's going on. I keep trying to figure out who dropped off those pictures? One of Antoine's fans? Somebody who has it out for me or him?" She rubbed her arms and glanced out the window.

Denise dropped her menu on the table. "Girl, I don't think we should stay here. Let's order takeout and go to my place. We'll have more privacy."

Jada rubbed her hands together. "Fine with me. I didn't want to change your plans."

Once they received their orders, Denise paid the bill, and they left. Jada was relieved with their agreement to have breakfast at her friend's apartment. In a distraught state of mind, a private conversation with her bestie would be helpful in case her anxiety escalated.

Denise drove north on La Tijera Boulevard and made a right on Centinela until she reached Beach Street in North Inglewood. She pulled up to the carport gate and hit the remote that led to underground parking.

"Okay, we're here," Denise said as they entered the elevator from the parking lot and rode to the second floor. Denise put her key in the door, and Jada walked in with her mouth open. Her eyes roamed her friend's neatly kept apartment, admiring the large multicolored decorative pillows on the gray couch and loveseat.

"You have new furniture."

"That's right," Denise beamed. "I forgot you haven't been over here lately. Ervin bought the couch and loveseat for my birthday. Nice, huh?"

"I love the color coordination." Jada took a seat at the dining table and removed her food from the bag.

"You want me to make coffee? I've also got orange juice or water."

"Water is fine. I don't need any more coffee. I'm already jittery about this morning."

Denise placed her food on the table and removed two bottled waters from the refrigerator. She handed Jada one of the waters and took a seat next to her. "Hmmm...I'm wondering if a jealous woman left those pictures. And if so, which one?" Denise picked up her water bottle and sipped. "It could be any woman, but likely somebody at the station. Who else has access to roam the station and drop off pictures?"

"I thought about that, too. We've been together for several months. So, why now? These pictures came out of nowhere. Really, who does that kinda stuff?" Jada opened a package of syrup and dribbled it over her pancakes.

"A *jealous* woman. There's plenty out there who'd love to sink their acrylic nails into Antoine. You really can't blame anybody without proof, though. I say wait and see if it blows over. If not, meet with Toni and request an investigation and additional security."

Jada pressed two fingers against her chin. "No, that might impact Antoine's career. He can't lose his job because of somebody's stupid pranks. Speaking of Antoine...he's been acting different lately."

Denise looked at Jada. "Girl, men are unpredictable. You know he's got a life outside of work and seeing you." She cut up her sausage and added ketchup to her hash browns.

"That's not my concern. I know DJs can make pretty good bank, but recently he's been spending a ton of money, and I'm sure he can't afford it."

Denise smirked. "He's your man, and you shouldn't mind him spending money on you."

"Well, I don't mind, but this was sudden, and he's usually frugal." Jada opened her purse and removed the ring box. She slid the ring on her finger and extended her left hand.

"Whoa! When'd you get that?"

"Sunday evening. We ate dinner and stayed at the Montage Hotel in Beverly Hills." Jada glanced at Denise.

"The *Montage Hotel?*" She lifted Jada's left ring finger. "Beautiful ring. Don't tell me he proposed already."

"No, he didn't." Jada pressed two fingers to her temples. "What I can't figure out is why the diamond ring, flowers, nice stay at the Montage, and then his strange behavior and pornography?"

Denise's eyes widened. "Exactly. Why don't you call and ask him?"

"At the moment, I can't. I'm afraid I might find out things I can't handle."

"Jada, what kinda things?"

"He can't possibly be earning that much money. We stayed in a suite, and you wouldn't believe the hotel bill. Plus, he offered to cover the attorney's fees for the dress shop." Jada stared at her food and remained quiet for several minutes. She leaned forward. "Where's all the money coming from?"

Denise waved her hand. "Forget it. We're not going there. What you should do is have a conversation with him. Ask him about the pictures, the finances, whatever you're not sure of." She sighed. "Keep in mind, DJ's pick up extra gigs."

Jada tilted her head. "I know. Maybe the pictures are tied into the money he's making. I hope he's not into porn. The naked woman in the photo bothers me." Jada bit a piece of bacon while waiting for Denise's response.

Denise's eyes drilled straight through Jada's. She put her fork down and folded her arms. "Porn? Girl, use your head. If he was doing porn, he wouldn't be asleep, and he sure wouldn't be wearing clothes. I get your feelings over the raunchiness but stay rational. First, those pictures might be photoshopped. Look at what happened with the USC admission scandals."

"What if they're not photoshopped?"

"And what if they are?" Denise studied Jada for a moment. "Look. What I'm saying is... give the brother a break. Antoine is not like Gordan, Tyron, or other guys you've dated."

Jada pressed her lips together. She understood where Denise was coming from, but the past two days had stamped a huge question mark on her forehead. At times, people were not who they appeared to be. No way would she be a sucker for another man.

"You love him, don't you?"

Jada caught Denise's gaze, then shifted her focus away. "Yes, too much."

"And from what you've said, you know he's over-the-moon in love with you." Denise stuck a fork in a piece of sausage and lifted it to her mouth. She shook her fork at Jada, "And all the braggin' about the way he makes you feel..."

Fiddling with her charm bracelet, her friend's comments reminded her of how much she talked about Antoine. "Shush, I wasn't bragging," Jada laughed quietly. If bragging is what she called the admiration she had for her man, that was okay. Antoine's name flowed from her mouth in almost every conversation. She daydreamed of him, thought about the similarities they shared. Kindred spirit is what Antoine called their relationship. Jada didn't know what it meant until he explained, and he made her believe in love again. She anticipated another escapade like the one they had this past Sunday. But now...

"You already know this. Antoine's a popular DJ, and like it or not, other women will be hitting on him. *All* the time."

"My friend, like I said, I'm not worried...Well, I should say I wasn't until somebody put those photos in my mailbox. Honestly, I'm conflicted and angry. But the other red flags I've seen are worse."

"Hey, I may be wrong. Nobody's perfect. From what you've told me, and his reaction in your office, I think another woman should be the last of your worries."

"I'm still not contacting him today. I haven't slept well for weeks but Sunday night... I did. We made love; he held me until I fell asleep." Jada shook her head. "Forget that for now. I need some me time; so I'm requesting vacation days for the rest of this week. Can I stay here a few days?"

Denise looked at Jada. "Yes, you can. I'm just saying... it's best that you communicate to eliminate the guessing and worrying. That's not healthy for you."

"It wouldn't make a difference. I'm overwhelmed and my anxiety is up. A lot of stuff is going on. The eviction, Kiley's getting on my nerves, now Antoine and those pictures. I may contact Valerie about a few therapy sessions. I'm supposed to do that when I feel they're needed."

"Really?" Denise folded her arms. "Hon, if it's that bad why didn't you talk to me? You know I got your back."

Jada pushed her plate aside, splayed her left hand and stared at the ring. "You're my ace. I thought things would calm down. They're not."

"Have you told Antoine about your anxiety? You know it's nothing to be ashamed of."

"I understand, but I can't. Now is not the right time."

Chapter 25

ANTOINE

Tuesday Morning

Glancing at the studio wall clock, Antoine chewed his bottom lip and wagged his foot, anxiously wishing he could speed up the time. Lina had already arrived for her shift, and he'd be free to check on Jada soon. Watching Jada cry wasn't cool. And what was up with Denise insisting that she needed her space? She must've OD'd on shopping and lost her mind to say something that off-beat. If Jada had a crisis, he should've been there by her side. Why wasn't she answering his texts? Denise had made him angry, and he was inches away from telling her off. Then he realized she was trying to support Jada.

Headset in place, he took a deep breath in preparation for his end-of-show remarks and leaned into the mic. Antoine rambled off the titles of the last three songs he'd played.

"All right, L.A., it's been a blast. You've been listening to 101.3 KTLM radio station. I'm DJ Ant, Prince of Romance, checking out for the day. Listen in tomorrow, same time, same place — six a.m. to ten a.m. Love and Peace. Ciao." "September" by Earth, Wind, and Fire played, but he didn't feel any kind of love and peace today, not after seeing Jada in emotional distress. He wondered if Kiley had upset her. Had she been bold enough to announce her pregnancy?

His eyes shifted to Lina, who stood behind him ready to take his seat. After briefly updating her, he moved so she could sit down. "I'm out after I finish up." He said, logging his playlist. He picked up his briefcase, put on his cap, and walked down the hall to Jada's closed door. He knocked and opened the door to Shamika sitting at Jada's desk.

"She went home sick," Shamika barely looked up.

"Thanks." Antoine was disappointed but still determined to see if Denise could update him on Jada's condition. He started to close the door but paused. "Do you know if Jada's all right?"

Shamika stopped typing and gave Antoine an annoyed look. "I wasn't here when she left."

"Okay." He closed the door and walked to the

Sales Department to see if Denise was there. No Denise.

"Hey, Antoine. Can I see you for a sec?" Griff asked, walking from the breakroom with a cup of coffee in his hand.

"Uh, I guess. I'm heading home."

"I won't keep you long."

He followed Griff into his office, watched him roll up his shirtsleeves as if he had to dig ditches all day.

Griff closed the door. "Take a seat."

"What did I do wrong?" Antoine chuckled lightly before setting his briefcase next to the chair. He crossed one leg over the other.

"Nothing. Have you talked to Jada today?"

He lifted his brows. "Briefly. Why?"

"Well, it's my understanding that she got sick this morning."

"Really? Is she okay? I've been trying to reach her."

Griff shot a suspicious stare at him as if he thought Antoine was lying. "This may be of comfort to you. I spoke to her." Griff's office phone rang. "I have to take this. Hi, Shamika. Yes, that's right. Good, so she called? I'm in a meeting, but I'll be there shortly. Bye."

"Did she hear from Jada?" Antoine asked.

"Yes, but as I said, I did too." Griff steepled his fingers. "Man, I understand you and Jada are close, and that's none of my business. But she's like family to me and I'm concerned about her." He stirred a sugar packet in his coffee and drank some. "Just thought you might have an idea of how she's doing or when she's coming back. It's unusual for her to take off. In fact, she never takes off." He paused and wrinkled his forehead. "She... She's not pregnant, is she?"

Taken aback by his boldness, Antoine's heart skipped a few beats. He pulled his shoulders back. "No... I mean, I have no idea." He extended both palms. "Why are you drilling me about this?" he said with an edgy tone.

A broad grin broke out on Griff's face. "I thought you'd be the first to know."

Antoine's anguish shot up to the sky. Hands clammy, stomach doing backflips, he wished he could shrink into the floor. He rubbed his chin. "Well, I'm not," he snapped. "Why didn't you ask her that question? I need to run."

Griff's phone rang again, he checked the number on the office phone. "It's Shamika. Sit tight and cool off. I'll be right back."

Embarrassed at being a little short with Griff, Antoine bent down, his elbows dug into his knees. He should've left right after he got off, and then he would've avoided this meeting with Griff and his intrusive questions. No disrespect to Griff. Antoine knew it was important to keep strong ties with the management team, but why was he snooping in their business? What he needed to be doing was checking on his secretary, Kiley, who obviously has major issues going on. *What makes him think Jada's pregnant? We made love for the first time a few days ago. So, that can't be true.* He thought of Gordan, frowned and sat up. *Or can it be true?* Griff entered the office a few minutes later and took a seat.

"Uh, man... I apologize for being short," Antoine pulled his earlobe. "But your question was surprising and way off base. This morning Jada was upset, then she bounced without saying anything."

"Hey, no explanation necessary," Griff ran his finger down his coffee cup. "Uh... What I will say is, Jada's like a daughter to me. Do me a favor and make sure you treat her like a queen. She deserves that."

Antoine's gaze met Griff's. "Absolutely. She means the world to me."

"If I hear from her again, I'll suggest that she call you."

"Thank you. I appreciate that." Antoine got up and offered Griff a brother-to-brother handshake and hug before he left. He strutted down the hallway and saw Kiley walking toward him.

She summoned him with an index finger. "Can we talk a minute?"

Don't answer—breeze right past her and leave now. His conscious kicked in, his mom raised him to be a gentleman. He glanced around and walked up to Kiley.

"What is it?"

"Call me this evening."

Antoine's lips tightened, he whispered. "That won't happen. Back off me or you'll hear from my attorney." He turned around and walked in the opposite direction, cutting through the breakroom to exit out the back door. A longer route to his truck was no big deal to get away from that woman.

Frustration made his mind spin as he rushed to his car. Griff asking personal questions. Kiley asking him to call her. He released the alarm, got inside the truck, and threw his head back against the headrest. *Kiley's lies about her pregnancy. Why was Jada so upset?* Griff's inquiry about Jada being pregnant still bothered him.

He removed his cell from his jacket and dialed Jada. The voicemail came on. "Babe, it's me. Call me back ASAP. I'm concerned about you. Let me know that you're safe. Love you." He waited, but when she didn't return his call, he tried again two more times. He retrieved his shades from the sun visor and decided to drive to her house and park in front.

Jada's car wasn't in the driveway, and neither was Celine's or Charmaine's, but he got out, walked to the door, and rang the doorbell. "Why hasn't she called me back?" He mumbled. *Maybe she went to the hospital.* No. A thought like that was worse than being hit upside the head with a bat. He was certain Denise would've called if that happened.

Antoine jumped in his truck, reared the seat back, and closed his eyes. He did something he hadn't done since he attended worship service with Jada at her aunt's church. He prayed, and then fell asleep. By the time he sat up, it was close to 1:00 p.m., and he was still sitting in front of Jada's house.

One last time, he stared at the gray house on 10th Avenue surrounded by flower beds and a well-manicured green lawn. Jada's home was near the Jefferson Park sector of an urban area, much like the Oakland neighborhood he'd lived in for the first thirteen years of his life. He was glad that he'd met Jada's Aunt Dee and Celine but had not met Charmaine yet.

He wrote Jada a message on a yellow Post It note and ran back up to the door and placed it on the screen. Antoine glanced down noticing the cracked gray concrete porch steps. He walked to the end of the porch and viewed the cracks in the long driveway leading to an old dilapidated garage that needed painting. According to Jada, they had stored many of their parents' belongings in the garage, and it was full. He twisted his mouth as sadness set in. This was the first time he'd noticed the defects that badly needed repairing. Other than picking Jada up for a date, he had only visited her home a couple of times.

He returned to his truck and blew out a breath, turning on the sound system. He waited until a commercial came on before saying, "Siri, call studio." He hoped Lina would pick up. He'd forgotten about two early morning deliveries that had come in today.

"Lina."

"Sorry to bother you. I need a favor. Two packages came via Fed-Ex this morning for Griff and Simon. Could you make sure they get them? Looks like promo stuff."

"Are those the ones in your inbox?"

"Yeah."

"Will do."

"Thanks so much. Bye."

He had decided to drive to Hermosa Beach for some time alone and to write when his phone chimed. The text from Joy read: **Call me when you're**

free. Did she really want him to call now? When he's free meant it could wait. Or could it? What she had to say might interfere with plans to relax on the beach. He tapped Joy's number.

"Ant? Can you talk?"

"Yes? Is something wrong?"

"It's about Jada's business. Touch of Class Dress Shop on Overhill Drive, right?"

"That's it."

"You won't believe this. That's one of our buildings."

"One of our buildings? No. That can't be right."

"Pop purchased that building about seventeen years ago. Her mother's name was...Oh, here it is. Ellen Carson. After her death, the children acquired the lease."

Antoine shook his head. "Man!" he tightened his grip on the steering wheel. "That's bad." This was not what he'd expected to hear. Of all the properties his father owned, he would happen to own Jada's family dress shop. "What can I do?"

"Wait a minute. How's that bad? Pop is no stranger to you, and if you talk to him..."

Joy's words resonated, but he didn't understand the rationale. Talk to his father? They barely spoke to one another. "Pops and I agree on zilch. Not even about me selling my own townhouses. So how am I supposed to negotiate the eviction?"

"Ant, that's different. The townhouses are yours to do what you wish. I keep telling you he's all talk."

"Sure. And if I sell without his approval, believe me, the consequences will be steep." His sister had no knowledge about the agreement their father made with Antoine concerning the townhouses. He could stay in one townhouse and oversee the other three leased townhouses or get his own place. Antoine felt it was his punishment for not working in his father's real estate business. He accepted the offer because he was granted ownership and income from the leases.

"Pop's out of town. He'll be back Thursday. Can you fly up this weekend? Explain the dress shop situation, see what you can work out. And bring up the townhouses again. We should try to resolve these matters quickly. Who knows, maybe this will bring you both closer."

Closer? Is that what Pop really wanted? He tossed his shades onto the passenger seat and stared at the street.

"Ant? Are you still there?"

"Yeah, uh. I'm not sure if I can do that. Let me give it some thought."

"You have no choice, and strongly consider bringing Jada with you. It won't be that bad."

"Jada flying up there won't happen. She's off this week. I'm not sure what's bothering her. She won't return my calls or texts."

"Mmm... Do you think she found out about Kiley?"

"I don't think so. But I hope she would've told me."

"Well, she needs to know, so work that out and bring her with you. She should be present at the meeting. Pop has been asking about you for months. Oh, and the private investigator is completing his research on Kiley. I'll text you when I hear from him."

"That's fine. Look, I'll get back to you on the trip." He ended the call.

He loved his baby sister with all his soul, and he'd never say or do anything to hurt her. Joy was right about Jada being present, and Joy was right about most issues she pursued. She was the chosen one — smart, a heavyweight in her league. Out of the three kids, she was the only one who revered Roland Bailey so much that she forfeited her dreams of practicing criminal law to specialize in real estate law and work for him. If anyone could persuade their father to the right on Jada's family business, it would be Joy.

Chapter 26

JADA

Thursday Morning

Exhaling a long breath, Jada pulled out the photograph and pressed her lips together. Every view of that woman sitting on Antoine's lap was worse than the one before. Her stomach churned; she couldn't sleep, and she wanted to scream. She'd vacillated between taking the photo to a photo shop to have the picture validated for authenticity or waiting. Finally, she decided to contact the shop.

What if it's not photoshopped, then what? This was the question her brain kept replaying like an old video.

She removed a pink and white sweat suit and tennis shoes from the closet and gathered her toiletries and hair products from her overnight bag. She checked her texts again, surprised that Antoine hadn't sent another round. Jada hadn't figured out her next steps yet, but she was grateful Denise allowed her to use her spare bedroom for a few days.

She walked to the bathroom and turned on the shower. As she removed her pajamas, she heard her cell. She slipped on her robe and ran to the nightstand.

"Hi there."

"Well, hello stranger," Celine said. "I got your text. Sissy, why aren't you coming home? We've missed you."

"Sorry for the long text. I was hot and not feeling up to a chat." Jada sat on the edge of the bed. "There's a lot of drama in my life right now."

"Yeah, I hear you. That stuff was bizarre. Did you tell Antoine what happened?"

"That'll come later; I'm not ready to face Antoine, but I got his note you left me. What are you doing later today?"

"I'm off, but I have to go to the bank. You wanna catch a matinee?"

"I might take you up on that offer. I have an appointment, though. Can you check for times around 2:00?"

"Why don't you stop by for breakfast? I'm cooking. I can check on movie times while you're here."

"After my appointment, I'll be there. Probably won't be until after 11:00. Just save me a plate."

"Okay, will do."

Jada brought her hands together in a quick prayer, then rushed back to the bathroom to ready herself. After gathering the items she would need for the day, she took a paper cup from the cabinet and poured herself some orange juice before leaving Denise's apartment.

She found a parking spot near the photo shop and added coins to the meter. Parking in Inglewood was horrible, and by the time all the shops opened, part of her parking fee would be exhausted.

Jada got back in the car and removed the picture from a manila envelope. Did she really want to take this photo in? Would it make her feel any better, and would it resolve the issue at hand? She turned the radio on, something she would ordinarily do on the way to work. Nostalgia swept over her, and she realized the emptiness of not having Antoine around. Provoked with intense cravings, thoughts of those bulky arms, Mr. Sweet Lips, and his dimpled smile that swung across his face compromised the serenity she desired.

"Good Morning, L.A. You're listening to KTLM 101.3. I'm DJ Ant, Prince of Romance, playing music for you – Monday through Friday, 6:00 to 10:00 a.m.

You've been listening to the sounds of Musiq – "So Beautiful," and Drake – "God's Plan."

Antoine's poetic voice cheered up her soggy mood. She stuck the photo back in the manila envelope, started the engine, and drove off. Pulling into the medical building parking lot on Santa Rosalia, Jada pushed the button for a ticket and found a spot close to the entry. She entered the elevator and exited on the fourth floor. After a brisk walk down the hallway, she paused in front of the door that read Valerie Purdue, MSN, R.N., DNP, FNP-C, PMHNP-C, Natalia Simms, MSN, RN, FNP-C, AGNP-C. She was relieved that her nurse practitioner agreed to a visit for a therapy session. She opened the door and entered the office.

The front office assistant greeted Jada with a smile. "Good morning."

"Good morning, I have an appointment to see Valerie," Jada said while she signed in.

The assistant checked her name and said, "Oh, yes. She's expecting you. Let's see, I believe your recent physical was faxed from your physician yesterday." She looked through a chart. "Yes, it's here. Here are couple of forms she wants you to complete, and I'll let her know you're here." She handed Jada the two forms with a clipboard and pen.

"Thank you," Jada said.

Jada completed the forms, and shortly afterward was escorted to Valerie's office.

"Hello. How are you?" Valerie asked when Jada walked into her office.

"Uh, I want to say okay, but that's not true. My anxiety is back." Jada sat across from Valerie.

"Yes, I see that your score is up on the Generalized Anxiety Disorder assessment form. It's thirteen. Ph-9 form score for depression is in normal range. I received your last physical, and everything is normal." Valerie browsed the computer as she spoke with Jada. "When you called, you said that you're having issues with sleep."

"My sleep is erratic. Some nights I can get a full night, most of the time I wake up several times."

"Are you taking a sleep aid?"

"Not now. I've thought about the Melatonin but wanted to see you first."

"Well, let's talk more, then I'll decide. Hydroxyzine is for anxiety and sleep. Or Buspar and a sleep aid might be helpful. I know you didn't want to take medication, but since your anxiety is elevated, that will likely be my suggestion to get the anxiety under control."

Jada's gaze met Valerie's. Medication was not an option. She didn't want to get bogged down with filling prescriptions nor did she want to rely on them as a crutch for managing her symptoms.

Valerie pushed her oversized brown framed glasses up on her nose and said, "I know this will be tough for you. I strongly encourage you to consider the medications to see if they'll work. We'll discuss that in more detail later." She went on to ask Jada multiple questions, and made suggestions about healthy diet, exercise, coping skills as she documented in her computer. "What do you think triggered your anxiety this time?"

Taking a deep breath and clasping her fingers, Jada said, "Everything. Work, a new relationship, dealing with my younger sister's personal issues."

"You have quite a few. Have you been using the coping skills we discussed previously?"

"Yes, often. Mostly deep breathing, and I try to avoid negative thinking. I mean...it happens, but I try not to stay in a slump."

"That's positive. Remember to assume positive outcomes. When you expect a negative outcome, it will prevent you from trying to reach a positive one. In addition to the other things we've discussed, try progressive muscle exercises along with deep breathing for relaxation. I have handouts regarding reframing negative thoughts, and deep breathing and progressive muscle exercise techniques. Read over them when you get an opportunity." She removed the handouts from a drawer and handed them to Jada. "Cut the coffee, unless it's decaffeinated."

Jada and Valerie talked for nearly an hour, and Valerie suggested Buspar for anxiety and Melatonin for sleep. Although she didn't want to take medications, Jada agreed to take the Melatonin for one week to see if it would help her sleep, and if not, she would start the Buspar and a prescribed sleep aid. Her next appointment would be in two weeks, but she'd call Valerie in one to report her status and whether she needed a prescription.

Chapter 27

JADA

Celine was in the kitchen cooking when Jada walked into the house. The aroma of fried fish caused her taste buds to sweat. "Hey, whatever you're cooking smells delicious," Jada laughed as she entered the kitchen. "You need help?"

"No, I'm almost done."

"I thought you'd eaten by now." Jada retrieved glasses and plates from the cupboard, and then opened the refrigerator and removed a bottle of cranberry juice. "Girl, you keep throwin' down the way you do, Darius is gonna to propose one day."

"Sissy, he's been talking about marriage. It's unofficial, though. I told him when he proposes, I want a ring not talk."

Jada slid into the chair and placed her purse on the table. "I know that's right."

"He knows that I've got to finish school first."

"Where's Char?"

"She should be up. I heard her in the bathroom not long ago. She's been helping Aunt Dee."

Jada lifted her brows. "Really?"

"Aunt Dee was swamped with formal dresses and alterations. Char volunteered." Celine sat a plate of salmon croquettes, hash browns, and zucchini squash on the table.

"That's great to hear."

"Did you have a doctor's appointment?" Celine asked.

"No. I went to see Valerie."

"The therapist Valerie?"

"She's a mental health nurse practitioner, and she does therapy. I felt I should start therapy again for a while."

"You've done well until recently. If you need therapy, that's a positive choice. How'd the session go?"

"Well. She wants to put me on medications."

"Remember, I told you at times medications are essential. You've been a little irritable lately. I know she told you mental health can affect physical health and vice versa."

"Yeah, she went knee-deep on the meds and health situations. I agreed to go back on the Melatonin for a week. If it doesn't help me sleep, she'll write a prescription for sleep and Buspar for anxiety. Talking to Valerie was refreshing."

"Bottom line is taking care of yourself. These fried hash browns and croquettes sure aren't helping us." Celine let out a soft laugh.

"Exactly. We eat enough healthy foods." Jada held her left hand up and wiggled her fingers.

Celine pressed a hand against her chest. "Oh, Sissy. He proposed?"

"No, he didn't. This is my three-month anniversary gift."

"Look at you. It's beautiful." Celine studied Jada for a moment. "You sure that's not an engagement ring?"

"It's not. We're not there yet, and I'm ashamed that I don't know what to say to him about my behavior." She picked up a croquette and scooped up hash browns and zucchini squash.

Celine sat down and fixed her plate. "Yup, your problem is complicated. You should give him a break, though. Also be upfront about your diagnosis and how it affects you."

Jada slanted her head. "Whose side are you on?"

"Nobody's. From what you texted, sounded like the picture was some fanatic groupie's prank. You're not sure, so why'd you get so angry?"

Jada poured a glass of cranberry juice. "I let my

anxiety overwhelm me. Now, I'm confused on whether I should apologize. I went to the photo shop to validate authenticity, but I changed my mind. What do you think?"

"Can I see the picture?"

Jada removed the picture from her purse and handed it to Celine. How had she allowed her disorder to misconstrue a senseless act that could've destroyed her relationship? Did Antoine know about the photos? The burden of guilt was frustrating, and regret filled her head. Why had she acted so foolish? Still...she was uncertain. *The pictures.*

"Huh. At least he's not naked. I bet this is an ex-girlfriend's shenanigans. And who took the picture? Ugh!" Celine scrunched her face. "Nowadays, great relationships are golden. Lord knows me and Darius have our ups and downs. Relationships are hard work, but a healthy level of trust, respect, and faith in God keeps the flame burning."

"It's just... that picture bothers me," Jada said.

"It should, but you can't let worry interfere with your life. Until you have proof that something is wrong, don't let circumstances or anybody blow out your flame. Pray, then you and Antoine need to get busy on those picture issues."

"You're right," Jada wiped her mouth. "Denise shared a similar opinion."

"Good Mornin'. "Charmaine walked in with her hair pinned up in a bun.

Jada quickly picked up the photo and stuffed it in her purse. "All right now. No hoop earrings, long hair down to your butt, or short skirt today?" Jada joked.

"No, ma'am. Not when I'm workin' with Aunt Dee. I don't wanna hear her mouth. Pin that hair up before it gets caught in the sewing machine, take off those hula-hoop earrings, and on and on," she mimicked her aunt. "Whew!" Charmaine spun around. "I look okay?"

"You'll pass Aunt Dee's dress code," Celine said. "No boobs showing, and you're wearing pants. Fix a plate before you leave."

"Nah, I'll wait. Aunt Dee brings food every day, and if I bring McDonald's or any food, she'll say, 'you knew I was bringin' food. Why waste money?' I'll take a croquette though." Charmaine laughed, lifting a croquette with a paper towel and taking a bite. "I'm leavin'. When you comin' home?" she asked Jada.

"I'll be here tonight, my overprotective sisters. Tell Aunt Dee I said hello." Jada said.

"I will. And yes, we're overprotective. I guess you and Antoine had a nice time." Charmaine smiled.

Celine raised her brows and looked at Jada.

Jada popped a fist to one hip. "Who said I was with Antoine, missy?"

"Who else would you be spendin' nights with? Not Gordan I hope," Charmaine said.

"Char, time to leave for work. Scoot out the door so you won't be late," Jada said, hand gesturing her to the door.

"See yah," Charmaine said, walking out. "Oh, by the way, Sissy, I found your hotel bill on the floor, so I put it on your dresser." She smiled so hard her face almost cracked. "Payback," she said, cackling all the way out the door.

Jada's eyes landed on Celine, whose head stayed down while she ate. She'd planned to keep her intimate life wrapped and in the closet, but Charmaine shot a bullet in that plan. Now Celine knew, and they'd have to chat about their differences. Jada hadn't reached the same magnitude of faith as her sister, nor was she sure that she wanted to. Celine needed to understand that while she was always striving to maintain a healthy life, emotionally, physically, and spiritually, she was still a work in progress.

Since Celine barely said more than a few words on

their way to the movies, Jada reflected on Celine and Denise's heartfelt pep talks. They had given her a lot to think about. She decided to let the issue related to the photos rest until she and Antoine discussed them. Nothing would blow out her flame with that man.

Chapter 28

ANTOINE

"Hey, L.A. This is your favorite champ DJ Ant, the Prince of Romance, getting ready to check out with Earth, Wind, and Fire's tune, "Imagination." Join me tomorrow, same time, same place from 6:00 to 10:00 a.m. KTLM 101.3 on your dial. Next is Lina Reshawn. Peace and Love. Ciao." Antoine removed his headset, jotted down a few notes, and turned to see if Toni was still in the hallway bending Lina's ear. As the general manager, Toni came in late and stayed late, she was rarely in her office before he left for the day.

Lina walked in. "Good Morning."

"How's it going?" Antoine said. "I see our GM is here. Why is Toni in early?"

"I'm not sure. Toni was venting like she does frequently." She removed a small hand mirror, stroked her short hair, and applied orange lipstick.

As the last word slid from Lina's mouth, his phone started buzzing in his pocket. He removed it. It was as though Toni had overheard his inquiry, which was next to impossible from the hallway. He viewed her text.

Please stay for a 10:30 meeting. My office. Thx Toni.

Then he vacated the chair so Lina could prepare to go on the air. He gathered his belongings and stared briefly at Lina. *What makes her brain function?* She didn't know about the meeting. Right. Standing in the hallway allowing the GM to vent, and there's nothing about to go down. *Tell that to the rookies.* Toni didn't come in early without a reason. Antoine couldn't blame Lina for not sticking her nose in the station's politics, but she could've given him a warning. His preference was staying on top of projected changes or issues related to his position, and he paid it forward to colleagues when necessary. Their team had a solid pact to work collaboratively with each another, and they worked extremely well with management. Being the new DJ on stage with the lowest seniority, it would be nice if Lina tried being more collegial with fellow employees.

He would try to catch Denise in reference to a note he'd left in her box. Griff normally had a sales meeting on Thursdays around 11:00, and she should be in soon. He flipped through the station directory for the sales team and found her number, then walked to another empty studio room and called her extension.

"Good Morning," Denise said.

"Hey, Denise. This is Antoine. How're you?"

"I'm well."

"Did you get my note?"

"Yes. Perfect timing because I got here a little while ago. When can you talk?"

"I'm off the air. Can you meet me in Studio Two? It'll be brief; I have a 10:30 meeting."

"I'm on my way."

Antoine drew in a steady breath, which had no impact on the fury he'd experienced for the past three days. He sat down and folded his arms, reminded himself to abstain from being too outspoken. He'd considered sending Jada a text saying their relationship was over. No return calls, no return texts, and he had no idea why. He loved her too much to let her go, but he would not get zapped in another relationship. A burning thought of Kiley telling Jada the lie she'd created would not leave his head.

He heard the doorknob turn and glanced up. It was Denise.

"Hi," Denise sat across from him.

He smiled and propped one leg over the other. "I've been calling and texting your girl ever since Tuesday. Also went by her house and she hasn't been home. You have any idea where she is?"

"I do. What should I tell her?"

"Absolutely nothing. I have an urgent envelope I want her to receive today. Can you see that she gets it?"

"Of course."

"After she reads the information, she should correspond accordingly via text only. No more calls or texts from me because I *might* go off," he said with an edgy tone. "Honestly, I'm a positive person, and I hate feeling like this," he interlaced his fingers.

Denise sighed. "You have a right to your opinion. But, Antoine, I think this may have started with you. She was feeling the same way Monday when she didn't hear from you." She looked at him. "Uh, I'm not in this, so you and Jada should straighten out your biz."

"Well, I disagree. FYI, I texted Jada twice and told her I had a business meeting."

Denise cleared her throat. "Let me get this straight. Jada should open the envelope and read what's in there. Then text you."

"Right. When we talk again, it must be in person. Minus whatever her problem is, I'm trying to take care of her business, and she has to cooperate." He removed the manila envelope from his briefcase and handed it to Denise; she accepted. "I'm leaving town tomorrow. I'd like to hear from her today."

"Antoine, I'm sorry about the bad karma between you and Jada. I thought she'd called you."

"Bad karma?" He shook his head. "Life is short. I don't allow *bad* in my life for long. They're catalysts for unhappiness and failure. She's being unreasonable. I'm in the dark, worried about her... I—" Antoine pushed an index finger against his temple.

"I know. I'll text her when I get back to my desk."

"Again. Please make certain she receives that soon. It pertains to her dress shop, and it's urgent. I started to send it Fed Ex but changed my mind. I think this is best."

"You know I'll take it to her." Denise stood. "Uh, I'm not at liberty to tell you much. Jada got bent out of shape because something funky happened."

"And suddenly she shuts down and stops talking to me?" He patted his chest. "That's not cool." He rubbed the side of his face. "I'm entitled to know what happened."

"I'm sure she'll explain." She leaned against the wall. "See, she's been through a lot in life, and..."

Denise stared at the floor and paused. "After you two talk, you'll understand."

Antoine held his breath, hoping she'd disclose what was on her mind.

"Let me stop; I've probably said too much already."

He bit his lower lip, and thoughts of seeing Jada in Gordan's car at church came to mind. Looking up at Denise, Antoine said, "Is she sick?"

"No, she's not."

"Okay. Another question...Is she pregnant?" This, he had to know. Because if she was, that would be another baby that wasn't his.

Denise laughed and clapped a palm to her forehead. "Jada pregnant? Now that...I would know, and so would you. Is that what you're thinking?"

"Um...No. Somebody asked me. I mean...I didn't know, and that's what I said." He smiled, happy to hear that response, then picked up his pen and wiggled it in between his fingers. Glancing at his watch, he said. "Thanks for your help, Denise."

"Yeah, watch for her text. If I must...I'll twist her arm and then she'll call you."

"After she reads the content in the envelope."

"That's right. I'll swing by her house after our Sales meeting. I've got a bone to pick with her anyway. She left my orange juice out on the counter this morning."

Antoine laughed at the look on her face when she made the comments. "Wow! Make her buy you a quart of O.J."

"More like a gallon."

Denise closed the door, and he checked his watch again, but it was not time for the meeting. He put on his headset, turned on his MP4 player and earplugs to Earth, Wind, and Fire, "Reasons," and kicked back.

Chapter 29

ANTOINE

Thursday

Watching the clock until a minute before his appointment, Antoine removed his earplugs and placed them and his MP4 in his briefcase. He opened the door to Studio Two and peered down the hallway, then walked to Toni's closed office door. He tapped and opened it. Toni, Simon, and Griff were already in there talking.

"Come on in. I was going to text you," Toni said.

"Oh, sorry. I was in Studio Two."

"You're all right. I asked Griff and Simon to come in before we started. You know...to chat."

Antoine walked in and sat in the only available chair in between Griff's and Simon's. Feeling apprehensive, he set his briefcase next to the chair and wondered what happened and why he was there.

Toni cleared her throat. "Okay, I'm going directly to the point." She tossed three photographs on the desk.

Antoine picked them up. "Whoa! Where did these come from?"

Pushing back in her seat, Toni shifted an intense gaze at Antoine. "We're hoping you can tell us. Two packages arrived with those pictures. Lina said she saw them in the studio inside your box. Can you share some facts on who delivered them?"

Lina. Suddenly, she's talking. "Yes, I placed them in my box. Will was doing the news; I saw a young man walking to the front door. I went up front; he showed me two packages, I opened the door," Antoine shrugged. "The return address was Gordan's and Air Mist Records, and they were for Griff and Simon."

"That's right," Simon turned toward Antoine. "I called Gordan, he denied sending any packages, though. Generally, Gordan stops by the office to drop off promos."

"Mmm...Someone hand delivered them. This is very bizarre," Toni swiveled her chair around to the desktop. She tapped in some information on the

RHYTHM BAY LOVE

computer. "Marisol hasn't emailed my notification that will go to the employees yet."

Griff frowned. "This stuff is childish and cut-throat. If somebody in Sales did this, I want first dibs on the consequences." He turned to Antoine. "Man, you know anybody crazy enough to send those pictures?"

Antoine rested his arm on the back of the chair. "The pictures are familiar. My ex was into photography, and I remember those snapshots. That was years ago." He twisted his mouth and forced himself to look at Toni. "The picture of her on my lap...I was asleep; she was playing around with the camera. I don't think she's behind this, though." The last problem he'd need would be Fiona coming after him, and he didn't believe she'd be that lowdown. But he suspected that someone else he knew would.

"Wow. That's deep," Simon rubbed his chin. "What about social media? Hackers are accessing Facebook and other accounts all the time."

"Nope! I'm not on social media a lot. In her defense, she's never done much social media. Fiona's a professional dancer, not a stripper," Antoine cracked his knuckles. His patience was wearing thinner than a piece of xerox paper. *Where are they going with this issue?*

"The next step is a plan of action." Toni removed

her glasses. "I'm sorry this happened to you, Antoine. We must ensure this doesn't go public. Negative publicity can hurt our ratings and yours. That can't happen."

Ratings? He hadn't given much thought about how this would affect his career. He was thinking about Jada. "I understand, and that's disturbing for me. What we should be discussing is an investigation into this matter. What else do you propose we do?" Antoine asked.

"I'm hoping we'll determine who was responsible for distributing the pictures." She paused before speaking again. "After Marisol finishes the email, she'll send it out to the staff today. I'm asking all employees who have photos to bring them to my office. "

"Approximately when will that email go live to the team?" Simon asked, crossing his legs.

"After I approve it, immediately. We're all professionals here. I won't tolerate these kinds of pranks," Toni said, writing notes on a lined yellow pad. "Sometimes, I feel like screaming."

Antoine lifted a hand. "Can I say something? Please don't mention my name in the email. I mean...who knows? Griff and Simon might be the only ones with pictures. Plus, shouldn't we evaluate hiring more security?"

Griff nodded. "I agree on the security, and don't worry. I'm sure your name won't be mentioned."

"No, it won't. My interest is in making employees aware, and collecting all those pictures," Toni said.

"We've got a close team. I think people will cooperate," Griff said. "The pictures came in express mail packaging and without postage. Think about it. Those packages could have contained rigged pipe bombs and blown this place to pieces."

"Griff, that was my fault, and I take full responsibility. I shouldn't have opened the door," Antoine said.

Simon leaned forward. "We've got to tighten our security measures."

"Toni, can you make that happen pronto?" Griff said.

Toni's weary smile and nod provided minimal assurance for Antoine. In her position, she had a heavy workload. Repetitive discussions about preventing the pictures from getting out to the media circulated from plan A to B, and back to A again. How did they plan to protect him and his reputation? He was the only one that could be identified, and that could possibly hurt his career.

The meeting didn't end soon enough for Antoine. He exited Toni's office with conflicting feelings. His first concern was whether Jada had received photos, and he was tempted to approach Kiley about the matter. If Jada had pictures, why would she avoid mentioning them? He'd attempted to answer that question repeatedly yet could not fathom a reasonable answer. *You need to calm down. There is still the roadblock of Kiley's potential blackmail to be crossed.*

Chapter 30

JADA

Thursday

Jada and Celine opened the door and walked into the siren-like sound of one smoke detector and smoke so thick that it resembled a forest fire.

"Char? What you burnin' in there?" Celine yelled, turning up her nose and propping the door open. She and Jada rushed toward the kitchen.

"I was cookin' a hamburger since I didn't see any food on the stove," Charmaine said, fanning the stove with a folded newspaper.

"That burger must be charred," Jada laughed. "You need to learn how to cook before you burn the house down."

"I second that motion. Cause one day you'll be cooking for yourself," Celine said. "Turn the fan on high and open the kitchen windows. Oooh...we need our smoke detector's serviced."

Charmaine opened the windows. "Right on the detectors. Only the one in here is working. Oh, Sissy, Denise brought you an envelope. It's on the coffee table," Charmaine said, walking out the kitchen with a plate in hand. "She said call when you get here."

Jada picked up the manila envelope with her name on the front. She went to her bedroom, closed the door, and turned the fan on before she called Denise.

"Hey, Jada. Did you open the package?"

"Celine and I just walked in. What's in here?"

"Girl, I didn't ask. It's from Antoine; he said read what's inside right away. I'll call back."

"Okay." Jada ended the call and opened the sealed envelope, in disbelief that he'd asked Denise to make a delivery. She removed a handwritten letter, two airline tickets, and money. "What's this for?" she asked with crinkled brows. She crossed her legs and read the letter, which started off with the salty words *"Is your head on straight? If yes, why are you messing with mine?"* She laughed. This was so like Antoine, and she was not surprised. By the end, he'd cleaned up the language with a beautiful poem that ended with "*My heartbeat, my love. I hope you'll join me in San Francisco. Love you, Ant.*" Her cell rang.

"Sorry. I was with a client," Denise said after Jada answered the phone. "All right spill the beans."

"He sent two airline tickets to San Francisco. One for an earlier flight, the other for a later one." Jada shook her head. "Now, see. This is what I'm talking about. Who can afford to buy two first class one-way tickets and two more to get back? He wants me to fly up to Frisco tomorrow. Can you imagine?" She kicked her shoes off. "At his command, I'm supposed to take off like a helicopter. I don't work that way."

"Go on up there. No excuses."

"You don't know Antoine. As usual, he's impulsive; he'll make plans and tell me at the last minute. Celine's hair stylist is doing my twisties tomorrow, and I'm not changing my appointment. It took forever to get one."

"Jada, stop! Do you really love that man?"

Silence.

"Answer me."

"Yes, I love him. More than the air I breathe."

"Then, cut the minor details, get your hair done and take a flight. He mentioned your dress shop."

"Yeah, his note said I have to be in a meeting."

Jaida picked up the tickets and stared at them. "That man. At times, he's off the chain."

"Can I ask you another question?" Denise said.

"Sure."

"We talked about this the other day. You said you'd call him after you worked through your feelings. Have you done so?"

Jada bowed her head and considered how to answer. "To some extent, yes. Am I ready to talk to him? I'm not sure, but I will."

"Awesome. Stop with the blaming and criticism and take my advice."

"I know, and you're right. I guess I'll pack this evening."

Jada ran her fingers through her hair and shook her head. Amazing as Antoine was, there's so much she didn't understand about him. Unconventional, talented, sweet, and complicated. She fell in love with him, and never had she ever desired a man so completely and infinitely.

Jada realized she hadn't been fair to Antoine. Should she tell him; how could she tell him about her anxiety disorder and be sure he wouldn't judge or leave her?

"You've got to fly up there to straighten—" Denise paused. "Ah, no!"

"What is it?"

"I'm scrolling through my emails. Have you checked yours?"

"No."

"Quick. Sign in now. Toni sent an email regarding the pictures."

Jada stuffed the letter and tickets back inside the envelope and reached for her iPad on the nightstand. She quickly opened the email. "Oh, great," she slapped her leg. "The pictures are floating around the station. I bet Kiley is doing this crap."

"Slow down and read this carefully. Her email says *Only* Simon and Griff have photos thus far. Antoine's name was not mentioned. You should call Toni. Let me ask you something...Could Gordan have done this?"

Jada frowned. "Gordan? I hadn't considered him. What reason would he do something that stupid? Nah, it's not him."

"I understand he's your ex. Don't rule him out, though. You'd be surprised at what some folks will do. I'm sure he'd love to see you and Antoine split up. "

"I've made up my mind. I can't resolve this, and I'm hopeful management will."

"Now's the time to hit up Toni for a private meeting before another incident occurs."

"For sure. Um..." Jada wound a strand of hair around her fingers. "What did Antoine say?"

"First, he seemed frazzled; a bit mad. He admitted it, but we didn't talk long. Oh...he asked me if you're pregnant."

Jada's lips puckered. "What made him ask that?"

"Girl, I don't know. He said somebody asked and didn't say who. I reassured him that you're not."

"Strange. Well, thanks for driving over here. I need to text him. Talk to you when I get back."

"No problem. Have plenty of fun in San Francisco. And girl, whatever's wrong, fix it."

"I'll work on it." Jada ended the call and tapped in a message to Antoine stating that she'd received his envelope and would take the 2:12 p.m. flight with him on Friday.

Chapter 31

ANTOINE

Friday

Antoine settled in a chair at the airport and worked on another poem in progress and his book. He tried not to think of Jada, although she was prime on his list, considering he expected to see her by now. Laying his iPad down, he scanned the area. Boarding would take place soon and he questioned why she hadn't arrived. *This is ridiculous.* He slammed his iPad shut and stuffed it inside the case, before exploring the waiting area and a couple of food businesses in the airport.

"Flight 1247 to San Francisco will depart on time. We will board in ten minutes," echoed in the airport. Antoine scuttled back to the gate to line up in the first-class section, constantly scanning the area with a watchful eye as he moved forward. He removed his cell, and as quickly as he pulled it out, he put it back in his pocket. *She's not coming.*

Within an hour and fifteen minutes, Antoine rested as the plane cruised low in preparation for landing. He was losing hope, and doubt gnawed at his feelings. *What happened? Is my relationship with Jada irreparable?* Once the plane landed, he turned his phone on and called an Uber. No texts or voicemails had come in from Jada. He thought the opportunity to introduce her to Joy, Ellis, and his wife would finally take place. An introduction to his father was less important other than to discuss a different resolution besides the Carson family's eviction. That might change the whole dynamic of his usual visit. He retrieved his computer bag from under the seat, opened the overhead bend and removed a small backpack, then hurried off the plane.

Inside the Uber, he tapped Joy's number.

"Hi, Ant."

"Hi. I'm here. Jada didn't make it."

"Does this mean it'll be us fighting for *her* business?"

"What can I say? I purchased tickets. She didn't show up. Any plans set up with Pop yet?"

"Yes, but I'm not rescheduling. Call Jada, tell her to get up here."

"Seriously? Give me a break. I'm not a miracle maker."

"Neither am I," she snapped. "She has to be at this meeting or there won't be one. Maybe you'll have a better chance if Pop meets her."

"I'll see what I can do." He ended the call and put on his shades.

Upon entering his townhouse, the fragrance of Pine Sol and fresh flowers filled his nostrils. Noreen, his housekeeper, had done the weekly cleaning; the house was spotless. That's why she'd kept her job for so long. She never failed to meticulously clean and bring him a fresh bowl of fruit and home cooked Jamaican food when he texted that he'd be in town. He smiled as he picked up a nectarine and washed it off. Taking a bite of the sweet fruit, he opened the refrigerator to Jamaican peas and rice, plantains, and jerk chicken. One of his favorite dishes.

Antoine walked to the downstairs bedroom, dropped his backpack in a chair and changed into a green camouflage t-shirt and olive-green shorts, then slipped on a pair of brown sandals. He couldn't believe Joy's harsh tone. Attempting to unravel issues that didn't make sense had become taxing. It was hard to focus, write, or think because his mind was so cloudy. Now his sister was on him. What did she expect him to do, go drag Jada to the airport?

He shrugged it off as Joy being under a lot of stress today.

He went to the kitchen, dumped the nectarine seed in the trash and got a bottle of water from the fridge, then walked back to the living room, and flicked on the big screen. He plopped on the burnt orange loveseat, adjacent was a matching ottoman, on which he kicked off his sandals and rested his feet. The aroma of Noreen's food almost forced him to make a plate, but he didn't want to go into a food coma this early. Writing would take precedence later, and he'd try to reach Jada.

A loud chime awakened him. He jumped up. The doorbell? No one knew he was in town, and how in the world had he fallen asleep this early? Sliding his feet inside his sandals, he rushed to the door and peeked through the peephole. *Jada?*

Antoine swung the door open. "Hey. What happened? You forgot how to get to the airport?" He twisted his mouth slightly to emphasize his sarcasm.

Jada tilted her head and glanced up at him. "Well, I made it safely; how are you?" She walked in with a shawl draped around her shoulders, pulling a small luggage behind.

"Here, let me help you." He picked up the luggage to avoid scratching the hardwood floors and set it against the wall near the hallway.

"You mean I came up here and don't get a hug or a kiss?" she folded her arms.

Antoine had no words; he stuck his hands inside his pockets and checked out Jada's reddish-auburn braided hair. A brown off-the-shoulder polka-dot dress that stopped mid-thigh and a new fragrance almost forced him to hug, kiss her, and never let go. He'd missed this woman so much. Even though it had only been a few days, it seemed like weeks since they'd last spoken. All he could muster was a half hug. "I'm being real. I need answers. What happened, and why'd you stop talking to me?" He rubbed his palms together.

"Jeez. Before you plow me in the ground, can I explain?" She walked in the living room, glanced at the high ceilings and surrounding areas. "I was delayed at the hair shop and missed the 2:12 flight. I caught a Lyft, and when I got to the airport, I had to run to catch the next flight."

"I'm up here taking care of your family's business. It would've been nice if you had updated me." He pushed his dreads back.

"I appreciate that, and I'm sorry. Remember, you chose to tell me at the last-minute." She placed her purse on the coffee table and laid her shawl on the couch, then walked over to the fireplace for a closer view of a large picture above the mantel.

"Synthia Saint James."

"The artist?"

He nodded, thinking of the day he and his mother went artwork shopping. "That's Masekelas Marketplace Congo."

"It's beautiful. I didn't know you're into art."

"Most anything that's creative, I love. She's a renowned African American artist. Mom's the expert, and she helped me out on the artwork."

He walked to the couch and sat down, never taking his eyes off Jada. "You still haven't answered my question. Why'd you stop communicating with me?"

"Honey, I'll explain."

"Talk. I think I'm entitled to know. Ever since we've been together, not one day have we skipped talking or texting."

"Except the day you left work without saying a word."

"Hold up." He waved his hands. "I'll admit, I was hasty that day. I answered your text, though."

"Yeah, much later," Jada said, massaging her scalp.

"I love your hair. But why're you doing that?"

"It's these braids. They're so tight I feel like my scalp is being pulled from my head."

"Oh, wow. It's that bad?"

Jada waved her hand and said, "Yes. I'll deal with

it, though. Listen, something happened that morning and today—" She paused.

"You read Toni's email."

"I did. It's way more than the email. I was up early, and now I'm beat. Can we put this conversation off for a few hours?"

Antoine pulled his earlobe. This was not what he'd planned. A long conversation to clear all the dirt from his tray and hers was required. Then, he understood what she meant about the fatigue, and she deserved to rest.

"A few hours are no problem."

"Thanks. These were great choices on the artwork." She scanned the other art on the walls and tossed a glance over her shoulder at Antoine. "Uh, whose place is this?"

"Mine."

She pursed her lips, "No. Who really stays here?"

"I said it's mine. Why would I lie? Better yet," he pointed at Jada, "I'm not delaying what I have to say any longer. Have a seat; I'll be right back."

Antoine skipped every other step until he reached the top of a wraparound stairway. He went into his office and removed a red folder with the deed and other documents. *It's time to be truthful.* He walked to the top of the stairs and stalled; leaning against the bannister, he smiled. His beautiful woman was doing a catwalk through the kitchen, exploring. She walked over to the glass door that led to the sun deck; he thought she seemed a bit dazed and stiff as she gazed out at the scenery.

He bounded down the stairs and handed her the folder. "Here's the paperwork for this property." Jada examined the paperwork, her expression changing from a smile to a frown.

"What's the matter?" Antoine said.

"You paid all this money for one townhouse?"

"Four townhouses. That's what they sold for back then. This one's mine, the other three in the building are leased out." He folded his arms, "These places are worth millions now, but I didn't buy them. My father did. He bought houses for all his children, except me. I got the townhouses. I had plans to bring you up here."

She arched a brow, "Why did you wait?"

"Why you looking at me like I have smut on my face?"

She handed him the folder. "I-I can't stay here. I'm going back to L.A." She grabbed her purse off the coffee table and her shawl, then started toward the door.

He followed close behind. "Babe, hold up. Why're you trippin' about this?"

She stopped and twirled around to face Antoine.

"I'm trippin'? You're trippin' if you think I believe this *Donald Trump* lie." With her hand on one hip, she said. "I wasn't born yesterday. A black man who's not playing ball. Not an entertainer, doctor, or lawyer, and you've got all this?" She shook her head. "Uh-uh. DJs don't make that kind of money. You've *got to* be dealing drugs or doing something illegal."

Antoine lifted his hands. "I'm not lying. I don't deal drugs. I'm not doing illegal stuff." He tried his best to avoid laughing.

"Oh, it's funny. What. Do. You. Do? And don't say you're a DJ."

"Can you step off the podium and take a seat so we can talk?"

"This better make sense. Or I'm outta here." She rolled her eyes.

Antoine flashed a grin. "It will. Let me get us some wine." He reached out for her hand; they walked to the couch, then he went to the kitchen and returned with two glasses of red wine and coasters.

"Where do I start?" he said. "A little more about the dress shop. In my note I mentioned my father has owned the building for seventeen years. I was unaware that he owned your building. This trip is to *try,* and I emphasize that, to see if I can work a deal with him."

"Do you foresee difficulties?"

He picked up his glass and drank a couple of sips. "I don't know. My father's not the easiest man to understand, and we don't always get along. But Joy is working with me on this project. She's his righthand attorney."

"Oh, I'm sorry."

"For now, we'll see what happens. Uh, I may have told you that I grew up in an urban Oakland neighborhood. At thirteen, my world collapsed when I learned we'd be moving. We were like the Jeffersons, moving on up. Didn't know nothing about our new neighborhood." He let out a laugh that trickled over to Jada. Antoine shared that he had no desire to leave his friends and neighborhood. Although their family became wealthy, his spirit stayed within the urban community that he loved.

"I was into social justice issues at UC Berkeley and continued after I graduated because I wanted to see a change. Still do. I'd planned to return to my old neighborhood in East Oakland, and help rebuild the area, so my people could live in affordable housing."

Jada gave him that look of approval with her broad smile, which always made him feel good.

"How sweet. Now that's something more people should do," she said.

"The homeless population is massive," he lifted one leg over the other. "And gentrification, the issue that everyone swore wouldn't happen, is driving black and brown people out of their neighborhoods."

"That's true. I know people who moved out of areas like Inglewood, and the Crenshaw district. It's a shame."

"It's affecting many areas. California, the east coast, down south, all over." Antoine swung his fist, "And what really bothers me...is a lot of working adults can't afford to become homeowners. Ellis and his wife lucked out and found a property a few years ago. And to think my father wouldn't hear of me buying in Oakland because he wanted me in this townhouse."

"That must've been tough. Is living here really that bad?" Jada took a sip of wine.

"This is Pacific Heights. I wouldn't mind, but I'm the only black person here. The African American population is approximately two percent in this area. I'm not prejudice, but I'd rather live in a more culturally diverse area that includes more black folks." He pressed his fingers against his temple, "The other tenants in this building are white. Most are cordial, but one woman stares at me like I have horns growing out my head." He paused and laughed lightly. "Funniest thing is, none of them know I'm the owner."

Jada laughed. "Get outta here. Seriously?" She crossed her legs. "You should shock her one day and introduce yourself."

"I prefer to keep things the way they are. Pop hired a property management company that handles the business here." He wrapped his arm around Jada's shoulders. "Babe, my main concern is not these townhouses or this area, and by the way, your property could use some repairs."

Jada shook her head. "Don't start. Our little house is standing, so for now settle your problems. That can wait."

"I'm letting you know, that's next. I have work to do in the community where I formerly lived, too."

"You've already started in Oakland. Think about how much you've done for Rashad." Jada rubbed his thigh.

"True, but not enough. And there are so many more Rashads out there. Black males are having it rough."

"Honey, we've traveled this afternoon. I promise to share what's on my mind." She put her hand over his. "Tonight, can we just relax and enjoy each other's company? You got any food in this fancy place?"

Breaking the images of what he envisioned in his old neighborhood, he kissed Jada's cheek. "I do. My housekeeper is from Jamaica, and she gets down in the kitchen. Let's go warm up some food."

"Oh, yeah! I love Jamaican food."

He desperately wanted to reveal everything to Jada and get the facts straight. He also needed to hear what she wanted to share, so they could move forward with their relationship. It was getting late, but he was wide awake thanks to his earlier nap. Jada was tired, even though she pepped up fast after they ate and toasted their wine glasses. Her first night at his place should not be full of personal confessions they could divulge tomorrow. They stacked the dishwasher and watched two movies.

Before the second movie ended, their lips were locked in hot passion. Antoine clasped Jada's hand and led her to the upstairs master bedroom, watching the shocked look on her face.

She glanced around. "This bedroom is bigger than my living room."

"Yeah, it's big." Antoine went to the bathroom and turned on the shower. He removed his clothes before returning to Jada, who was patiently waiting, arms raised above her head. Taking Jada's clothes off piece-by-piece was the quickest way to arouse her, and he preferred to simultaneously stimulate her body with tender kisses at the same time. Her dress fell to the floor, followed by the bra, then she stepped out of her panties. He caressed both breasts, gently sucked and planted kisses on her nipples and breasts.

Antoine and Jada ran to the shower and stepped into the fragrance of a honeysuckle-pineapple shower gel. They kissed and rubbed each other down with the gel and rinsed off the suds. Antoine slid his tongue up and down her neck, kissing droplets from her forehead as he explored her body with his hands, igniting an erection and desire for her luscious body. She lay against the shower wall, arms above her head, moaning with pleasure. He pressed his buffed body against hers, lifted her and they became one, pleasuring each other with hot steamy passionate lovemaking.

Chapter 32

JADA

Saturday

With one droopy eye open, Jada pried the other open with her finger and batted both. That wine was delightful and sweet, but it gave her quite a buzz as did her man. She rolled over to the pleasant sight of Antoine sprawled across the bed. He was dressed, smelling like men's Aramis soap on a rope. "Morning. What time is it?" she yawned.

He lay on his side with his head propped up with one hand. "Time to rise and shine. It's a little after 7:00. How'd you sleep?"

"Better than ever. Can't remember sleeping this well in months."

"I'm glad. I talked to Joy after I worked out, and we should be at Pop's by 4:00. I stopped for Starbucks;

it's in the kitchen. If you're hungry, I can run down the street for turkey and swiss croissants."

Jada pulled the sheets up to her chin to cover her nakedness. "After all that Jamaican food we ate last night, my stomach might pop open." She snuggled up to him. "Starbucks or food isn't what I want at the moment." Lifting a loc that had fallen in his face, she planted a light kiss on his lips.

"Babe, I could make love to you all day and night." But today, that *ain't* happening. Remember, we need to finish our chat and get out early so you can see the city. But tonight, I promise you it'll be on." He kissed her forehead. "I'm going out for food."

Dang! He caught on. Any time that man refused to make love, something was up and popping. Jada sure wasn't ready for a long conversation this early, nor did she look forward to meeting Antoine's family. There was so much to consider. His father owning her family's building; the anticipation of being introduced at a family gathering. And most important, keeping her anxiety under control when the eviction was discussed. Jada needed a prayer and a miracle to get through this day. She tossed back the blanket and swung her feet to the floor.

Thirty minutes of stretches, twists, and sit-ups followed by meditation and a short prayer, increased her energy. Jada picked up a short peach silk nightie she didn't get a chance to wear. She slipped it over her head and put on the matching robe. After she made up the bed, she sat on the side.

During the heated passion with Antoine, she hadn't paid much attention to the décor in the bedroom. Her eyes scanned the room. African masks on the wall, paintings, a set of highboy dressers. A huge bookshelf filled with books traveled across a long wall. Jada adored the writing desk and chair by the window, and the black and maroon Asian rug that covered shiny hardwood floors. This was a room fit for a king. Her king Antoine.

A while later, she picked up the remote to the big screen, then tossed it on the bed. She was not in the mood for TV. *What's taking him so long?* She reached for the cell on the nightstand and texted Antoine.

Where are you?

Antoine texted back. **Down the street at the deli. You want a sandwich?**

No, I want you.

Got it. One order of me to be served hot and tasty tonight. Lol.

She threw her head back, laughed out loud, and texted.

Can't wait!

Twenty minutes later, another text chimed. It was Denise.

Hey girl, how's it going?

Awesome! Chillin' in a townhouse that cost 7 digits.

Stop playing. You and Antoine okay?

Yes. Not playing – 7 digits!

Call me. ASAP!!!

The front door buzzed. She texted. Got to go! Jada swung her legs up on the bed.

Antoine entered the room holding a cup holder with two coffees and a white paper bag that exuded the pleasing aroma of hot food.

"You're finally back," Jada said. She untied her black silk bonnet; it had fallen off more than it had stayed on her head last night.

"Yeah, the deli was busy. I warmed our coffee in the microwave. There's another turkey and swiss in the bag. I figured we could eat and chat. You ready? "

"I guess. I have no choice." She hesitated and then blurted out, "I suffer from generalized anxiety disorder that started after my parents died. The reason I didn't tell you is...I thought you'd break up with me."

"Babe, I can't believe you didn't tell me." He handed her the coffee and a small bag with cream and sugar. "Why'd you assume the worst? Plenty of people have anxiety, and I've heard it's treatable."

"It is. Mine comes and goes based on the severity of my stress." She added cream and a pack of sugar to her coffee and stirred. "I went for talk therapy that lasted six months, and I was fine until recently. My stress level got out of control. So, I'm back in therapy for several weekly sessions. I don't take any prescription medications, but I take one over-the-counter sleep aid called Melatonin. I use therapeutic techniques to manage my stress and anxiety, and if that doesn't control it, I've decided to try an anti-anxiety medication. The email from Toni about the pictures? I have three. That's what upset me that morning."

Antoine sat on the other side of the bed. "I'm your man. If I can't be there during hard times, what good am I?" He opened his sandwich and took a bite.

She splayed her fingers. "I couldn't share. I was already dealing with other stressors. Baby, that picture of a naked woman strapped across your lap? I—I just lost it. When you walked in, my heart was beating fast, I was a mess. That's why I called Denise to come help me." She sighed and looked at Antoine. "I didn't mean to block you out. I needed time to revamp, and Denise drove me to her place."

"I just wish you'd told me this sooner. I really

would've been by your side. Toni's working on that picture issue because Griff and Simon received some, too. She's also working with Will and the news team to prevent this from getting out to the media."

"I know. I called her from the airport; we're meeting on Monday." She picked up her cup and stared at it for a long time before taking small sips of coffee. She shouldn't drink it, but right now, she required the boost. "Who do you think sent them?"

Antoine wrapped the half-eaten sandwich and placed it in the bag. "I'm not sure, but I'm hoping to find out today. Joy hired a PI to investigate. We think it might be Kiley."

"Kiley?" Jada squinted, with tight lips. "It better not be her."

"We'll see, so don't get uptight. Uh, I have a few more things to disclose, and they'll come out at Pop's."

"Why can't you discuss them now?"

"Trust me. It's complicated, and Joy may present information that I don't have. The woman on my lap is Fiona. For some reason, she decided to set up a camera to snap those shots years ago. I don't think she did this, but I'm not sure."

"Doesn't she have the photos?"

"At that time, she did." He slung one leg up on

the bed. "There's a lot of fishy stuff floating around. Fiona showed up at my last spoken word poetry session. She asked me to go out with her. I think you should know she got pregnant while we were together, but she lost the baby. She begged me not to break up with her, but as I've explained to you, I couldn't stay with her."

"I didn't know that information. Fiona was pregnant; she asked you out?" Jada folded her arms, shifting her gaze to the floor.

"Hey, I turned her down, and the pregnancy wasn't planned." Antoine ran his hand through his dreads. "I'm over her; you're the one I love."

Jada listened to Antoine's story about how Kiley, along with a few other females at the station, had flirted with him from the day he arrived. He emphasized that Kiley was the one who strongly pursued a relationship with him, even after he'd asked her to back off multiple times.

Gordan's comment about Kiley instantly brought back a memory. She wondered if Antoine was one of the several men Denise said Kiley had dated at the station. Antoine went on to explain about his mother's health and the ongoing discord in their family.

By the time he'd finished, her stomach was more twisted than a pretzel. A stream channeled in the corners of her eyes, ready to swim down her cheeks. She siphoned the vulgar words about the women who'd tried to steal her man and wiped the tears with an index finger. *Not this time. This is not about me.* Exposing personal conflicts that unlocked pain and anger must've have been difficult to withstand. If anybody knew, she did. She'd dealt with those issues for ten years.

His eyes filled with sorrow. "I swear I've never been attracted to Kiley. She's the first person I suspected sent those pictures, but that's strange. Where did she get them?" He lay his head back against the dark brown leather headboard.

Jada didn't answer; she sensed his emotional distress and pain as though it were her own. She waited a few seconds, and then laid her head on his arm. "I believe you."

He glanced at her with a relieved look on his face. "Thanks, Love."

"What's next after Joy's report from the PI?"

"We'll find out this evening." He wrapped his arm around Jada and embraced her for a long time. "Two more points to mention. I love your hair. Can you guess how much I love you?" He lifted both arms up and stretched them as far as possible. "This much."

"Uh, uh. Thank you for the compliment, but you can't beat me," Jada laughed as she got on her knees and lifted her arms over her head. "See? This is how much I love you."

They laughed when she tumbled down next to him and planted her head in his lap.

Antoine stroked Jada's face with his finger. "We're equal on the love joy. Can we make a pact to always communicate with each other despite whatever happens?"

"Yes, my sweet man."

"Cool," he pressed his lips against hers. "Get ready so I can show you the Bay area. First stop, Oakland. We're going to Souley Vegan in Jack London's Square."

"Souley Vegan? They don't have meat?"

"They have other dishes like sweet potato waffles, blueberry pancakes, zucchini crab cakes... "

"Say no more. I'm sold. What about the sandwiches you bought?"

Antoine shook his head. "After the conversation we just had, I'm not hungry anymore. My appetite will come back at Souley Vegan."

Chapter 33

ANTOINE

Saturday

Antoine glanced in the mirror and inspected his two-piece beige Armani. It was perfect for the beginning of a summer day and fit for his father's taste. He also remembered to switch out the Apple Watch he loved for the Rolex, a gift from his father after he finished UC Berkeley. He grabbed his keys and walked downstairs. Jada was sitting on the couch reading a book. She looked hot in the low-cut fuchsia top and purple capri leggings, but it was a little too casual for the meeting with his father.

"Hey, babe, I'm ready. Are you taking a bag with your clothes for this evening?"

Jada glanced at him. "Nope. And why're you dressed up and I'm casual? Are we going two separate places?"

"I don't think so. I hadn't planned to come back here."

"Come on, honey. We have to come back. I love the suit, but the weather is supposed to be eighty-four today. We'll be all sweaty," Jada turned up her nose. "I don't even wanna be funky when I meet your folks."

"Talking about a catastrophe, that would be one. I'll go up and change."

Antoine changed to a pair of Levi's, a yellow Polo shirt, and tennis shoes. He grabbed his windbreaker from the closet and headed downstairs. After he set the house alarm, he and Jada caught the elevator down to the parking garage and walked to his truck.

Jada saw the black Mercedes G-Wagon with custom rims and removed her sunglasses. "Woot, woot. A G-Wagon? Go on, boy."

Antoine tapped the alarm release, "Ah right ah right, woman, get in this truck," he shook his head. "I've had this truck for over four years."

"Doesn't matter," she climbed in and fastened her seat belt. "Looks brand new to me."

Antoine started the G-Wagon and cranked the sound up to blast "Sunshine" by Earth, Wind, and Fire. He sped out of the garage and headed to the Golden Gate Bridge. "This bridge was built in the late 1930's to connect San Francisco to Marin

County," he told Jada. "Before that, people had to cross over in boats."

"For real?" Jada said, "This view of the water is amazing." She held her phone up and snapped the Golden Gate Bridge and the ocean.

"I agree," Antoine glanced at the dark blue water in the Pacific Ocean while he drove across the bridge. "The ocean is deeper and larger than any ocean in the world. And did you know Pacific means peaceful?"

"No, but I can see why."

"The Pacific Ocean, the atmosphere... this is why I love the Bay Area. Our time is limited, and I can't show you much. But next time you come up, we'll do more."

"Honey, don't worry about it. I'm satisfied being here with you."

"That's encouraging." He reached for her hand. "You've got to meet Ellis and his wife. And if I can catch up with Rashad, him too. I didn't know if I'd have time to get with him this time around."

"You're up here earlier than usual, right?"

"True."

You might want to check in, see if he's okay."

Antoine nodded. "I'll call him before we go in the restaurant."

They arrived at Souley Vegan at 10:30. Antoine

called Rashad, and they entered the restaurant. Seated shortly after they arrived, Jada ordered blueberry pancakes, and Antoine chose zucchini crab cakes and sweet potato waffles. Within ten minutes, the waitress brought out the steaming hot food.

"Can I get you anything else?" The waitress asked after she set the food on the table.

"I'm straight," Antoine said.

"Me, too," Jada smiled at the lady. "Thank you." Jada poured maple syrup over her blueberry pancakes and cut them up. "Where are we heading after breakfast?"

Antoine rolled his wrist to check the time. "Hmm, it's almost noon. "Why don't we go Uptown? You want to do some sightseeing and shopping?"

"Boy, no way," she laughed, pointing her fork at Antoine. "You think you're slick. I don't want you to buy me anything else; the tickets and money were enough. Besides, I don't want to haul anything back on the plane."

He lifted a brow. "That's not a problem. I can have the items shipped."

"Shipped? Honey, you know I appreciate you," she ate a bite of pancake. "But I don't think so. I shopped enough before I left."

"I appreciate you too, babe." Antoine kept his eyes

on Jada attempting to rationalize why she didn't want to go shopping. Didn't all women like to shop?

"Let me get this out my system," Jada placed her fork on the plate. "At this point in our relationship, you don't have to prove anything to me."

He cocked his head to the side. "What do you mean?"

"I bet you already know." She held up her left hand and wiggled her ring finger with the flashy diamond ring. "The ring, hotel, expensive gifts. I don't love you to get anything from you. I fell in love with you, not your money."

"I see. Now that you know I have money, I can't spend any on you?"

"That's not what I said, Mr. Bailey."

Leaning forward, he clasped his fingers and lifted them to his chin. "I wasn't sure about exposing my wealth. But the way your face lit up at the Montage, I thought I'd hit ten jackpots. I want to make you happy."

"Frankly, I was happy before the Montage. You told me you were frugal and that was impressive."

"I am frugal. Not with my woman, vehicles, or my clothes. Remember? I live with Derrick?"

"Yeah, yeah. Probably to throw people off. Be yourself, that's all I want. And breakfast is on me today."

He raised two thumbs. "I hear you on breakfast. I love Derrick; unfortunately living with him drives me mad sometimes. That's why it's temporary."

She laughed, pressed her fingers to her lips and blew him a kiss.

"Got it. Okay, next up. We'll ride through Uptown so you can see the area, and then to my old neighborhood in East Bay Oakland. I touched base with Ellis and told him we might swing through later."

"I'm loving the tour already, and whatever you decide, I'm ready. Do you think Rashad was disappointed that he won't see you this time?"

"He's cool. Rashad is mature and he understands. He really wanted to meet you, though."

"Aww... I want to meet him too."

After they finished eating, Jada paid the tab and tipped the waitress, which was different for Antoine. The divas he'd dated expected him to be the big spender on every date, but he understood where Jada was coming from and would try to consider everything she'd said.

Nothing in the world could ever replace a relationship based on love, respect, and honesty. That's why it was so important to him that this ongoing situation with Kiley was eradicated. He hadn't been able to function at full speed because of this irritating blotch on his life. And holding it back from Jada made it worse.

They rode around Oakland for almost an hour as Antoine showed Jada some of the infamous hot spots for socializing and restaurants. They viewed the Cathedral Building, the tallest building in Oakland, and he explained the history of the city. He also drove down to the Oakland Palestine Solidarity Mural.

Jada snapped a picture on her phone. "There's a bunch of artistic talent in that mural."

"I thought you'd like it. It's a cultural mecca that draws folks. Like I said, I'll show you more next time. You've gotta come back for poetry night and check me out. The Power of Words Lounge is boss."

"Oh, I'm definitely gonna see your spoken word night."

Antoine nodded and drove to Skyline Street. He parked near a high school and turned off the engine. "Here we are," he gazed at the school. "Skyline High School."

"Don't say nothing. This is where you went to school?"

"For a while, yes." He hit the control that made the windows go down and propped his elbow up. "Right there...I played basketball for the Titans, was on the Honor Roll, had a zillion friends. Out of nowhere,

Pop comes home, tells us during dinner, we're moving in a month. I went berserk, yelled, threw things." Antoine turned and stared at the school. "My mom...she calmed me and my sisters down. She taught at Oakland High School, and she worked it out so I could stay another year. My sisters went to the private school, then I was later transferred there. That was a huge bomb in my life. Ellis graduated from this school."

"Changing schools is never easy. How'd your sisters take it?"

"Hard. Not as hard as I did, though. We'd lived in that area all our lives." Antoine shifted his gaze to Jada. "Uh, babe, before I forget... What I told you earlier is strictly confidential. Only Simon knows my family's background. We worked together at a station up here. Actually, his referral got me hired at KTLM."

"Oh, I didn't know that," Jada lifted both brows.

"Yep, and that's confidential too."

"I got it, baby. I bet it's tough being a rich kid," she smiled while watching him from her periphery.

He peered over the rim of his shades. "What are you saying, smarty pants?" He started tickling her.

She twisted and jerked while laughing hysterically. "Okay, stop! I'm joking."

"You better believe it's rough. That's why my

personal life is private. Some people like me because I'm wealthy. Haters don't like me because I have wealth and they don't. Other haters just hate. It's hard to comprehend if you haven't lived it."

"Oh, I know. After I received a scholarship to Pepperdine, some of my friends hated me, too. My bestie, Madelynn, stopped hanging out with me," Jada waved her hand. "Jealous because she didn't go to college. Me and Denise are tight; we share our ups and downs. She knows many things I don't even tell my sisters."

A quizzical look crossed Antoine's face; he glanced at Jada, who stared at him as if she'd expected a smart-mouth response.

"Ah hah! You told Denise, didn't you?"

"Not everything, honey. She's my bestie; she won't share."

"I know she's close to you, like Ellis is to me." He put his arm around her shoulder. "But scouts honor you won't leak this out to anybody else. Okay?"

"I won't."

Antoine's cell vibrated in his jacket, and he checked his texts. "Oh, man. Ellis worked today. I thought he'd be home by now, but he's still at work. He suggested we stop by his crib tomorrow or join him and Sherrie at Osete Bar and Cafe for brunch. What do you say?"

"Either is good for me. What time is our flight?"

"It's at 5:50. We'll have plenty of time."

"Great. Let's do it."

Antoine started the car and let it idle. He glanced at his old school and sighed with relief. There were so many fond memories. Awesome teachers who encouraged him to go to college, playing sports, making captain of the Debate Team. His best memory was developing a close friendship with Ellis....and Skyline was where he met his first girlfriend.

"What's up, Daydreamer?" Jada said, scrolling through the pictures she'd taken.

He grinned. "Just reminiscing." Placing the car in gear, he headed home.

Chapter 34

ANTOINE

Saturday

Antoine strutted into the living room and draped his suit jacket over the back of the sofa. "Alexa, play "Work" by Drake and Rihanna." He reflected on their day while bobbing his head and snapping his fingers. It had been fairly productive, minus Jada's chance to meet Rashad and his friends. He picked up his manuscript notes from the table, sat on the couch and read.

Dancing her way out of the room, Jada popped her fingers, rolled her shoulders and shook her hips to the beat of the music. She wore a straight A-line royal blue and beige dress with beige heels.

"Nice," Antoine said. He got up and danced over to her.

"Which dress? This one or the multicolored one?"

Antoine scanned Jada up and down and made a circular motion with his finger. "Twirl around."

Jada made a few steps and spun around, then posed with one hand on her hip.

"That's the dress. The multicolored one is boss, but it's too dressy."

"We agree, so this it is. I'll be ready in fifteen minutes."

"Perfect. I forgot to ask if we should take a dish or dessert. I'm calling Joy."

"Okay," Jada said, entering the bedroom.

"Siri, call Joy," he said. She picked up on the first ring.

"Yes, Ant. You on the way?"

"Jada's getting ready, but we'll be on the road shortly. Hey, are we supposed to bring food? Or drinks, dessert?"

"No. Just be there at 4:00 p.m. Eddel has caterers handling dinner."

He snapped his finger. "Ah, man, she always uses caterers. I don't believe she can cook. Right?"

"Ant, please. You know she doesn't cook," Joy said, chuckling. "This is a heads up on the plan. Introduce Jada to Pop and Eddel. You'll meet with him first, so speak up. At the end of your meeting, text me. If everything appears favorable, I'll bring

Jada in. If not, I'll step in to intercede. Eddel and Merlon will keep Jada company. Will that work?"

Antoine scratched his chin. "I guess. You've mapped this out like we're meeting with the POTUS."

"Knowing your father, that's fairly close."

"Uh, on the other hand; I don't know. Jada may want stay with me."

"Can she be out your sight for thirty minutes? We don't bite, you know."

"No, but Pop barks. That's who I'm worried about."

"Maybe at you sometimes, but he certainly won't act that way around Jada."

Their father was an excellent provider, but his weakness was socializing. He hated it. Their mother worked full-time, maintaining a level of normalcy in the house. While their father worked six days a week, she made sure they attended Sunday services, went on vacations, and supported her children's interests.

"Yes, but...this is her intro to the family. I'll check with her. What's the chances of Pop swaying to the right on the eviction?" Antoine put on his shades and stepped out on the deck.

"I'm not certain. To start, I think a hug and handshake might help. You know what? I catch your shows sometimes. I know why you're the hottest DJ around. Use your ingenuity and that mellow voice to bring a positive vibe into the meeting. Stay in that mode; you'll get Pop's attention and respect."

"With my audience, a positive vibe flows naturally. Pop is another story."

"Whatever. I'm saying, it's time for you and him to bury the swords and make peace. You'll have kids someday, and they should know Roland Bailey."

"True. I'll keep that in mind." He allowed his sister's advice to resonate. *Kids?* With all the madness going on with Kiley, he'd pushed that aside. He did want kids with Jada someday, and his father's role as a grandparent was something to consider.

"After you meet with Pop, Merlon and I will update you on the investigation. Will Jada be present?"

Rolling his eyes upward, he rocked his head back, "You told Merlon?"

"Merlon is my husband; we're partners. He compiled a lot of this information, so watch your tongue."

"Okay, okay...my situation is embarrassing enough." He paced the deck, "This info is confidential, and the media can't even get a sniff or I'm burnt toast."

Joy shared practically everything with her

husband, and Antoine hadn't thought of that when he asked for help. But to tell Merlon about Kiley was stepping outside the boundaries of their sister-brother bond.

"Exactly. Guess what? We'll be on the air reporting your business on the 6:00 a.m. news. Ant, surely, you can't believe we'd betray you."

"No, baby sis. I didn't mean to come at you like that. Management is in my business, and they're concerned about those pictures. So am I." He'd have to force himself to flow with her decision to tell Merlon.

"Stay calm, we'll work through this. See you soon."

"Ciao." While a stream of light brought warmth, a mild Bay breeze grazed Antoine's face, bringing a level of relaxation. He and Jada had disclosed a lot of heavy information this morning, and he sensed one apparent fact that bothered him. She wasn't ready to meet his family. If they could sit on this deck, clear their heads, and enjoy time alone, this trip would be perfect. He stepped back inside the living room.

Jada sashayed out, dazzling the room in the beige and royal blue dress.

"I'm ready," she draped a beige wrap over her arm.

"Okay, fine woman. Let's roll to Piedmont."

Chapter 35

JADA

Saturday

Antoine made a quick right on a street that resembled Paradise City, and Jada gasped. He continued to drive up secluded hills, but the area was so extraordinary, she missed the street name. In awe of the caliber of homes, it was unbelievable that black people lived up here. She'd have to be on top of her game to impress Antoine's family. What if they didn't like her? She didn't come from a wealthy family, nor did she know anybody who had this kind of wealth.

Antoine swerved into the circular gray cobblestone pavement and parked. "You ready for this?"

"As ready as I can be. I'm a little nervous." She shifted her attention to the two-story house, green trees, sculptured lawns and bushes. The multicolored flower bed landscape expanded around the property and beyond her view. "Jeez, this house is awesome, like the others on this block. Where'd you say this is?"

"Piedmont, it's in Alameda County, close to Oakland. Wait until you see the inside. Pop's girlfriend, Eddel, can't cook, but she's charming. They're using a caterer for dinner. Hopefully, it's Ethiopian food."

"Oh, Ethiopian food. I've never had it."

"Trust me. It's delicious. That's where Eddel is from. FYI – Pop likes younger women these days, and Eddel is about our age. Joy and Merlon will love you, and my father...well, you'll see how he is."

"I'll see how he is?" Jada jutted her chin. "Please explain what you mean."

"Don't worry. Before we leave, you'll know him well. It'll be all right. By the way. I have a private meeting with Pop. Are you cool with my absence for about a half hour?"

"Yes, but you don't think I should be in there?"

"Not until I meet with him first." He stroked her face and kissed her cheek. "Let's get going."

"When will I meet your mom?" Jada knew this was a touchy area, but she wanted to meet his mother before her illness worsened. Joy mentioned their mother hadn't felt well for the last several days. A visit might ease Antoine's tension.

Antoine gazed at her. "You must've read my mind. I'll be sure to let you know."

"One month's notice is required for *every* trip."

"Got it." He unlocked the car doors and removed the key from the dashboard.

The lengthy walkway to the expansive front door made Jada regret wearing three-inch heels instead of pumps. Antoine rang the doorbell, and a lovely young woman with a pretty smile answered.

"Welcome! I'm Eddel."

"Eddel, this is Jada."

"I'm so happy to meet you." She hugged Jada, and then Antoine.

"It's a pleasure to meet you, too," Jada said.

"Is Joy here? I didn't see her car," Antoine said.

"Yes, I'm here," Joy walked into the room. "Merlon left, but he's coming back."

"Joy, this is Jada," Antoine said, with a broad smile.

"Well, I finally get to meet you, lady," Joy said, with a mouth full of snow-white, perfect teeth and a smile.

"Yes, nice to meet you, too," Jada hugged Joy, admiring her print A-line dress, gold chain and cross. She resembled Antoine and carried the same personal warmth.

Joy pressed her hands together. "We changed the plan. Pop's been detained; he's on the phone with a client in New York. And Merlon...he'll be here before dinner. So, we have hors d'oeuvres and drinks on the table. Help yourselves."

"Is Cheyenne here?" Antoine asked as they walked to the dining room.

"No, she's with the babysitter. When you're up here again check in. Either we'll bring her to your place or you come to ours. I hope Jada will be with you."

"Oh, she'll be up here again." Antoine shifted his eyes to Jada.

"Definitely, I love the atmosphere in the Bay Area."

Eddel followed the caterers with another tray of food for the table. They made their plates and she guided everyone out to the patio. The backyard was spacious. It had a large pool and lots of green plants, flowers, and trees that created a scenic environment. Joy and Eddel were engaging and friendly, and Jada blended in with the family.

"Well, well, if it isn't my one and only son." Antoine's father walked onto the patio.

Antoine hugged his father and shook his hand

before introducing him to Jada. His dad smiled and that made her comfortable. Merlon breezed in five minutes before dinner and introduced himself to Jada. Antoine's family treated her well and everyone was extremely pleasant. Hoping for a positive solution to the eviction, Jada could not wait to get past this evening.

Chapter 36

ANTOINE

Saturday

Pleased with the flow of conversation and comradery between his family and Jada, the evening couldn't get any better. The fact that his father wanted to shoot a few rounds of pool after dinner was not surprising; pool was his favorite game for winding down. Antoine and Merlon went along, even though Antoine's hope was to get straight to their meeting. Jada had acclimated to his family and was chatting with Joy and Eddel. She seemed comfortable with the men fleeing to the game room in the back of the house.

Pop had a shot at the ball; he drank a sip of rum and Coke and stepped up to the pool table. "All right let me dunk this ball." Pop picked up the pool stick, and his olive brown, clean shaven face appeared brighter than a full moon. He smoothed his silver hair back, studied the table carefully, bent down, and made his shot. "Yes!" he pumped his fist in the air. "Straight in the pocket. I'm done. You young bucks take over."

"What?" Antoine shook his head. "Pop, you can't quit in the middle of a game."

"Nah, I'm tired. Finish up. I've gotta make a few calls anyway." Pop picked up his drink and left the room.

That was just like his father to quit while he was ahead of everyone. Antoine caught the smile on Merlon's face; neither was surprised by his father's actions.

"Brother." Merlon laughed. "I guess it's just me and you."

While they played, Merlon seemed preoccupied.

"Hey, bro', are you okay?" Antoine said.

"Yes. Just ready to get the meeting done."

"You? That's all I've thought about this evening. How's everything looking?"

"Uh, man, I have to be honest." He paused, and then shot the ball, which did not go inside the pocket. "This situation is perplexing, we'll run it by you."

Antoine rolled his shoulders and picked up the pool stick. Merlon's facial expression and words, literally summed up part of his findings. Antoine analyzed the shot, but his mind was not on the game. A plethora of possible solutions, but not one that he could see as alternatives, stuck in the back of his head. Well, he was minutes away from receiving the lab results and private investigator's report. At least he'd have some closure.

Eddel entered the room, "Hey guys, Roland's ready when you finish this game."

"Cool, we're almost done," Antoine said. He walked around the table, assessed, and found the vertical center of the cue ball. He hit the ball with the pool stick, and the ball rolled into the pocket. "Whoa! Best shot this evening."

"Yeah, that was a super shot," Merlon clapped Antoine's hand.

They cleared the table and placed the pool sticks on racks before heading down the hallway. Antoine peeked in on Jada, who was watching a movie with Joy and Eddel. Merlon removed the cell from his pocket and disappeared. Antoine glanced around and started toward his father's office. His steps were slow and steady, but it seemed as though he'd never reach the office. Or was it that he purposely delayed his arrival? He knocked.

"Come in."

"You ready?"

"Yeah. Have a seat. I called Nikki; spoke with your mother earlier."

"How is she?" Antoine took a seat across from his father.

"She's a bit better today. The doctor came out and she's on antibiotics. I, uh...flew up to D.C. last month and visited her."

"What's the antibiotics for?"

"She's got a respiratory infection.

"I talked to mom yesterday; Nikki didn't mention that. Joy told me."

"Yeah, well, she probably forgot. Say...is Jada the girl you knocked up?"

Antoine's mouth gaped open. "Who told you that?"

"I've got my sources. Son, you've gotta stop bangin' all those women. Get one pregnant; it'll cost you plenty."

Attempting to simmer down before he responded, Antoine rolled his shoulders. "Fiona was the only girl who got pregnant, and she lost the baby. That wasn't planned. You know the story, so don't sweat me about it."

The silence in the room was so thick, a machete knife wouldn't slice through it. Pop lifted a cigar out of a box labeled Arturo Fuente. He flicked a cigarette lighter, lit the end of the cigar, and drew in a long puff before blowing smoke through his mouth. Swiveling his chair, he turned on the fan that sat on the credenza, and then stared hard at Antoine. "Think about what I said."

Antoine pressed his fingers against his jaw and stared back at his father. "Jada is the *only* woman I've been intimate with in almost two years. Nobody else. She's not pregnant."

"Then who's the other woman?"

"Some chick at the station who's trying to set me up. Joy and Merlon are on top of that."

"Yeah. You better hope they are. Because your *hide* is grass if they're not."

"Can we get to Jada's business?" Antoine didn't want to argue with his father; he'd done that for too many years. Drilling him about the women in his life was not what he'd anticipated.

Pop thumped ashes in an oval crystal ashtray. "Ellen Carson. Astute businesswoman, paid her rent on time. She died; her kids acquired the dress shop."

Talking fast as usual; Antoine often questioned how his father had made so many major real estate deals using rapid, choppy speech. His mother's eloquence and giving spirit in contrast to the fast-talking businessman's arrogance and selfishness left many questions circulating as to why she was drawn to him.

"That's correct. And they'd like to stay at their location. Why would you want to throw them out after they've been there twenty-one years? They have nowhere else to go."

"Not the point. Their rent's been low, and I've lost money for years. Got a buyer who's interested in the building."

"Yeah, but Pop, why that building? I'm sure you have tons of buildings other than the dress shop." Antoine extended his hand.

"To make money, son. Jada seems nice. But your priority... handle your business with that pregnant girl." He puffed the cigar and blew out a whirlwind of smoke. "Pay for an abortion, if necessary. And does Jada work or is she making clothes like her aunt?"

Antoine's thoughts hit the brakes. "An abortion? That would be like admitting I'm the father. I'm handling that, okay? Jada's a college graduate, and she works at the station. Can I ask you to help her family? Even if it means raising the rent. You know...give them some slack and let them stay."

"Humph. So, Dee's still cranking out clothes, huh? Thought she'd retired by now."

Antoine propped his leg up over the other. "Are

you serious?" he said with a light laugh. "You knew Mrs. Carson and you know Aunt Dee?"

"Yeah, I knew them well. Your mother referred them some clients."

"Well, you know they've worked hard. Her family's business is stable. Their aunt's kept things afloat, and that business is her livelihood. Twenty-five years in business, twenty-one in your building, and you have no empathy for this family?"

"Empathy? That what you want from me?" Pop frowned. "I didn't get this far off empathy. Didn't want it. Didn't ask for it."

Antoine tilted his head and pulled his earlobe. "I take it that's a no."

"There's three months left. Find them a new location."

Antoine opened his mouth to speak. An inner voice said, *Don't. Keep your mouth shut, even if you feel like saying words that will force him to jump from the seat like his pants are on fire.* Challenge him, call him the son of a— No. He rubbed his temple with two fingers. *I've got to stay in control.*

After moments of reconsideration, calmness overpowered the disgusting words in his head. He was better than Pop. He'd followed all of Joy's suggestions, remained calm and mellow, but to no avail. But it was okay. He was tired of fighting, tired of attempting to reason with a bull-headed man who cared about nothing but wealth and money. He'd have to figure out a way to help Jada and her family. Removing his phone from his pants pocket, he texted his sister.

Joy, it's a no go.

A few seconds later she texted, **I'm on my way.**

Let Jada know I'll be out soon.

"Who'd you text. Jada?" Pop asked.

"Joy. She's coming in here."

There was a quick knock, then without waiting for an answer, Joy stormed in and sat next to Antoine.

She crossed her legs. "Pop, you're saying you won't help Antoine's girlfriend?"

"Help? What's wrong with you two? The Carsons have...wait a minute." He tapped information on his desktop and read through it. "They've got a couple of months left."

"Is that reasonable?" Joy asked. "Jada's like family now. And you shouldn't have given them an eviction notice anyway. They've paid you on time, never skipped any payments or violated the lease. You can extend the lease, but what you should do is let them stay where they are."

"They had six months."

"No, they didn't," Joy said. "Jada didn't get the letter right away. Please be lenient."

Antoine didn't want to hear any more of Joy coaxing their stubborn father. It was useless. He got up and started toward the door.

"Ant, stop! Don't leave," Joy folded her arms.

He stared at Joy with a look of defeat. She pointed to the seat next to hers. Again, salty words formed in his mouth. He grappled with restraining himself. If he expressed what was in his heart, he'd ruin any potential chances of obtaining favor on this eviction.

"Sit. We're not finished," Joy said.

Antoine shuffled back to the chair, stretched his legs out and pressed a palm against his face. If his father said no to him, he would likely say the same to Joy. So why waste time?

"Is dessert here yet?" Pop asked.

"Who's thinking of dessert after you made this appalling decision?" Joy frowned.

"Joy, this is business, and you should understand." Pop steepled his fingers. "I have a buyer. I'm done."

She bobbed her head up and down. "You're done all right. Effective Monday, you'll have thirty days to find a new lawyer. I'm resigning to work for Merlon's law firm."

Antoine jerked his head around to face Joy.

Their father's eyes widened. "What? No, you can't do that. You're my lead attorney."

"Watch me," she said with a sly grin.

"For what reason? You get paid well; you have flexibility."

She waved both hands in the air. "No, no, no! You don't understand. It's not about pay. We're wealthy. I've prayed daily, and this is about giving back. My interest was in criminal law, and what did I do? Sacrificed my preference to help you all these years. And here you are...too ornery and greedy to help your own people."

"Darling, slow down. A buyer made an offer for the building."

"That's no excuse," she snapped. "You must've listed it for sale if a buyer made an offer. Pop, please reconsider your decision. You have a long-term tenant in the building, they may lose clients...their business."

Antoine saw a change of expression on his father's face as he listened to his youngest daughter. He didn't expect Joy to go this far in his defense, but better her than him. He would've kicked him out the office by now.

"I said I'm done. My decision is final." Pop puffed his cigar and leaned back in his chair.

Joy shifted her attention to their father and said,

"*Timothy 6:10: For the love of money is the root of all kinds of evil.* Thirty days. Now, I'm done." She touched Antoine's hand. "Let's go."

Immediately after Antoine and Joy exited Pop's office, water in the corners of Joy's eyes made him feel guilty that he'd accepted her help. He hugged his sister.

She quickly wiped her tears away. "Ant, I'm sorry. I don't know what else to say or do."

"You did the best you could. I'll work things out."

Joy summoned Antoine to follow her. She opened the door to another bedroom, and they went inside.

"Lady, you shocked me. You resigned?"

With one finger, Joy brushed a strand of hair from her face and smiled. "It's time for a change, but I'd planned to give Pop a three-month notice. I've been doing some part-time work for Merlon's law firm for over a year. Pop doesn't know that."

"Are you really leaving in a month?"

"I have to. Some of his decisions are off the wall. But this one...it's ridiculous and gut-wrenching. It's getting late. I'll find Merlon and see if Pop will let us use his office."

"Okay, I'll get Jada."

"Jada?" Joy said with a surprised look.

"Yes, she'll be in the meeting. She's gotta know what happened."

"Why not wait and talk to her in private after you get home?"

There was a momentary lull as Antoine considered his sister's recommendation. Her point was valid, but he felt certain Jada would prefer to be present.

"I'm sure she'll be okay," he said.

Chapter 37

JADA

Saturday

The second Antoine ambled into the den; Jada suspected his father hadn't approved the lease renewal. He tried to hide his feelings, but she picked up on the change in his mood and his distinct swagger. The dejection seeped through his dimpled smile, a cover-up for whatever had occurred behind closed doors. He reached out and lifted her hands to his lips.

"Time to meet with Joy and Merlon," he said. They strolled down the hallway to a door that was slightly open where Joy and Merlon were seated and waiting.

Joy moved one chair over so that Antoine and Jada could sit together.

"Ant, Merlon's going to discuss the labs first, and

then the PI's findings. I'll interject comments as needed," Joy said.

"I'm okay with that. First, I want to thank both of you for pitching in," Antoine said.

"No problem, brother. We're always here to help." Merlon put on his glasses and opened a file folder. "I hate to say this, but you may be the victim of a date rape drug. The lab report showed a fairly high amount of Rohypnol and a small level of alcohol in your bloodstream."

Jada sucked in a breath so hard her chest hurt. She made brief eye-to-eye contact with Antoine.

Antoine shook his head. "Nah, how is that possible? Where'd the Rohypnol come from?"

"It is possible," Merlon said. "Both men and women get date raped. Most men can't perceive a male being date raped, and many don't report it. The drug Rohypnol is a powerful drug that's used to incapacitate people. Scopolamine is another one that's used. Once the victims ingest one of the drugs, they become dizzy, confused, and exhibit other symptoms; some go into an unconscious status. You said while you worked on Kiley's sound system, she served food. I believe tea and cake."

"That's right."

"Did you have cocktails at Kiley's?" Joy asked.

"No. I had one glass of wine at the event where I

was the MC. And I never left the table, so nobody could have tampered with my drink. Man, I remember feeling dizzy, nauseated one minute. I had the kind of chills a snowstorm would cause. I couldn't remember where I was either, and then I remember laying on her couch."

"What?" Jada repositioned herself to face Antoine.

"Those symptoms are congruent with drugged date rape victims. How to prove that happened at Kiley's is the problem," Joy said. "Consumption of alcohol and the drug Rohypnol combined could've killed you."

"In fact, if there was a date rape, a possible pregnancy could have occurred," Merlon said.

"I don't see how. I woke up with my clothes on."

Jada's mouth dropped open. "Date rape? Pregnancy? What the heck is going on," she asked Antoine. "Is this what you couldn't say earlier?"

Merlon's eyes widened. "I apologize. I thought you knew."

Antoine glanced at Jada. "Babe, I'm sorry. I was trying to wait for the labs and PI reports to come back. Kiley, accused me of..." he twisted his mouth, "of being the father of her unborn child. I've never willingly slept with that woman, ever." He wiped his moist forehead.

Jada clapped a hand to her mouth; her mind trailed off to one person. Gordan. Conflicted and unsure of whether to bring up the information that he'd mentioned, she remained quiet. How could she disclose Gordan's relationship with Kiley if she had no specific information? She knew something happened that made him angry enough to break off the engagement. Did she tell him she was pregnant, too? What if she'd told the other men she'd dated the same?

"Well, since that's established," Antoine folded his arms over his chest. "What can I do?"

Merlon, lifted a small paperweight and laid it back on the desk, apparently pondering an answer. "Has she asked for money?"

"Lately, yes." He let out a deep breath and looked at Jada. "She called yesterday while I was at the deli. That's the reason I was gone so long. This woman is trying to destroy my life. Calling my cell, harassing me, now she wants ten-K for prenatal care."

"As Merlon said, there's a chance you might be the father. You were sedated with a hypnotic drug, and you can't remember much." Joy crossed her legs.

"I get that. It's still unbelievable. There's no way I can prove I'm not the father?"

"A DNA test can be done. Sweetheart, did you hear from Jeanie?" Merlon asked Joy.

"Not yet. She'll text before the weekend ends." Joy looked at Antoine. "She's an OB doctor, so she can clarify if the DNA can be done before childbirth. We're not sure."

Merlon closed one folder and opened another one. "Last, Kiley's married, but she's separated from her husband. There's a chance that he's the father."

Antoine scooted to the edge of the chair and leaned forward. "I'd like to get this resolved ASAP. What if I agree to pay the ten-K if she agrees to a DNA test and stops harassing me."

"That sounds like a reasonable option. We can help you with the agreement. Before you do that, we should find out if you can get a DNA test before the baby's born."

"What if you're the father?" Jada said.

He glanced at Jada, dropped his head and stared at the floor. "Then I'm the father, and I'll take care of my child."

His child? And Kiley's child? Hearing that response was worse than taking a dive off a twenty-story building, tumbling slowly, and then crashing on the pavement. All Jada's beautiful dreams shattered in a million pieces. Her man fathering a child with Kiley was unimaginable.

Joy touched Antoine's hand. "We'll discuss this again after we find out about the DNA test."

"Cool."

"There's more. Mr. Dearden's report. He's the PI, and his findings are interesting," Merlon said.

Jada held her breath. What else did they discover?

"We asked that he thoroughly research a few people that might be involved." Merlon scrolled through the report and looked at Jada and Antoine.

"Fiona Harris? Your ex, right?" Merlon asked.

Jada changed positions, frowned and glanced at Antoine, who appeared to get more agitated by the minute.

"Yes, but she wouldn't do this. She has no reason to."

"You don't know that. It's not untypical for ex-spouses, girlfriends, boyfriends to get revenge." Merlon glanced at Antoine. "Are you aware that she's Kiley's cousin?"

"What the hell—" Antoine shouted, pounding a fist against his thigh. "Crap! Kiley and Fiona set me up."

Jada rubbed his back. "Baby, take it easy." She was shocked by the outrageous information that was disclosed but was even more shocked to hear Antoine use foul language. However, if Kiley was involved, outrageous behavior wasn't a surprise. When would this end?

"You think Fiona set you up after all this time? Don't jump to conclusions," Joy said.

"Yeah, but muddy water doesn't clear up right after it rains. Fiona showed up at my spoken word session when I was up here last time. Now I'm thinking she might be the linchpin in this scheme."

"I know you're angry. It's just... you can't speculate that Fiona and Kiley plotted together. Where's your proof? Remember you went in her apartment," Joy said.

"I don't have any. But if I had to guess, those two are the culprits." Antoine shook his head.

"They're cousins, but that doesn't prove you're right. Here's the PI's notes and your lab results. Read through them, make your own assessment and draw your own conclusions before you approach them. Don't talk to Kiley until you hear from us regarding the DNA test."

Jada raised her hand. "Can I speak?"

"You sure can," Joy said.

Somewhat nervous, Jada glanced at Antoine, and then faced Joy and Merlon. "Antoine doesn't know this, but I have information that may help him."

Chapter 38

JADA

Saturday

On their way home, a bitter wind swept in a crisp breeze, much different from the sunny-filled day of warmth. Jada threw her shawl around her shoulders and glanced at Antoine. He'd kept his eyes on the road and hadn't said a word since they got in the car. Maybe he was upset about Gordan. She'd mentioned calling him with good intentions of obtaining information that could be useful.

"Hello. Calling Antoine to earth," she snapped her fingers. "Are you mad at me?"

"Don't be ridiculous. I'm tired." Keeping his eyes on the road, he twisted his mouth.

Jada gazed at him. "Too tired to talk to me?"

He rocked his head from side-to-side. "I'm not in the mood for talking, maybe later."

He turned a jazz tune up so loud it could've ruptured their eardrums. Was he trying to drown her out altogether? This sudden change of behavior was strange, but she chalked it up to the events of tonight. Nothing had panned out in his favor, and her heart went out to him. She hoped Gordan would willingly share information about what happened between him and Kiley.

Antoine made a quick right on his street and drove up into the carport of his townhouse. He remained silent in the elevator; his eyes stuck to the elevator lights that indicated each floor number. The bell chimed, and they exited on his floor. He rushed to the door with Jada a few steps behind. When he entered, he pushed a button on his keychain to disable the house alarm.

"Can you slow down for a minute?" Jada trailed him to the kitchen.

"What's up." He opened the refrigerator and grabbed a bottled water.

"My guess is you're upset about tonight, and I would be, too. I'd like for us to talk, but if you don't want to, I'm going to bed."

"I can't talk right now," he said with his head down. "I'll be upstairs in my music studio."

Jada nodded.

Antoine started up the stairs, not bothering to

show her where the studio was located. She had no idea there was one in the townhouse. They'd been so busy; he'd likely forgotten that she missed the grand tour. She walked upstairs to the master bedroom and closed the door. No more begging for communication, at least not tonight. After a warm shower that eased her tension, Jada put on a lavender slip gown, brushed her teeth, and removed a novel from the nightstand. She wasn't ready for sleep. How could she sleep when her man was so miserable?

A few hours later, she checked the time. Antoine still wasn't in bed. She placed a bookmark in her novel, got up and slipped her arms into a robe. She swung the door open and slowly pattered barefoot across the hardwood floor, searching for the studio. Of the three upstairs bedrooms, one door at the end of the hallway was partially open, so she tiptoed to that one.

Edging closer to the door, she swayed back and forth to Earth, Wind, and Fire's song, "All About Love." Antoine said their music was musical poetry at its finest. That man loved him some Earth, Wind, and Fire, and she'd planned to surprise him and buy tickets for a concert, which was coming up soon. She loitered at the door before peeking in at Antoine, who was sipping wine and bobbing his head to the beat of the music while writing in a notebook. Wearing his signature white muscle t-shirt and plaid shorts, his preference over pajamas, he appeared more relaxed. He was probably working on his manuscript. She remembered that he told her sometimes he wrote chapters and had them typed later.

Jada could've rested her eyes on him forever. She twirled around and slowly walked back toward the room.

"You looking for me?" Antoine appeared in the doorway.

"Uh, no. It's late; I thought I'd check on you, but it looks like you're busy."

"Come join me. I don't think I showed you my music studio."

"No, you didn't." Jada ran a hand through her braids. "Uh...you sure? You're writing and—"

"It's cool," he summoned her with an index finger. "I'm ready to call it a night anyway."

She walked back to the studio and followed him inside. Stunned, her eyes roamed over what appeared to be a full studio — electric piano, large speakers, tons of other equipment that she could not identify. "This is fly," Jada said.

"It is," he took a seat in front of his desk. "Have

a seat. This place eases my mind, but music, writing, and *you*... have that effect on me, too."

"That's nice to know." She walked around, touched the synthesizer, admired photographs of Antoine posing with famous entertainers.

"That's the synthesizer," he pointed when she touched it. "It's operated by a keyboard, produces a wide variety of sounds and frequencies. Perfect for producing music. There's a portable keyboard in that corner, and of course lots of Bose speakers for dynamic sounds." He grinned, "This is my dream room; I usually write in here."

Jada sat in a red and black chair and gazed into Antoine's face. "You mean you write music, too?"

"At one time, I thought I wanted to. I prefer to play it now."

"I'm glad I help you relax," she looked around the room. "This studio is so cool."

Antoine licked his lips. "I didn't mean to drag you into this Kiley mess."

"No, don't say that. We've got to support each other."

"I'm speaking truth. You don't deserve this. If you ever walk away, I wouldn't blame you," he draped his arm over the chair.

"What are you saying?" The negative vibe he pitched at her was outlandish. Was he losing hope already or was something else on his mind? This was not the optimistic, persistent Antoine she knew.

He picked up his wine glass and sipped. "My aim was to make you happy, not throw you in a lion's cage. Pop said no; those reports from Merlon and Joy..." he sighed, "blew me away."

Pressing fingers to her jaw, Jada tried to understand his sudden shift from optimism to pensive sadness. "The PI's report is progress, and you should be okay after the DNA test. You know this whole situation is about money. I plan to call Gordan tomorrow."

"Nope. That's another issue. I don't want you calling that dude or riding in his car. Why are you talking to him anyway?" He snapped.

With pouty lips, she stared at him with the intent of snapping back but took a deep breath before speaking. "He attends my aunt's church. I ran into him there one Sunday; we talked briefly...He apologized."

Antoine's eyes had turned red, and his unreasonable behavior meant that he could be drunk. She should've read her book and gone to bed.

"Yeah, an apology means Gordan wants you back." Antoine rocked back and forth in his chair. "I canceled our lunch with Ellis and Sherrie."

"Aww, Ant. For what reason?"

"Right now, I'm not socializing; my focus is to clear my name. You feel me? Fiona and I need to talk before we leave." He picked up a pen and started jotting down more notes.

Jada frowned. "Hold on. What's the deal with you? First, you're excited about introducing me to your friends, then you cancel. Now, you're going to see Fiona? Should you do that without consulting with Joy or Merlon? If she's involved, she may try to set you up again."

"She won't have time. I'm showing up on her doorstep unannounced."

"Oh, no." Jada jumped up. "Boy, I'm going to bed. You've leaped overboard on this one."

"Look, I don't need my sister and brother-in-law telling me what I should or should not do. And why you trippin'? You're meeting with Gordan," he said in an edgy tone. He sipped wine and continued writing.

"Yes, I'm calling Gordan to get information for you." Jada lifted a brow and crossed her arms. "By the way, how many glasses of booze have you drank?"

"Not many."

"Uh, huh. Too many. Stop with the pity party and try faith. Goodnight, Antoine." She was done. No way could she persuade him to not visit Fiona. In the morning, she'd encourage him to call Joy before he did something else that he'd regret.

Chapter 39

ANTOINE

Sunday Morning

A loud blowhorn alarm blasted the studio room. Antoine sprung from the chair, arms flinging in the air; he stumbled and almost fell. Dazed and momentarily confused, the blowhorn transitioned to a soft jazz song, while he found his bearings. Antoine plopped down in the chair and pressed several fingers against his pounding forehead. He'd forgotten to cut off that stupid alarm. 4:52 a.m. Why was he still in here and not with Jada?

He looked over his manuscript notes; he'd aced his word count, talked to Jada, and— He closed his eyes in the middle of a thought. "Man. That was wrong." His behavior, the way he treated her. He kicked his foot against a bottle of Moscato that had fallen underneath his desk and spilled on the floor.

Stooping down, he grabbed it. The bottle was almost empty, and only one wine glass was sitting on the desk. *Unbelievable. I drank nearly the whole bottle.* With the bottle and glass in hand, he bolted out the door and downstairs to the kitchen where he discarded the bottle and placed the glass in the dishwasher.

It was time to get his act together. Fast. Antoine made a cup of instant coffee and drank it black. He opened the refrigerator and picked up two bottles of Perrier water, guzzled half of one bottle. If his head would stop hurting, he could figure out what to say to Jada before she awoke. Embarrassed and guilty, he'd screwed up.

After Antoine showered, he put on a pair of green and white shorts and made his way upstairs to the master bedroom. He quietly opened the door and eased in bed, gently pushing his body against Jada's. He placed one arm around her waist; she lifted her head and faced Antoine.

"Good morning, sleeping beauty."

"Mornin'," Jada said in a groggy voice. Whew!" She fanned her face with one hand. "What's with the coffee breath?"

He huffed a breath in his palms. "You smell coffee? I brushed my teeth."

"Yeah, smells like you bought out Starbuck's whole stock and drank it all."

"Babe, I owe you an apology."

"Hmph. Apologize to yourself 'cause you don't owe me a thing." She turned over and dropped her head on the pillow. "It's too early for talking; I'm going back to sleep."

"Hear me out. Uh, I drank a little too much last night. I was down, felt like I'd failed you. Said some things I shouldn't have." He blew air through his mouth. "Now I have a freakin' hangover I'm trying to hide."

He rested his chin on her shoulder and tugged her closer. "Babe, can you forgive me?"

"Forgive yourself. Kiley's messing with your head, and you're too smart for that. If I survived what I've been through, you can, too." She rolled over and snuggled against his hairy chest. "*We* got this, okay? And about Gordan, I believe he has some important information that could benefit you. He was briefly engaged to Kiley before he broke it off."

Antoine raised up. "Are you serious?"

"Rumor is... she dated other men, some who work at the station."

"You mean she slept with other men and claims I got her pregnant? And that date rape drug..."

"I tried to tell you last night," she tapped his nose.

"You got buzzed instead of talking to me. Focus on now and the future."

"You're right," he kissed her forehead. "This puzzle gets more twisted every day. It's important that I talk to Fiona, though."

"Consider this. If she's involved, will she admit it?"

"Babe, I don't know, but I plan to find out. She might give me what I need. The best way to deal with Fiona is face-to-face."

"But not at her house," Jada said, side-eyeing him. "No, I'll go anywhere except there."

He was running out of time, and although he cherished Jada's suggestions, he'd meet with Fiona before they left. His gut instinct may prove that his suspicions were valid. Either she knew something, or she didn't. Antoine and Jada reached a truce. He would meet with Fiona, and she would call Gordan.

They slept in for several more hours, then readied themselves for an early breakfast on Fisherman's Wharf. After they walked along the wharf, Jada wanted to ride the trolley cable car.

"Okay, this is what we're doing. Seats might not be available, and the cable car has no doors. So, we'll jump on the trolley and hold the pole while the car is moving. Don't jump off until it stops," Antoine said.

"I hope we can hang from the side of the car," Jada said. "That looks like fun."

"We'll see."

When the trolley car stopped, they ran and jumped on a crowded car, found positions on the side of the car where they held onto the poles and rode up and down the hilly streets of San Francisco for over an hour. The trolley came to a halt, and they hopped off, along with a group of people.

"How'd you like the tour?" Antoine said, with hopes that their outing would make up for his ridiculous behavior last night.

"It was awesome," she said, with a thumbs up. "I don't understand how people drive on these steep streets. Me? I'd be taking Ubers or Lyfts to work every day."

"No, you wouldn't. You'd adjust. If you can drive on that wild 405 Freeway in L.A., you can drive here." He checked his watch. "I think we should get back. It's almost time to meet with Fiona."

"Yeah, it's about that time."

Jada seemed distracted as they walked to the parking lot.

"Where'd you decide to meet her?"

"Starbucks. Not far from the house." He unlocked the SUV and they got inside. "Open the glove compartment and get my other house key. I left the alarm off."

"You're not going in?"

"No, I won't have time."

Antoine drove home and pulled in the carport. He placed his arm over the passenger headrest and glanced at Jada. "You know this means nothing, okay?"

"What are you talking about?"

"I mean this meeting. It's solely business."

"Hey, I'm fine with that," Jada said, gazing out the window. "We already talked about this. I trust you; it's Fiona that I don't trust." Jada kissed his lips, got out of the truck, and closed the door. "Don't be gone too long," she said, giving him the side-eye.

He hit the automatic window button, and the passenger side rolled down. "Pretty girl, I'm crazy about you."

She smiled, offered him a wave and walked into the elevator.

Chapter 40

ANTOINE

Sunday Afternoon

Walking into Starbucks, Antoine scanned the coffee shop and spotted Fiona standing next to a table waving at him. He strutted across the room with his hands in both pockets, somewhat ambivalent after Jada's heedful warning. The second he checked out Fiona's attire, his eyes bulged at the short pink halter dress, exposing way too much cleavage and bare legs. But then...that was Fiona, always ready to show off her tits and fine body. This meeting would be brief, and neither had strict dress codes.

She smiled and threw her arms around his neck. The hug between them lasted longer than expected. Antoine stepped back to avoid getting too cozy or implying false notions.

"It's so great to see you again," Fiona surveyed him up and down. "Hey now. I like that UC Berkeley shirt. I see you've still got movie-star looks."

"That's nice of you to say. I'm not sure about movie-star looks, though." He tugged at his earlobe. Fiona had always been intrigued by his appearance, clothes, vehicles, money, and whatever his money bought.

"Are we ordering drinks or snacks? I think we should if we're taking up space," Fiona applied lotion to her hands and rubbed them together. She smelled like fresh peaches out of an orchard.

"I'm straight, but order, and I'll cover it."

"No, I'll pay." She bent to remove the wallet from her bag but seemed to have a hard time finding it.

Antoine's eyes dipped in her bosom for a half second before he moved his attention away from her size thirty-eights. Surely, she must have known that he was on to that losing the wallet gimmick to get his attention. He'd be mindful about keeping his eyes above her chest during their conversation. Removing his cell from the jean jacket pocket, he busied himself with text messages and social media.

"Be right back," she said, returning to the table within a few minutes with a Venti-size cup. "What did you get?"

"Iced green tea. It's too hot for warm beverages.

Come on with it. What's this meeting for?" Fiona tossed her long ponytail off her shoulder.

"It's like this...I'm caught up in either a blackmail, a set-up, or both. I thought you might know why."

She smiled, raised a brow and said, "Are you kidding? We're not together. I don't keep track of your life."

"Well, why didn't you give me a heads up about Kiley? Personally, I would've done that for you." He gave her an intense stare.

Fiona's smiley face disappeared in seconds, and she stared at Antoine. "I had no idea. Remember, I live in Oakland. Where would I get information about Kiley working at the station?"

He brought his hands together on the table. "How do you know she's working there?"

Her lips puckered. "Look...what I meant is if she's working there, I didn't know."

Antoine had already begun to lose patience. He had hoped Fiona would cooperate and give him the information he desperately needed. He sighed and leaned forward. "Well, where'd she get those pictures of you sitting on my lap while I slept?"

She reached for her drink and sipped but said nothing.

He rubbed his shadow beard, waiting for a response. "No answer?"

'LIAR' should have scrolled across Fiona's face. Crossing and uncrossing her legs as she sipped tea, her body language clearly demonstrated guilt. Old habits don't die, and that's when he knew he'd nailed her. She never was a good liar and with minimal prompting would eventually confess to gain a clear conscious.

Avoiding eye contact, she bowed her head and squeezed both arms. "I gave them to her," she said softly.

Bingo! He was right. Leaning forward with flared nostrils, he stared through her shallow countenance as if she were glass. Angry enough to tear down the Great Wall of China, he didn't speak, restraining himself from sputtering foul language. *Take your time and stay calm.*

With both hands on top of his head, Antoine said, "I need answers. Why'd you do that to me?"

"I wanted you back, Antoine. I missed you so much I—"

"Stop," he hit the table lightly with his palm. "I can't focus on that. What's important is Kiley. I want anything you can share about her. When she moved to Oakland, L.A., whatever you can offer to resolve my dilemma."

Fiona wrung her hands. "Kiley separated from her husband, moved here from St. Louis, and stayed with me for several months. Then without notice, she took off. I didn't know where that girl went." She shrugged. "I swear...at first, I had no clue she was in L.A. Until she flew up here one weekend and told me she got a job at the radio station. I asked for a favor and gave her two sealed envelopes. She was supposed to place the pictures and my notes in your mailbox. That's all."

"That wasn't all. What she did was make copies and distribute them to management." He explained all the tricks Kiley had played, and how they affected his life. "Now management knows, and I'm walking a tightrope trying to save my job and relationship."

She sighed. "That heifer is up to no good. The photos were meant for you only," she said with a sad expression. "My cousin is a little weird at times. When she claimed you got her pregnant, I was furious. Then...I figured out she was talking trash. You wouldn't date her."

"Question? After she told you all those lies, you couldn't text or call and warn me?"

She cupped her chin. "Didn't think about it. I—I was busy prepping for a gig to dance in Brazil. Kiley was dating guys in Oakland; her husband came out here a couple of times, too."

He told Fiona what had transpired at Kiley's place

and her accusations. By the time he'd finished speaking, she'd blinked back a few tears.

"Date Rape? That's awful, and you getting her pregnant is nonsense. I think she has mental health issues. You know... I still have much love for you, and I'm sorry this happened."

"Well, thus far, my managers don't know that part about the date rape and pregnancy allegations. Recently, she asked me for ten-k."

Fiona's mouth dropped open. "What? I wouldn't give her a penny," she said in a haughty voice.

"If you're sorry, do me a favor." He bit his lower lip. "Talk to your cuz; tell her I know what she did and to back off me or my attorney's coming after her, meaning jail time for what she did."

"Oh, don't worry. I'm calling her *today*. I have some words for her behind. She opened my envelopes. Expect a text from me after I speak with her." Fiona's gaze moved to Antoine. "So...you're in another relationship now?"

His eyes softened as he caught her gaze. "Yes, I am. That's the main reason I'm on top of this. I don't want to lose her."

"I'm glad you're happy." She attempted to force a smile, but the sorrow on her face was apparent. Antoine knew this would come up if he met with her, but their relationship was over.

"This means a lot to me, and I appreciate it. I've got to bounce; we have a flight to catch. Take care of yourself and find some help for Kiley." Antoine rose and kissed her cheek. "Ciao." Strolling toward the door, he tossed a quick glimpse back, catching Fiona's sad look. He turned and kept moving.

Relieved that he may be closer to accomplishing his goals, Antoine disarmed the car alarm and climbed inside. He hoped he hadn't been too assertive with Fiona, but his desire was to let her know he was serious. To some extent, she was responsible for this whole fiasco with the pictures. Was she truthful? Possibly. If she wasn't, she knew what he knew. And that should influence her to have a conversation with Kiley. His iPhone signaled a text that came from Joy.

Per Jeanie, Yes re: DNA test now.

He texted back. Awesome. Any info on where to go?

Yes, after you speak with Kiley, send 2 dates.

Will do.

BTW – Pop called. Extending Jada's lease for 1 year. Take it. Offer to buy building after you marry her.

Antoine's eyes widened, and he laughed.

He texted, Marry her? Are you kidding? Lol.

No, I'm not. You can't fool me. You're in love. Sweet girl.

He texted, Super sweet and smart . We're in love. Can't wait to marry her and have babies.

Yes, and that means a new house.

That was incredible news, and Joy most likely played a major role in that decision. It was also great that his finicky sister liked Jada. Joy was protective and seldom connected with his former girlfriends, especially Fiona. But she and Jada seemed to get along well.

Chapter 41

JADA

Sunday Afternoon

"Hold on, J. Pizza Hut is at the door," Gordan said.

"Okay, I'll wait." Jada slid her feet into a pair of flip-flop sandals and walked to the sliding glass door to the deck. She adjusted the Bluetooth, pushed the sliding glass door open, and stepped outside. A halo of sun rays beamed in the slow rhythm of blue water pooling near the sand. Inner peace heightened her outlook as she stared at the Pacific Ocean and listened to the waves.

Jada sprawled on the chaise lounge chair and propped her feet up. She hoped this call to Gordon wasn't a waste of time.

"You still there?" Gordan said.

"I'm here."

"Truthfully, I want to forget that woman. Our relationship was warped and I must've been tore up when I proposed to Kiley."

"You must've been *tore up* every day to date her and *tore up* when you bought that ring." Jada chuckled.

"That's not funny. My life would've been squashed if I'd married her."

"Remember, I work with her. So, yeah, you're right, and she would've squashed your bank account. I promise what you tell me won't be shared. I also need you to keep what we discuss confidential as well."

"Of course. You said management is aware of the pictures. How can you be sure they don't have other information?"

"I'm not sure, and neither is Antoine. Here's the scoop on KTLM. I talked with Toni, and she's going after whoever passed out those pictures of Antoine. That could hurt Antoine and the station's ratings."

"Well, that's true. But there's more to the story. Why should I give you info about me and Kiley? KTLM is part of my region; I don't want my personal life floatin' through the station."

"Number one. They don't care who people are dating. I know Kiley may be trying to blackmail

Antoine. My question is... did she tell you she was pregnant before you broke up with her?"

Silence.

Jada tilted her head. "Gordan?"

"Yeah. How'd you know that?"

"I didn't. Is that why you broke off your engagement?"

"Yeah, that's why. And I'm only saying this to you. If I hear it again, I'm denying it."

"If anyone finds out, it didn't come from me. Think Kiley."

"We dated briefly; one day, she told me she was pregnant. I said I'd marry her."

"Is the baby yours?"

"No. I started thinking...we'd only been dating a couple of months. Her due date didn't add up. So, I asked for a DNA test; she said no. I pushed until she had no choice. I told her I wasn't dishin' out no more money without a DNA test. The test came back showing I wasn't the father. I got my ring back and told her to take a hike."

"At least she didn't try to blackmail you. So, one DNA test down, and that likely means no more until the baby is born."

"After Simon called and asked if I mailed some pictures, I was hot. Putting my name on packages and making me look bad. Who else would've done that but her?" I warned her if she even looked my way, I was hiring an attorney."

"Good for you. This seems to be a vicious cycle. I guess by now you know she dated other men. Antoine wasn't in that group."

"I'm not surprised. I hope it all works out for him. Say, I've gotta eat before my pizza gets cold."

"Okay. Take it easy and thanks."

The door slid open, and Antoine walked out.

"When did you get back?"

"A few minutes ago. I saw you on the phone."

"That was Gordan. Kiley did the same thing to him. DNA test showed he wasn't the father. Do you still plan to take one?"

"I'm pondering, but I think I should. I'll never know everything that happened that night, unless the DNA test is positive. Fiona fessed up about the photos, and I'll share what she said. Despite the negativity, I have great news, and I'll reconfirm, but Touch of Class Dress Shop's lease might be extended for a year."

Jada glanced up at Antoine, who was standing over her. "Did I hear you say the lease is extended?"

"Yes, Joy texted me. She must've done a karate chop on Pop. If Joy told me, there's a 99.9% chance it'll go through. That'll give us some leeway for planning, but don't share with your family until the paperwork is finalized."

Jada got off the chaise and hugged Antoine. Thank you, baby. I love you."

"Love you, too. I bought Thai food and changed our flight to a later time. Now we have time for a few other things."

Jada smiled at his gargantuan grin that stretched over his whole face. She winked an eye and said, "I can't wait."

Antoine warmed the the takeout and brought it out onto the deck. He shared about his meeting with Fiona. When he finished, she told him about Gordan's experiences with Kiley and asked that he not share the information with anyone else.

After the food, Antoine reached for Jada's hand; they walked to the bedroom and undressed. She laid across the bed and moaned. The Thai food was sumptuous, but Antoine's tongue navigating around her nipples was food for a cheerful soul. "Baby," Jada said in a breathy voice, rubbing his back.

"Yes," Antoine answered, continuing to kiss and massage her breasts. He ran his tongue down her neck, then rolled off her and extended his hand.

"Let's take a shower together."

He rolled off her and extended his hand. "Let's do it."

They got up off the bed and pranced to the bathroom in naked splendor. He adjusted the shower settings, and they stepped into a soothing warm flow of water. They soaped each other down and rinsed well several times.

Antoine planted kisses on her mouth, neck, and breasts, then her navel. "Mmm...you feel and smell so good," he told Jada. His tongue slid from her navel down her inner thighs to the G-spot, stimulating the kind of excitement that made her quiver. *How did this man learn to make love like this?* With her eyes closed, she let out a deep moan. He moaned, they moaned, his manhood exploded to a full size. Spreading her legs, he eased inside her moist space, and they made sweet, passionate love.

Chapter 42

ANTOINE

Sunday Night

The American Airlines flight to LAX touched down at 7:47 p.m. Once the flight attendant announced all passengers could retrieve their items and leave, Antoine reached up and opened the overhead bin, removed their duffle bags, and they exited the crowded plane. Shortly after they reached the customer transportation loading zone, a large black SUV pulled up. The driver called Antoine, who waved to get the man's attention.

The gentleman loaded their bags in his trunk and introduced himself. "Hello, I'm Freddy. I'll be your driver this evening. How was your trip?"

"It was nice," Jada said.

"I have two addresses. Which should I go to first? Don Miguel Drive or 10th Avenue?"

They answered simultaneously. Jada said, "Don Miguel." Antoine said, "10th Avenue."

Jada touched Antoine's arm. "Baby, you have to be at work at 5:00."

"Nope, we're going to your house first."

"Okay, it's 10th Avenue," the driver said, pulling away from the curb.

Traffic wasn't busy, and the flow was smooth. The driver took shortcuts to Jada's house, made a left on 10th Avenue. Several police cars were lined up in front of a house two doors down from Jada's. The driver parked in front of her house and popped the trunk. He scurried to the trunk and opened it.

"Oh, wow. I wonder what happened down there," Jada said, getting out of the car.

"Whose house is that?" Antoine said.

"Mrs. Bennett's. I'm sure she'll announce this to the neighborhood. The police are always messing with her sons, especially Lakeel. He used to sell drugs but cleaned up his life years ago."

Jada got out and walked to the trunk for her bag, where the driver cautiously peeked from behind the lifted trunk. She walked back to the side of the car and watched.

Antoine frowned and let the window down, "A drug dealer?"

"Yeah, but he's working now." Jada leaned down and kissed him.

"Babe, are you all right with going home?" He lifted his head, the police had cuffed a young black man as more police cars pulled up. "Aww, man, they need this many police for one man? Who's the man they handcuffed?"

The driver closed the trunk and got inside the car. "Uh, I think we should go," he said with a nervous look.

"That's Lakeel. I'm okay. He'll probably be home tomorrow. You should leave."

The driver shifted to drive.

"Hey, Bro', wait until she gets inside," Antoine demanded. His eyes shifted between Jada walking up the path to her front door and the police, who'd assembled on the sidewalk. After she opened the door, he gave the driver a cue to leave. That was senseless if the police harassed the man and he hadn't done anything, but it didn't have to make sense. That was common in urban neighborhoods.

He twisted his mouth, and frowned when he saw one officer shove the man in the car. Memories of similar incidents in the urban neighborhood where he once lived had never faded. He thought of Rashad. The boy's safety was of great concern. Antoine offered to move his mother and siblings to a better area, but she declined. He understood. Leaving wasn't always easy nor was it the answer for resolutions. True to his word, Antoine taught Rashad many techniques on how to behave when approached by the police, and his mother re-emphasized them often. *One more year and he'll be off to college.* Antoine let out a shaky breath.

Lights were on in the living room when the driver stopped in front of Derrick's house. It was possible that Derrick didn't have company. And even if he did, after a long day of activities and traveling, Antoine was set on relaxing in his room and calling Jada.

"Thanks for the lift," Antoine handed the driver a fifty-dollar tip. The man deserved it.

"You're welcome and thank you." The driver lifted the trunk, and Antoine picked up his bag.

He walked to the door and put his key in the lock; chatter and laughter emanated from the dining room area. He strolled in.

"Well look what the wolves drug in," Derrick said with a drink in his hand.

"What's up?" Antoine said.

"Not much. How was your trip?" Romero asked.

"I think it was productive." Antoine placed his bag on the sofa and removed his jacket.

"We had dinner and Romero made martinis. You want one?"

Antoine sat down. "No alcohol for me. I have to be up by 4:00."

"Any positive news regarding your situation? If you don't mind talking in front of Romero."

Romero rolled his head around to face Derrick. "Oh, I can go in the other room."

"Bro' you're cool," Antoine crossed his arms over his chest. Whatever Derrick hadn't told Romero didn't matter. Surely, he'd given him the whole spiel by now.

"What I will say is...I have a lot more information. Kiley has slept around with a lot of guys, and she gave me a date rape drug. Now, I have to take a DNA test."

All the color drained from Derrick's brown face, and Romero looked the same but with his mouth gaped open. Antoine found it fascinating that they both reacted similarly as if they had telepathic qualities.

Antoine lifted his bag and jacket and started walking to his room.

"Oh, no, you can't walk off. Was that a joke or part of the book you're writing?" Derrick cocked his head to the side.

"Believe me, I wish it was a joke, and I'd never

include that in my book. I'm tired. We had meetings with Pop, Joy, and Merlon all weekend, and then I met with Fiona. She provided a lot of valuable info, but...this is a tangled web, and I'm not sure what's next."

"Well, Joy and Merlon didn't have suggestions?" Derrick said.

"No detailed legal advice, but options and the PI's findings. I'm okay with that. I just want to figure this out so I can move on. I have people I care about, and my responsibility to them is to be at one-hundred percent, not half-cocked."

"How's Jada taking this?" Romero asked.

"Oh, my girl is supportive. I couldn't ask for a better woman."

Derrick smiled. "Uh, I told you so. Listen, Ant. You know I'm here if you need me. I'm glad you listened to me about Jada.

"Yeah, you waved your magic wand on that one. "I'm checking out. Goodnight."

His phone rang after he walked in the bedroom. He removed his cell from the jacket pocket and answered. It was Jada.

"Hey."

"Are you standing or sitting," Jada said.

He sat on his bed. "I'm sitting now. What happened?"

Denise just called me from the station. She's there putting together a client's package. Kiley came in and cleaned out her office but didn't say why. She may have quit or got fired."

Antoine dug his fingers into his thighs and didn't move. He sat perfectly still for a minute, not sure of how to react. Was this positive or negative?

"Talk to me. How do you feel?"

"I don't know how to feel. I found out everything except if I'm the father of her baby."

"I may be wrong, but this could be best."

"How? I don't see it that way now." He chewed his lower lip, "What if...there was another human being in this world that could be a part of you? Would you want that person in your life?"

"That depends on the circumstances. Honey, I get where you're coming from. If it's that important to you, we'll find Kiley. If we locate her, and the DNA test is positive, consider how this pregnancy happened."

"I've done that already. Is Denise still there?"

"She was a few minutes ago, but I'm not sure for how long. Call her."

"No, I'm going down there." Antoine pulled on his jacket.

"This late? You'll be there early tomorrow."

"I won't sleep until I make sure Kiley didn't play any games before she left. See you tomorrow."

He quietly walked out of the door without being noticed, hopped inside his truck and drove to the radio station. The big question was what transpired and why? Had management discovered that Kiley arranged the delivery of the pictures. Or did she really do that? As he pondered, a deep feeling of concern for an unborn child that might be his became a reality. He'd have to figure out a way to get the DNA test and to get back his peace of mind.

Antoine drove into the parking lot and parked close to the entry. He hit the alarm and made his way to the building as Denise was exiting.

"Antoine? You workin' tonight?"

"No, I talked to Jada. She told me Kiley's gone. What happened?"

"Honestly, I don't know. I was working when she came in with boxes. I asked why she was here. She barely said two words. Said she's leaving and had a strange look on her face."

"No indication of where she was going?"

Raising her brows, Denise said, "No, when I called Griff, he didn't know what was up. He said she hadn't notified him. I checked all the mailboxes after she left." She looked at Antoine. "Uh, yours is the only one with an envelope. I just texted Jada to inform you."

Denise's words *"had a strange look on her face"* sparked tension. Heart racing, he turned the corner and headed for the mailroom. Did he really want to know what was in the envelope or should he discard it? Staring at the mailbox, he paused and then removed the manila envelope with his name handwritten on the front. He held his breath and let out a long sigh while he opened the envelope. What appeared to be a sonogram of a fetus was distinct. Inside was an eight by eleven piece of paper that was folded in half. He unfolded it and read the giant red marker letters – 20 WEEKS – IT'S A BOY!!

He stuffed the sonogram and paper in the envelope and rushed to the door. This was too much. Now he was on the verge of giving up hope. So many raw emotions started circulating — ambivalence...fear...disgrace... Jada. She was sitting in the lobby.

She walked over to him. "What did she leave you?"

Antoine handed her the envelope and looked off into space as if in a daze. Jada removed the sonogram and paper, checked them, and handed everything back. She turned away, covered her face and cried.

He placed his hands on her shoulders, "Babe, please don't do this. I promise, we'll be okay."

She shook her head and glanced into his eyes. "I'm not crying for me. I...I'm crying for you. You deserve to know the truth."

A tear hit Antoine's cheek; he flicked it away and gently cupped Jada's face between his palms. He had deep love for this woman, and watching her cry was painful. "Babe, we still love each other, right? Nothing will stop us from being together."

She nodded. "I know."

"When I was growing up, my mother always said, love never fails. We can't forget that." He pulled Jada closer and they embraced.

Chapter 43

JADA

Two Months Later

Jada entered her office, and when she saw what was on her desk, she was elated. A large bouquet of red roses was in the center of her desk with a card attached. Antoine. What had this man done now? Their sixth-month anniversary of dating, and she already had an idea there was something he'd planned other than just dinner. She lifted the card from the roses. *Good morning, Love. Happy 6th month anniversary. I love you! Ant.*

Rosa strolled in, and her eyes widened. "Welcome back. How was your vacation, and what's the occasion?"

Jada wore a shy smile. "Two weeks flew by, but I enjoyed my time off. And this is a gift from my man for our sixth month anniversary. Aren't they nice?"

"You got a real special man. My husband remembers birthdays, Mother's Day... uh, let me see. Oh, and Christmas." Rosa sniffed the flowers. "You look pretty in that dress. I love black dresses for evening wear."

"Well, thank you. We're going out after I get off."

"Good morning," Ervin said. "Flowers? Someone sent you flowers? Who might that be?" He laughed.

"Quit playing, you already know. Where's Denise?" Jada said.

"She's at her desk. Just stopped by to say it's great to have you back."

"Hi, Jada, welcome back," Will, the News Director waved as he walked by.

"Thanks, Will. I guess I was missed."

Jada removed her burgundy coffee cup from a side drawer and walked to the closed door of the lounge. She smelled coffee, but when she turned the knob, it was locked.

"Hey, girl," Denise said. "That's off limits today. The coffee's in the kitchen."

"What happened in there?"

"I don't know. Whatever it is, they'll be here to fix it soon."

Jada walked to the kitchen and poured a cup of coffee.

When she walked back to her desk, she opened

her computer and started working, but within an hour, seven more people had stopped by her office. Darren, one of the sales execs who was rarely in this early, along with Alisha and Denise, for that matter. *Must be a meeting today.*

Toni stuck her head in the door. "Good morning, Jada. It's nice to have you back. How are you?"

Toni's here? "Uh, I'm fine. Is there a meeting? I don't recall getting a notice."

"No meeting. Just checking on you," she said with a smile. "Those flowers are lovely."

Suddenly, a voice that sounded like D.J. Rocky's came over the intercom. "Jada Carson, please come to the studio. Jada to the main studio, please."

Jada tilted her head "Me?" *Okay, why is DJ Rocky calling me?* She checked her watch. *9:40 a.m. Antoine is still on the air.* Jada got up from her desk and rushed toward the studio. *Is something wrong with Antoine?* The hall was packed with people from Sales, the new sales secretary, Linda, and others. She'd never seen that many people in the office at the same time, unless they had a meeting. *Something must have happened.*

"Excuse me, I was summoned to the studio." Jada zigzagged around employees who divided into two sides, creating an open entry faster than Jesus parted the Red Sea. When she got to the studio, she was out of breath and sweating. Lina was in the room, and several people had cameras. "What's going on?" she asked Ervin, who smiled.

Antoine opened the door. "Hi, babe."

"Why was I called in here?" She pulled two Kleenex from a box and patted her forehead.

"I have something for you. Take a seat right there," he pointed to a chair.

Jada still didn't understand what was going on. "Why are all these people here?"

"You'll see in a minute."

Jada ran her eyes over Antoine who was dressed up like he was going to a party. *That sharp burgundy suit fits him well. Dress shoes, too?*

"All right, L.A. You're listening to KTLM 101.3 on your dial. I'm your favorite champ, DJ Ant, the Prince of Romance, playing oldies but goodies with a splice of romantic tunes for your pleasure. You've just heard – "You Got it Bad" by Usher; "Girl on Fire" Alicia Keys. It's almost time for me to check out soon, but before I leave, I'm sharing something special today. My lady, Jada is here in the studio. "Hey, babe, stay tuned. Next is our favorite dance song – "Work It" by Drake and Rihanna."

Attempting to figure out Antoine's plan seemed pointless, so Jada rocked back and forth to the music and waited. *Guess I'll find out in a minute.*

"Hey, L.A., as you may know, I'm a die-hard fan of Earth, Wind, and Fire's musical poetry. This next song is dedicated to my girl, Jada. "Love's Holiday.""

Jada rolled her chair next to Antoine's. She smiled and waved at the employees peering through the studio window, and then asked, "Boy, what are you doing?"

"Babe, sit tight. You'll find out shortly." He faced her, rolled his chair closer, never taking his eyes off her, started singing the song to her along with the record.

She looked up, and the managers, Griff, Simon, and Toni were chatting with the employees. *Oh, we're in trouble now.* She knew something was up when Celine, Charmaine, and Darius walked in and waved at her.

"L.A. are you ready to hear my special announcement? Antoine pulled out a light blue Tiffany & Co. ring box from his pocket and dropped to one knee. "Jada Carson, will you marry me?"

Her mouth dropped open as all the employees cheered. "Uh, yes." He slid the ring on her left fourth finger, gave her a quick kiss on the lips and moved over to his seat. "I'm overjoyed. She said yes. This is DJ Ant, the Prince of Romance, and you're listening to KTLM radio station, 101.3. on your dial. Until tomorrow, peace and love. Ciao!"

Jada was speechless as she stared at the large diamond on her hand. She got up and hugged Antoine. "Babe, you've got to meet Char and Darius." They exited the studio to applause and congratulations from all the staff and managers. Cameras flashed, they shook hands and received congratulations from their co-workers.

The man with the camera said, pose by the door. She and Antoine did as he asked, and he shot four poses that Antoine said would be announced in the Los Angeles Sentinel Newspaper. Then she introduced Antoine.

"Baby, this is Darius and Char, and you know Celine."

"Nice to meet you. Hey, Celine," he said, hugging and shaking hands.

"Alrighty, folks, we have breakfast in the lounge to celebrate Jada and Antoine's engagement," Denise said.

"Baby, I'm going to the office for a minute," Jada told Antoine. She rushed to her office and opened the desk drawer, removed a white envelope, then rushed to the lounge where everyone had started helping themselves to bacon, sausage, eggs, and pancakes.

"This is our six-month anniversary, and I guess it's your engagement gift now." She handed the envelope to Antoine who was surrounded by well-wishers. His whole face glowed when he pulled out two tickets. "What? Earth, Wind, and Fire Concert tickets. This is boss. Babe, you didn't have to do this."

"Yes, I did." She grabbed his hand. "Excuse us. We'll be back in a minute." They walked back to her office.

"What's wrong?" Antoine asked with a concerned look on his face.

"I'm happy, and this ring..." She looked down at the sparkling diamond. "It's gorgeous."

"Don't tell me I spent too much money."

"No. You could spend whatever you wanted on my engagement ring." She laughed. "But announcing our engagement at work?"

"Now that was cool. It's out in the open, so no surprises. I told your sisters, Derrick, Rashad, and Joy, who informed my family members. This is only the beginning. We're having engagement parties in the Bay Area, L.A., and in D.C. So, get ready."

"Antoine Bailey. You're a sweetheart."

"It's all about love," he said kissing her lips. They walked hand-in -hand back to the lounge to have breakfast with their co-workers.

The End

(Stay tuned for the sequel – Rhythm Bay Love II)

Patricia A. Bridewell

About the Author

Reading and daily journal entries were the catalyst to Patricia's first novel, *Reflections of a Quiet Storm*, published by an independent publisher in 2009. An avid reader, her previous published work includes two books, multiple short stories, monthly health care columns for an online magazine, and several health care articles for a local newspaper. She also enjoys reading Women's Fiction and Romance novels, which occupy many seats on her bookshelves.

Patricia is a Family Nurse Practitioner and a Psychiatric-Mental Health Nurse Practitioner, she holds Adjunct Nursing Faculty positions at two universities. She is a member of the National Black Nurses Association/Council of Black Nurses – L.A., Sigma Theta Tau International Honor Society of Nursing, Black Nurses Rock, California Association of Nurse Practitioners, and International Black Writers & Artists. Patricia's church home is Greater Zion Church Family in

Compton, CA. She considers music, reading, and prayer as the keys to relaxation and creativity, and she loves spending time with her family.

Patricia's short story appears in the Brown Girls Books Anthology *Single Mama Dating Drama,* an AALBC two-time Best-Selling book. *Two Steps Past the Altar* is her third novel. *Rhythm Bay Love* is her fourth novel. She is currently working on her fifth book.

Visit her online at http://www.patriciabridewell.com/

www.ingramcontent.com/pod-product-compliance
Lightning Source LLC
Chambersburg PA
CBHW030359180626
46812CB00005B/1840